D1052959

Goatsong

Also by Tom Holt:

Lucia in Wartime
Lucia Triumphant
Expecting Someone Taller
Who's Afraid of Beowulf?

NATIONAL UNIVERSITY
LIBRARY   SAN DIEGO

Goatsong

Volume One in the *The Walled Orchard* series

Tom Holt

St. Martin's Press
New York

NATIONAL UNIVERSITY
LIBRARY   SAN DIEGO

GOATSONG. Copyright © 1989 by Tom Holt. All rights reserved. Printed in the United States of America. No part of this book may be used or reproduced in any manner whatsoever without written permission except in the case of brief quotations embodied in critical articles or reviews. For information, address St. Martin's Press, 175 Fifth Avenue, New York, N.Y. 10010

Library of Congress Cataloging-in-Publication Data

Holt, Tom.
      Goatsong / Tom Holt.
          p. cm.
      "A Thomas Dunne book."
      ISBN 0-312-03838-0
   1. Athens (Greece)—History—Fiction. 2. Greece—History—
—Athenian supremacy, 479-431 B.C.—Fiction. I. Title.
PR6058.0474G6   1990
823'.914—dc20   89-24097
                                           CIP

First published in Great Britain by Macmillan London Limited.

First U.S. Edition
10 9 8 7 6 5 4 3 2 1

To James and Hilary

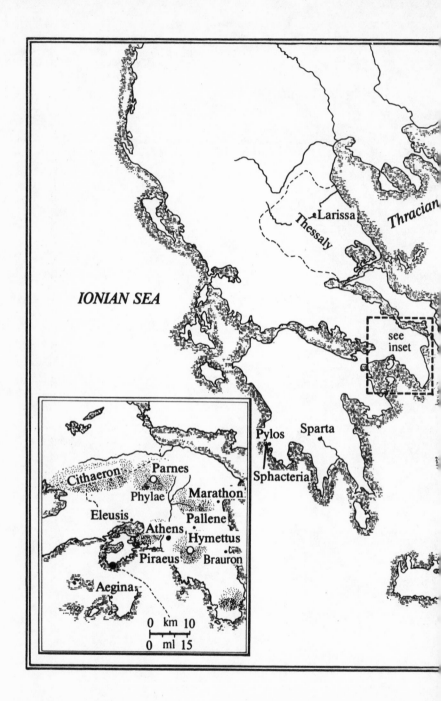

IONIAN SEA

Thessaly

Larissa

Thracian

see
inset

Pylos

Sparta

Sphacteria

Cithaeron

Parnes

Phylae

Marathon

Eleusis

Pallene

Athens

Hymettus

Piraeus

Brauron

Aegina

0   km   10

0   ml   15

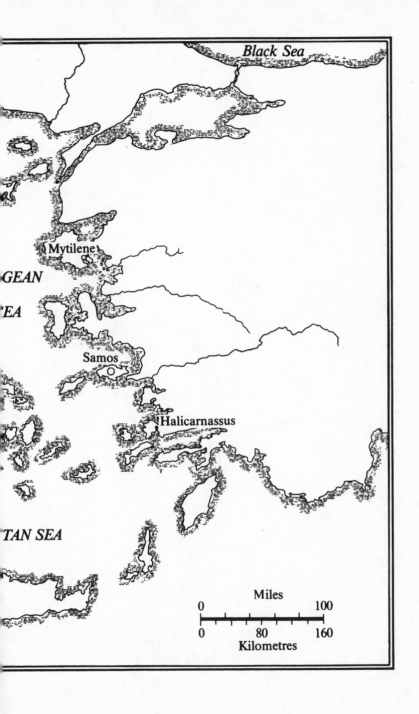

Black Sea

Mytilene

GEAN

EA

Samos

Halicarnassus

TAN SEA

Miles
0   100

0   80   160
Kilometres

Chapter One

 🔲🔲🔲

Athens is a large city situated in the middle part of the
country we call Greece. To the north lies Thebes, Corinth
is due west, and Sparta some way to the south. The City
is surrounded by the region known as Attica, a miserable
rocky district where very little can be persuaded to grow.
That is all I have to say, for the moment, about the City
of Athens.

Well, almost. The first really memorable cockfight I
ever saw took place in the City of Athens, outside the
Propylaea, where the little path that leads up from the
right joins the main stairway. It was a quite unbearably
hot day, the sort of day you get when your early barley
is wilting for lack of rain and your grapes are turning
into raisins on the stalk, and I can't have been more than
nine years old. I have no idea what we were doing in the
City at that time of year, but I remember that my father
had had to come in to see to some business or other and
had taken me with him. This was supposed to be a treat,
and in the normal course of events it would have been;
but what with the heat and the crowds of people I was
as sullen as only a nine-year-old male child can be, and
if Zeus himself had chosen that moment to come down
to earth in a fiery four-horse chariot, I doubt if I would
have taken very much notice. But this cockfight was
something else.

Of course we had cockfights in our village, and I
didn't think much of them, although I imagine that I
was every bit as bloodthirsty as most normal small boys

1

of that age. What this cockfight had that all the others had lacked was atmosphere.

From what I could gather, the challenger, a huge, brightly coloured bird with the magnificent name of Euryalus the Foesmiter, was taking on the southern Attica area champion, a rather tattered-looking creature called Ajax Bloodfoot, and the best part of a hundred drachmas was riding on the outcome. Although I knew little of such matters, I soon guessed that the Foesmiter was expected to make extremely short work of Bloodfoot, who was coming towards the end of his useful life as a fighting-cock and was widely regarded by the better informed spectators as little better than a self-propelled kebab. Had anyone asked my opinion I would undoubtedly have sided with the majority view, since Bloodfoot was considerably smaller than Foesmiter and something drastic had recently happened to his left wing. The Master of Ceremonies – a short man with a neck like a log – announced the two combatants in a loud and glorious voice, such as one imagines Homer must have had, and recited their various pedigrees, contests and victories. From this catalogue of ancient valour what emerged most clearly was that Bloodfoot's most notable achievements had all taken place well over two years ago, whereas Foesmiter was nicely at the peak of his form, having practically disembowelled a creature called Orestes the Driver of the Spoil only a fortnight ago, and had been living on a diet of ground wheat and lugworms ever since. Then the log-necked man announced that this was the last opportunity for staking money on the contest, and withdrew to the edge of the chalk circle.

At that time, my most prized possession was a single obol. It was the first piece of coined money I had ever possessed, and it was not a beautiful object at that. Some time before it had come into my possession, a previous owner had been extremely sceptical about the nature of the metal it was made of, and had taken a chisel and cut no less than four deep slices in it, three across the owl on the tail side, and one, extremely blasphemously, along the line of Athena's nose on the obverse. Be that as it may, I loved that obol, for I had traded for it three good-quality hare skins and a broken sickle-blade I had found in the bed of a small stream. When the Master of Ceremonies made his announcement about wagers I can remember saying to myself that I was far too young to start gambling, and that if my father ever found out he would quite rightly skin me alive. But then I seemed to hear the little obol crying out from its resting-place under my tongue – we used to carry our small change in our mouths in those days, before they started issuing those silver-plated coppers which make you ill if you swallow them – and it was saying that it was feeling terribly lonely, and here was a unique opportunity for me to acquire some other little obols for it to play with. There was no risk involved, said the obol; all I had to do was wager on Foesmiter at three to one, and I would have quite a little nest of owls rattling up against my teeth when I went home that evening.

So, when the mob of eager gamblers had subsided enough for me to squeeze my way to the front, I picked the obol out of my mouth, dried it carefully on the sleeve of my tunic, and wagered it solemnly on Euryalus the Foesmiter. Then the trainers each slipped their respective charges a small lump of garlic, which makes them fierce, and thrust them into the circle.

It took Ajax Bloodfoot about thirty seconds to dispose of the challenger. I think that what did it was the mindless ferocity of his onslaught. There was none of that careful walking round the ring and clucking that I was used to back home in Pallene; Bloodfoot simply stuck out his head, made a sound like tearing linen, and jumped on his opponent's neck. His entire strategy seemed to consist of getting his claws round the other bird's throat and pecking his head off, and this is a most unorthodox way for a cock to fight. A properly brought up, well-educated bird will fight with his spurs, as a heavy infantryman uses his spear; he disdains the other weapons that Nature has armed him with, just as an infantryman prefers not to use his sword unless he absolutely must. The orthodox fighting-cock is

3

therefore at a loss when a small but agile enemy attaches itself to his neck and refuses to let go. I had scarcely got back to the shelter of the edge of the crowd when the Master of Ceremonies was standing in the middle of the chalk circle holding up a rather disordered bundle of feathers, lately known as Euryalus the Foesmiter, and declaring that the champion had retained his title at odds of seven to one. The crowd then seemed to melt away, and I was left standing there with nothing but the grandeur of the Propylaea to look at, and no obol. In the end I walked away and found my father, and explained that I had swallowed my obol. He sympathised and said that it would work its way through my system in a day or so, and be none the worse for its experience. This worried me tremendously, since obviously it wouldn't and then he would guess that I had gambled it away and be seriously annoyed with me. Luckily, however, he forgot all about it, and I was able to earn a replacement obol by scaring crows by the time I had to account to him.

In many respects I feel a certain identity of experience with both of those birds; for throughout my life I have found that things which one would naturally expect to be easy have proved very difficult for me, while I have successfully survived trials and ordeals that have finished off much taller and more splendidly plumaged men than myself. If I stretch the analogy to its absolute limits, I can also claim that that cockfight is a nice epitome of the story of Athens during my time; Athens, of course, being Euryalus the Foesmiter. Unless your memory is as bad as mine has become over the last few years, you will remember that the Foesmiter had led up to his last encounter with a string of victories over extremely impressive opponents, and that it was the final battle, against an opponent that he was universally fancied to sweep aside, that finally did for him. Add to that his great size and the magnificence of his feathers and crest, and there you have Athens as it was in my childhood, just two years before the outbreak of the Great Peloponnesian War.

*

Dexitheus the bookseller, who has paid me good money to write this, would far rather that I started off in the correct manner with something like 'These are the Histories of Eupolis of Pallene, written down so that the glorious deeds of men shall never wholly be forgotten,' and then went on to narrate the genesis of the Gods, the birth of the Divine Athena and her founding of the City, the childhood and heroic deeds of Theseus and the second foundation of Athens, the reforms of Solon, the tyranny of Pisistratus, and the part played by the Athenians in the Great War against the Persians.

Here is where Dexitheus and I part company. Dexitheus believes that a book describing itself as a History should have plenty of history in it. I maintain that my readers will either be Athenians and know all that sort of thing already, or else they will be barbarians and outlanders who know nothing at all about our City, and that any prologue capable of putting them in a position where they can hope to understand everything I am about to say would be likely to be twice as long as the book itself and not particularly entertaining. I therefore propose to plunge straight into my story and let my readers sort things out for themselves as they go along. I believe that they will soon get the hang of it, and if Dexitheus doesn't like it, he can find someone else to write something to go on all that Egyptian paper he bought so cheaply last summer and has had on his hands ever since.

That still leaves me with the problem of where to start my story. You see, what I intend to do is to tell the story of my life, from my birth in the village of Pallene, thirty-eight years after the battle of Salamis, down to the present day. Nobody has ever been sufficiently egotistical to do anything like that before, and I must admit that the prospect alarms me rather. So I am tempted to skip over the events of my early life and concentrate on the period I can best remember, which nicely coincides with all the most fascinating parts of the history of Athens. But if I do this, and you know nothing about Athens beyond what I have just told you and what you have read on the necks of wine jars, you will soon be quite lost and very upset at parting with a solid silver drachma for such an obscure book; whereas if I start at the beginning and work my way doggedly through to the end, my readers will have lost patience by the time I describe cutting my first tooth and will be following Dexitheus round the Market Square loudly asking for their money back.

All I can do, then, is give you my word as an Athenian and a servant of the Muses that once this book gets nicely under way it will be extremely entertaining, moving and informative, and ask you to bear with me while I deal with all the tiresome material that has to be seen to first. Imagine, if you will, that you are at the Theatre on the first day of the Great Dionysia, and that you have walked in all the way from Marathon or Eleusis on a hot day to see the latest play by that celebrated Comic poet Eupolis of Pallene. First, you must sit through three apparently interminable Tragedies on such mundane and hackneyed themes as the Fall of Troy, the Revenge of Orestes, or the Seven Against Thebes. But you are prepared to make this sacrifice of your time and patience, since you know perfectly well that a Eupolis Comedy is worth waiting for, and when the Chorus come trooping on in their marvellous costumes singing their opening number you will enjoy yourself all the more because of the dreary stuff that you have endured before.

It has just occurred to me that some of you, being young and ignorant, may not have heard of Eupolis of Pallene, the great Comic dramatist. You may never have heard my name before. You may never even have heard of the Great Dionysia, or been to a play in your life. I don't really know what to say to you if that really is the case, except that the Great Dionysia is one of the two annual dramatic festivals we have at Athens, when for three successive days new plays are presented and the best example of Comedy and Tragedy is awarded a prize by the panel of judges, and that in my youth I frequently won the prize for Best Comedy, although most certainly not frequently enough. In fact, before we go any further, I think we should deal with this question once and for all, and then at last I can get on with telling the story.

There are a great many things in this book which would conceivably need explaining, and I am certainly not going to explain them all. That would be insufferably tedious. If, therefore, I refer to something which you do not understand or have not heard of, I advise you to keep quiet and use your intelligence to try and work out from the context what is going on, as I have had to do all my life. Pretend that this is not a book at all, but some enthralling conversation you are eavesdropping on in the Baths or the Fish Market.

And now, at last, I shall start my narrative, and soon you will be so completely enthralled by my powers of story-telling that all these problems I have been agonising over will melt away like bad dreams on market-day.

Athens, as it was in my childhood. Now I cannot imagine that you don't know at least something about the great days of the City, between the Persian Wars and the war with Sparta. 'They were giants in those days,' as that buffoon Teleclides says in one of his plays, for it was the time when the plays of Aeschylus were still recent enough to be remembered, and Sophocles was at the height of his powers, and a young man called Euripides had just started to make an impact; when Pericles was laying the foundation-stone of a new temple every other month, and the tribute-money from the Great Athenian Empire was rolling in like a flooded river.

That, at least, is how it seems in retrospect. Now, I was born and bred in Attica, and the City of Athens was always there in the background; but I had little to do with it in those days when the great men you all know so much about were carving their names on the walls of history. My early boyhood was not spent in the company of great men; in fact, it was spent mainly in the company of goats. My father was reasonably well off, and a fair percentage of his wealth consisted of a flock of hardy but troublesome goats which needed looking after. Goatherding is not difficult, but neither is it particularly stimulating and pleasant. Accordingly, as soon as I was old enough to be out on my own, I was appointed Chief

7

Goatherd and turned out on to the sides of Hymettus.

Although I disliked goats (and still do), I preferred goatherding to education and soon became as proficient at the business as it is possible for a small boy to be. At Pallene we were between two mountain ranges, so that pasture was available at no great distance from home, and since the beasts themselves were generally docile I was able to devote most of my time spent on goatherd-duty to what was, even then, my greatest passion and preoccupation; the composition of iambic verse.

At first I composed Tragedy, since Tragedy, and in particular the works of the celebrated Aeschylus, was what was mostly recited at home and in the village. Most people had at least a few passages of the great man's plays by heart, and one old man, who made his living mostly by paying visits and staying to dinner, claimed to know all the seventy-four plays. He had been (so he said) a member of the State Acting Corps; and he certainly had a fine reciting voice, which I used to carry in my head when deciding whether a line would sound well when spoken.

But I soon gave up Tragedy; the long streams of polysyllabic compounds and arcane kennings that make up the high Tragic style seemed to me both difficult and ridiculous. As soon as I saw my first Comic play – it made such an impression on me that I cannot now remember who wrote it or what it was about – I decided to compose only Comedies; and, with one exception which I shall tell you about in due course, I have kept that vow all my life. The Comic style, after all, is closely based on the patterns of speech of ordinary people, so that the greatest compliment you can pay a Comic poet is to say that you didn't realise that his characters were speaking verse at all. In fact, I maintain that Comedy is far harder to write than Tragedy (nobody believes me, of course) since Tragedy has a language all of its own which is expressly designed for writing plays in, whereas ordinary speech was never meant to be chivvied into an iambic line and neatly broken up with caesuras. Fortunately, I was born with the knack, and my mother used to say

8

that I spoke in verse virtually from the cradle. Coming from my mother, that was not a compliment; she came from a minor political family and had been brought up to despise satirists.

From the age of nine onwards, then, I took to warbling childish *parabases* and *stichomythiae* to the goats and the thorn trees. I had not as yet learned the art of writing on wax tablets or Egyptian paper, and so I carried the lines, once finished, in my head. I still do this even now, and only write a play out when it is finished. After all, actors have to learn their parts, and if the author cannot remember the play, how can the actors be expected to?

By the time I was eleven, I had started composing choral lyrics, which in fact I have always found easier than iambic dialogue, and soon I had completed my first Comedy, of which I was absurdly proud. It was called *The Goats* after its Chorus and first audience, and it was awarded first prize in the Pan-Hymettic Festival by the old white billygoat whom I had elected as chairman of the twelve judges. Since my play was the only entry that year, I don't suppose he had much choice in the matter, and shortly afterwards he butted me very painfully when I was trying to pleat his forelock, which gave me an early and invaluable lesson in the fickleness of audiences.

The Chorus, dressed as goats, represented the People of Athens, and their goatherd was the glorious Pericles, the great statesman who led Athens at the time. No Comedy worth the name was complete without a vitriolic and obscene attack on Pericles, and *The Goats* was no exception. One day, the goatherd is pasturing his flock on the fat uplands of the empire when a band of Spartan bandits waylays him and steals from him the cheeses he has himself stolen from his master the Treasury. I am rather better at allegory now, I am pleased to say; at the time, I thought this the height of subtlety.

Enraged at this cowardly attack, Pericles resolves to declare war on Sparta and build a wall of trireme ships all round the empire to keep the Spartans out and the goats in. There was a nice scene in the Goat Assembly, where Pericles proposes the motion; his speech, the *agon* of the play, was a parody of all I could remember of a speech by the great man that almost everyone in Pallene had learned by heart, while the counter-speech by Tragosophus ('Wise Goat') was a close imitation of the reply by one of his opponents. There was also a good Chorus scene where the Potidaean goat tries to break through the wall to escape, and is sacrificed and eaten by Pericles and the other goats (that was for my father, of course). To this day I could quote you the Prologue speech, the first I ever composed ('This goatherd now; he's quite another thing/We think he means to make himself our King'); but I have acquired a certain reputation as a Comic poet, and it is not quite worthy of me.

Then came the outbreak of the Great War against Sparta, and my idyllic life of poetry and goatherding was interrupted every year by the annual invasion by the Spartans, which involved two unpleasantnesses; going to school to learn oratory and the poetry of Homer, and having to live in the City while the Spartans were about. On the whole, I thought Homer more of a nuisance than the Spartans, because inside the City there were men who had recently been in a Chorus and so could recite the latest Comedies. Since there was nothing for men to do in the City between Assemblies and trials, with most of the population cooped up inside the walls for months at a time, everyone had time to spare for a small boy who said he was going to be a Comic poet as soon as he was old enough to be given a Chorus. The only condition was that I should give Pericles a hard time in my first Comedy; little did they know that I had already done this.

The leading Comic poet of the time was the celebrated Cratinus, whom I was privileged to meet when I was twelve years old. There are few people in this world who truly merit the epithet Disgusting, but Cratinus was one of them. He was a little, stooped man with a leering smile, and his hands never stopped shaking, even when he was relatively sober. There was always vomit on his gown somewhere, and his interest in small boys was not that of a teacher. Nevertheless, he was always an honoured guest, at least for the early part of the evening, and in spite of his unfortunate personal habits, such as wiping his fingers on his neighbour's hair when he sneezed, I never met anyone (apart from other Comic poets) who really disliked him. He was a born politician, and he loathed and despised Pericles with every ounce of his small, frail, unpleasant body. It was therefore quite easy to win his undying friendship, and my mother's uncle Philodemus, who knew him quite well, instructed me in the art when I said that I would like to meet him.

To endear yourself to Cratinus, all you had to do was this. As soon as the conversation turned to politics, you had to look troubled, as if you were on the point of making some dreadful confession. 'I know it's very foolish of me,' you would say, 'and I know he's made this country what it is today, but in my heart of hearts I think Pericles is wrong about . . . ' (Here insert the leading issue of the day.) 'I can't tell you why,' you would continue, looking sheepish and if possible mumbling slightly, 'it's just a feeling I have.'

This was Cratinus' cue. He would break in and start explaining, very forcibly and with many gestures, exactly what was wrong with Pericles' latest policy. During the exposition, you would frown and nod reluctantly, as if you were being forced, against your will, to accept some great truth. Cratinus would then believe that he and he alone had converted you to the right way of thinking, and you would be his friend and political ally for life.

After several rehearsals I was judged to be word perfect, so a drinking party was arranged and a cheap second-hand dinner-service was bought from the market, in case Cratinus started throwing things when he got drunk. It was my job to be Ganymede and pour the wine, and my uncle invited a couple of old friends with strong stomachs to be the other guests. As usual, Cratinus was unanimously appointed King of the Feast (which means he had the right to choose the drinking-songs and topics of conversation and declare who should sing or speak first), and the food was quickly and messily eaten. Then I was brought forward to play my scene, which I did perfectly.

11

Cratinus swallowed the bait like a tunny-fish, and started waving his hands about furiously. If only, he exclaimed, spilling his wine over my uncle's gown and tilting the neck of the jar I was carrying over his cup, all in the same movement, the voters of Athens had the common sense of this clear-thinking brat!

'You'd think,' he said, quivering with indignation, 'that if the idiots award first prize to a play entirely devoted to obscene and scurrilous attacks on a man, then they don't like him. It stands to reason, surely. Not in this miserable city it doesn't. Every year I put him on the stage and those imbeciles in the audience wet themselves laughing at his expense. Then they go home, change into something clean, and troop off and elect him for another term. I don't understand it; it's almost as if having the piss taken out of him makes the bastard more popular.'

'Maybe it does,' said my uncle. 'Maybe all you're doing is giving them an outlet for their natural frustration. If they didn't have that, maybe they wouldn't vote for him so much.'

'And anyway,' said one of the other guests, a neighbour of my uncle's called Anaxander, 'so long as you win your prize you don't care, surely?'

Cratinus nearly choked. 'What the hell do you take me for?' he snapped. 'I wouldn't give you a dead frog for all the prizes ever awarded. What do you think I want out of life, for God's sake?'

'Come off it,' said Anaxander cheerfully. 'All this crusading stuff is just for the audiences. Everyone knows that as soon as the Chorus have left the stage, the poet and the politicians go off and get drunk with each other, which is why we have all those pools of curiously coloured vomit in the streets the day after the Festivals. I bet you fifty drachmas that if Pericles died tomorrow you wouldn't know what to do with yourself. He's your meal-ticket and you're his pet jackal.'

Cratinus went as purple as the wine and started to growl, so that I was quite frightened; but my uncle just smiled.

12

'That's just the sort of crap I expect from a voter,' said Cratinus at last, when he had finally managed to control his fury. 'I'll bet you fifty drachmas you voted for the little sod at the last election. Well, didn't you?'

'As a matter of fact,' said Anaxander, 'I did. What of it?'

Cratinus leaned over and spat into Anaxander's cup. 'Now we're even,' he said. 'You foul my cup, I foul yours.'

Anaxander didn't think this was terribly funny, and my uncle started to frown.

Just then, it occurred to me that I might be able to save the situation, so I cleared my throat timidly and said; 'But isn't what Anaxander said right, up to a point? Isn't winning the prize, or at least writing a good play, what it's all about? Just because the <u>audience don</u>'t get the point, that doesn't make the play any less good.'

Cratinus turned on me and scowled. 'The boy isn't quite so sensible after all,' he said. 'If I wanted to write good plays, I'd be a Tragedian, and then perhaps I wouldn't get thrown out of quite so many polite parties. If all I wanted to do was write good iambics I wouldn't fool about with Comedy, which is mostly hard work; I'd write Oedipuses and Sevens against Thebes and all that kind of crap, and then I'd win all the prizes in the world, and nobody would have the faintest idea what I was on about, and neither would I. You listen to me, and I'll tell you something. If ever you want to be a Comic poet – God forbid you should, it's a really rotten life, I'm telling you – find yourself someone to hate, and hate them as much as you possibly can. For me it's easy, I've got Pericles and I actually do hate him. That's why I do Comedy better than anyone else. But you're young, you probably don't hate anyone enough to want to eat their guts warm off a meat-hook. In which case, you'll have to imagine you hate him. Picture him in your mind's eye killing your father, raping your mother, pissing down your well, smashing your vine-props. When you cut your little toe, say "That's Pericles' fault"; if it rains during harvest, say "Pericles has made it rain again." Everything that goes wrong in your life, I want you to pin it on this enemy

13

of yours. That way you'll get a sort of lump in your intestines like a slowly forming turd which you've just got to squeeze out, somehow or other, and then you'll start writing Comedy. At first, you'll just write hours and hours of vulgar abuse, like "Pericles has got balls like a camel", but then you'll realise that that doesn't do any good. You'll find that if you want to hurt you've got to write well, so that when the audience laugh they're siding with you and against him. Now I'm still not good enough to be able to make them do that, but it's too late now. One of these days I'll have his nuts, and then I can retire and grow beans.'

'You'll never manage that,' said my uncle. 'Or don't you know anything about Athenians?'

'I've been a Comic poet for fifteen years,' Cratinus replied. 'I know more about Athenians than any man living.'

'No you don't,' said my uncle. 'All you know about is making Athenians laugh, which is a trade, like mending buckets. You obviously don't know what makes them work, or you wouldn't still be trying to put a message across in the Theatre. If you knew the first thing about your fellow citizens, you'd have realised by now that what they love above all things is the pleasure of words. The Persians love gold, the Spartans love bravery, the Scythians love wine and the Athenians love clever speaking. The fact of the matter is that an Athenian would far rather listen to a description of a banquet in the great king's palace than eat a nice bean stew, and he much prefers voting to annex the silver mines of Thasos to harvesting his own winter barley.' He paused, took a long gulp of wine, and continued. 'Why do you think we invented the Theatre, for God's sake? Come to that, why do you think we have a democracy? It's not because a democracy makes for better government; quite the opposite, as you well know. It's because in a democracy, if you want to have your own way, you've got to make the best speech, and then all the farmers and the sausage-merchants and the men who work in the dockyards go away from Assembly in the morning

14

with their heads full of the most glorious drivel and think they own the world. That's how your beloved Pericles got to be Zeus' favourite nephew; by clever speaking. And it's the likes of you that keep him there, because just as soon as the fumes of all that oratory have worn off and the voters start wanting to see some public expenditure accounts, along you come with your incredibly funny plays and your brilliant speeches, and soon they're all soaked to the skin in words again.'

'Hold on a moment,' interrupted Cratinus. 'I write cleverer speeches than anyone in Athens. If they always do what the best speaker says, why aren't Pericles' nuts roasting on a spit on my hearth this very moment?'

'Because it's just the Theatre,' said my uncle, 'and so they don't take any notice; they've worked off their anger against Pericles by having you make a monkey out of him, and the next time he stands up in Assembly and proposes an expedition to conquer the moon, they stand there and gobble up his golden phrases like spilt figs. The Theatre is the place for making fun of Generals and Assembly is the place for voting for them. I'd have thought you'd have worked that one out ages ago.'

'So you're anti-democracy as well as pro-Pericles,' said Cratinus irritably. 'Don't bother asking me here again.'

My uncle laughed. 'What makes you think I'm anti-democracy?' he said. 'Just because my nephew here is an idiot doesn't mean I don't love him, and just because my city does a lot of very stupid things doesn't mean I want to overthrow the constitution. I love the democracy and I hate tyranny. Which is why I get irritated with people who don't understand the nature of democracy, and people who abuse it.'

'If we're going to start discussing democracy,' said Anaxander, yawning ostentatiously, 'I'm going home. I've got vines to prune in the morning.'

'You stay where you are and shut up,' said my uncle. 'You're just as bad as the rest of them really. Just now you provoked a quarrel with Cratinus just to see if he'd say something funny when he got angry, and then when he spat in your cup you didn't like it at all. That's typically Athenian. We all like a nice juicy crisis because it makes for such entertaining public speaking, so we all vote to annex this city or make that treaty, and when some smart-arse politician makes a good speech we feel so proud of ourselves that our little tummies swell up as tight as wineskins. Then when the crisis turns into a war and our vines get burnt we want to kill someone important, and we execute the first politician who catches our eye – probably the only one who really wants what's best for the City and is trying to clear up the mess. And then the whole circus starts up all over again, with factions and political trials and more and more and more speeches, and in the meantime we've sent five thousand infantry to some god-forsaken rock in the middle of the sea to fight a load of savages we've never even heard of. Now all this comes from us Athenians being the cleverest and most intelligent race on earth, and loving the pleasures of the mind more than the pleasures of the body. That's why Cratinus here is our most popular playwright, why Pericles is our most popular politician, why Athens is the greatest city in the world, and why one of these days we're all going to meet with a nasty end.'

'The hell with you,' said Cratinus, after a long pause. 'When I go out to dinner, I expect to do all the talking.'

'Exactly,' said my uncle. 'That's why I asked you. But then you got all incoherent, so like a good host I provided the entertainment myself. Where's that boy with the wine? I've got a throat like stone-mason's sand after all that pontificating.'

Anaxander emptied his cup out on to the floor and held it out to me to be refilled. 'If I'd wanted to hear you speaking,' he said, 'I wouldn't have come half-way across the City on a wet night. I propose that we don't give Cratinus anything more to drink until he's given us a speech from his latest play.'

'Steady on,' said my uncle. 'You'll give him a heart attack.'

'You can keep your lousy wine,' said Cratinus. 'After

everything you've said about me, it'll take more than this goat's piss of yours to get me to do any reciting.'

'I've got a jar of quite palatable Rhodian out the back there,' replied my uncle. 'Now I know it would be wasted on you, but I'm such a typical Athenian that a really good speech might induce me to part with some of it.'

Cratinus grinned, displaying his few remaining teeth. 'Listen to this,' he said.

Which is how I came to be one of the first four people ever to hear the great speech from *The Lions* in which Pericles' descent, conception and birth is described in loving and exquisite detail. It is quite the most revolting thing that Cratinus ever wrote, and will be remembered when everything I have written is long forgotten. Cratinus said later that he wrote the whole thing at a sitting while the barber was lancing a particularly objectionable and inconveniently situated boil. Of course we all fell about with laughter, stuffing cushions into our mouths to stop ourselves choking, while the great man sat there with a face as straight as a spear-handle, timing each line to absolute perfection, and when he had finished he got his Rhodian wine and shortly afterwards passed out. But my uncle was right, of course; if anything, it made me feel fonder of Pericles than I ever had before, if only because he had afforded me such glorious entertainment. To this day I believe that Comedy has very little effect on the part of the human brain that makes political decisions – God only knows what does.

It was not long after that dinner party that Pericles died in the Great Plague, and sure enough, Cratinus was inconsolable for months afterwards. He felt that Pericles had tricked him yet again, slipping quietly out of the world before he had had a chance to savage him properly. He had to tear up the Comedy he had been writing, which he swore was the best thing he had ever done, and immediately started on a new one, in which Pericles is brought up before the Judges of the Dead and condemned to the most frightful punishments, in most of which horse manure plays a prominent part. But he gave it up before it was finished and wrote

17

a miserable little farce about Heracles and Alcestis instead. He dashed it off in a few days just before the deadline for entries for the competition, and to his unutterable disgust it won first prize at that year's Lenaea.

Chapter Two

And now I think it is about time for me to justify the boast I made at the beginning of this book, when I claimed that in my lifetime I have seen all the most remarkable events in our city's history, and tell you about my experience of the Great Plague. After all, that's something you're bound to be interested in, even if you can't be doing with Politics or the Theatre; so we might as well make the most of it. It is, with one exception, the most interesting of the events which has shaped my life, and so I can get on and describe it without having to be clever and witty to retain your attention. This will be a great relief to me.

Mind you, it doesn't necessarily follow that because an event is of great historical importance it will have any significant effect on the lives of the people who were there at the time. I remember there was one very old man in our village when I was a boy who had been in the City when the Persians came. Now you would imagine that seeing the City burnt to the ground and the temples of the Gods levelled with the dust would profoundly affect a young man's character and development; but this was not so at all in this man's case. He was a tomb-robber by vocation, and he had only gone back to the City after the general evacuation to see if many people had left any articles of value behind in their hurry to escape, and when he found that the place was swarming with weird-looking savages with red faces and gold-plated armour, he very sensibly hid in a charcoal heap until they had gone past. When the burning started, he slipped out and escaped through a gap in the Wall with a sack full of small gold and silver statuettes he had found in a house in the Ceramicus, which later provided him with the capital to set up in business as a part-time blacksmith. The great event in his life, which entirely changed his perceptions of the world and the behaviour of mankind, was when the owner of these small gold and silver statuettes caught up with him and had him thrown in the prison.

The Great Plague, then, came early in the war and lasted for two or perhaps three years. I must be honest and confess that my memories of that period are all inclined to run into each other, so that I tend to look back on the plague as happening in the space of about a week; but then, I was young and it's remarkable how quickly you get used to things when you're that age. Recently I heard an account of the war by a very learned and scholarly gentleman – he had been a general at one time, and got himself exiled because of a terrible blunder; whereupon he retired to some safe little town in neutral territory and started writing this monumental *History of the War*, so that when everyone's memories were getting as bad as mine is now he could read them his book and show them that everyone else had been at least as incompetent as he was and probably more so – and he claimed that Pericles died of the plague in the third year of the war, which surprised me very much. But I suppose I prefer to remember the years before the plague to those immediately after it, and so I have made that time seem longer than it actually was. Now I come to consider it, I'm probably not cut out to be a Historian.

Of course, everyone you meet in Athens claims that he had the plague and survived it; somehow it's regarded as a mark of great moral and spiritual merit, as if you have been tried and acquitted by the Gods. Even the little general who wrote the book says he had the plague, and to be fair to him his account of the symptoms is at least recognisable. Mind you, he also gives you the impression that he was there on the spot when all the famous and significant speeches were being made, and since some of these took place simultaneously in opposite corners of Greece, I doubt very much whether he was sitting there with his wax tablets on his knees taking down every word as it cleared the speaker's teeth. I do know for a fact that I did have the plague, and that only the intervention of the Gods saved my life.

The plague arrived in Athens on a grain boat, and was soon making its presence felt in the Corn-Chandlers' Quarter. At first nobody took much notice, since most corn-chandlers are resident foreigners and one more or less makes no great difference to anyone. But soon it began infecting citizens, and then we all realised that we had a major problem on our hands.

My own experience of the plague was this. I had been on a visit to my aunt Nausimache, and there was gossip going around the City that she was having an affair with a rich corn-chandler called Zeuxis, who came from somewhere near Mytilene. In fact, if you have a copy of Cratinus' *Ants* (I don't; I lent it to someone years ago, like a fool) I think you'll find there's a reference to that affair in it. Anyway, the plague was one of those diseases which you can catch from other people, and my guess is that she caught it from Zeuxis and I caught it from her; I distinctly remember her giving me an auntly kiss when we arrived, and wiping it off with the back of my hand when she wasn't looking.

A day or so after this visit, I started getting these quite unbearable pains in the front and sides of my head, as if some idiot had knocked over a brazier inside my brains and they had caught fire. Then my eyes started to itch, just as though I had been peeling onions, and something horrible happened to the inside of my mouth. Even I could tell that my breath smelt like rotten meat, and my tongue was swollen and tender.

My grandfather, who I had gone to live with after my father died – I think I was about twelve at the time – took one look at me, diagnosed plague, and had me locked up in the stable with the goats and donkeys. The last thing he needed, I remember him saying as he put up the bar on the door, was a house full of plague, and if that was the Gods' way of rewarding him for taking in orphans he was going to have to think very seriously about his theological position. Luckily we had a Libyan housemaid at the time, and she had got it into her head that her black skin would protect her from the disease. She reckoned that if she fed me and looked after me and I got well again, my grandfather would be so pleased that he would set her free and let her marry his understeward, and so she brought me out the scraps from the table and a jug of fresh water every day.

So there I was once again, entirely surrounded by goats, and the disease went into its next stage. For about a day I could not stop sneezing and coughing, and I vomited up bile of every imaginable colour; there was one peculiar shade of yellow that I have never seen since, except in some rather expensive Persian tapestries that someone was selling in the market. Then my skin broke out in little blisters which itched unendurably; but I think some God whispered in my ear not to scratch, and I managed not to, somehow. The worst part of it was the thirst, which I simply cannot describe, and here I think my grandfather's treatment of me saved my life. You see, I had only a few cupfuls of water each day, and sometimes nothing at all when the maid forgot or couldn't get away, whereas I have heard since that the people who were able to drink as much as they liked invariably died. In fact, my belief is that once the God saved me from the disease itself, this lack of water stopped me from catching the murderous diarrhoea which killed more people than the plague did, and which inevitably follows the disease itself, like a stray dog following a sausage-maker. After all, what with no food and no water, there was nothing inside me to come out, and so my body was spared the convulsions of the diarrhoea and I survived.

I fully appreciate that I must have been an unlovely companion while the disease was on me, but from that day to this I have not been able to forgive the attitude of the goats and donkeys towards me, which was little short of downright offensive. Did they come and bleat reassuringly over me, and soothe my fevered brow with their tongues, like they are supposed to do in the old stories? Did they hell. They all backed away into the far corner of the stable and didn't even come across to eat the leaves and bean-helm in their mangers, and the hungrier they got, the more they seemed to blame me. This made me feel absolutely dejected, as you can imagine, and for a while I felt like giving the whole thing up.

On the seventh day of my sickness the maid stopped bringing food and water and I resigned myself to death, which was not a concept I had given much thought to previously. I remember thinking that it would be nice not to have to go to school any more, but that it would be rather a shame that no one would ever see one of my Comedies. However, I consoled myself with the thought of meeting my father again beside the waters of Styx, always assuming that I could recognise him after so many years. Then I started worrying about how on earth I was going to pay the fare, since Charon the Ferryman takes nobody across the river unless he pays his obol. Then I remembered hearing somewhere (I think it was in a Comedy) that Charon had finally retired and that an Athenian had bought his pitch, increasing the fare (naturally enough) to two obols, but letting Athenians across for free. This comforted me greatly, since I had been greatly distressed at the thought of spending the rest of time on the wrong side of the river with all the murderers and parricides and people who hadn't been buried properly, and so I settled back to die in peace.

Now I hadn't slept at all since the disease started, and I think I must have fallen asleep then, for I swear I saw Dionysus himself standing over me, leaning on his vinewood staff and wearing a Comic mask and boots, with the floppy leather phallus which all the actors wear in the Comedies dangling from his groin. He seemed very big and fierce and jolly, but I wasn't frightened by him, or particularly surprised to see him there at all.

'Cheer up, Eupolis of Pallene,' he said, and the whole stable seemed to shake, like those caves down south that are supposed to vibrate to the pitch of your voice. 'Pull yourself together and stop snivelling; you'll have to put up with far worse things than this before you see the last of me – in the front row of the Theatre when they hiss that clever Chorus of yours, and in the walled orchard, of course. But remember, you owe me some prizes which you must pay, and I've hand-reared you from a puppy to write me a Comedy or two. If you die now and leave me to make do with that idiot Aristomenes, I'll never forgive you.'

I wanted to promise but I couldn't speak; so I nodded, and kept on nodding, and then I was definitely asleep, because I remember waking up. And when I did wake up, I knew that I was going to live; just as you can feel when you walk into a house whether anyone lives there or not. I know that I just lay there for a very long time, filled with a joy that kept me warm and made me forget how hungry and uncomfortable I was; not because I had escaped death and was clear of the pain of the disease, but because I had seen the God of Comedy and been promised success. It had been well worth the disease, I reckoned, to get that promise.

After a long, long time I remembered that I was starving hungry, and I thought it was time to do something about it. I started shouting at the top of my little voice that I was well again and wanted to be let out, but nobody came; so I assumed that nobody believed me, which was reasonable enough. So, as soon as I felt confident that I had my strength back, I examined the door of the stable, which was barred on the outside and wouldn't budge. Now, after surviving the plague and being promised a Chorus by the God, a little thing like a stable door wasn't going to get in my way, and so I sat down on the manger and thought hard. Unfortunately, probably because the war kept interrupting my education, I had never been taught how to get out of locked stables – unless you count that bit in the *Odyssey* where Odysseus escapes from the Cyclops' cave, which I had been made to learn by heart. But I say that doesn't count, because the circumstances of that case were quite unique and highly unlikely to recur. Just as I was starting to feel baffled, I caught sight of my uncle's old black donkey, and I had an idea.

As soon as I was cured, the animals (who were just as hungry as I was) had resumed eating and drinking, and had finished off all their fodder. They were now getting extremely restive, and I saw how that could be turned to my advantage. You see, this old black donkey of my uncle's, which he kept for hauling olives and ploughing in the season, had the sort of temper you only usually come across in bath-attendants and the commanders of naval vessels, and hunger had not made him any sweeter natured. I'll swear that donkey hated everything and everybody in the world; but what he hated most of all, with the possible exception of other male donkeys and hard work, was being prodded in the ribs with a sharp stick. I happened to have a sharp stick handy – it had been in with the fodder in the mangers – and so I wrestled him over until his hind legs were almost touching the door of the barn. Then I took my stick and gave the donkey the most terrific poke and sure enough he lashed out with his powerful legs and gave the door a tremendous kick. I waited until he had settled down again and prodded him once more, and once again; and that was about as much as the stable door could take. The bar snapped, and at once I shooed the donkey away and threw myself at the door. It gave way, and out I rolled into the blinding sunlight of the yard. As I picked myself up, I saw that the little finger of my left hand had snapped clean off, just like a dead twig, although I hadn't felt a thing. I picked the finger up and stared at it – it had shrivelled away into a little white stick and it smelt quite disgusting – and I tried to fit it back on, but of course it wouldn't stay. Eventually I gave up and threw it away, and a crow who had been busy with something behind the muck-heap fluttered over and took a very tentative peck at it. Apparently, the loss of fingers and toes and even whole hands and feet was quite common among people who had survived the plague, but of course I didn't know that at the time and it startled me considerably.

Well, there I was, safe and sound, and I wanted to see the expressions on everybody's faces when I walked in and told them I was well again. Being a horrible child in many ways I thought I would give them a surprise, so I crept over to the back door and tiptoed in to the inner room, where I expected my grandfather would be sleeping after his midday meal. But he wasn't there; instead I saw my mother, sitting bolt upright in her chair in front of her spinning-wheel, as dead as Agamemnon. I could see from the state of her and the horrible expression on her face that she had died of the plague; typically she had stayed at her household duties to the last, so that Hermes would be able to report to the Judges of the Dead that she had died as a woman should. That was my mother all over.

I found our Syrian houseboy doubled up in the corner of the inner room – he had taken off his sandal and bitten clean through the thongs – while the Libyan maid was lying in the storeroom. The pain had clearly been too much for her to bear, poor creature, and she had cut her own throat with the fine ivory-handled razor my mother used for shaving her legs and armpits. However, I could find no sign of my grandfather anywhere in the house, and I began to hope that he had somehow survived, and maybe even gone to get help. But I found him, too, a little way down the street, which was utterly quiet and deserted, the way an Athenian street never is. He was in one of those big stone troughs set up to catch rainwater in the dictator Pisistratus' time, and I guess that he found the thirst so unendurable that he had jumped in and drowned. It was a sad way for such a man to die, for he had been at the battle of Plataea, when the Athenians and the Spartans had defeated King Xerxes' army and killed his great general Mardonius.

It was a most peculiar feeling to come out of that stable and find that all my family and household had died without letting me know. While I had been ill, I had assumed that I was the only person in the whole of Athens to be afflicted, and that if and when I ever got out of there the world outside would be roughly the same as it had been when I went in. As I stood there looking at my grandfather floating in the rain-trough, I must confess that

I felt little or no grief or sadness, and ever since then I have never been able to take the Choruses in the Tragedies very seriously. You know what I mean; the Messenger bustles on with the news of the great disaster, and at once the Chorus start moaning and singing *Aiai* and *Hottotoi*, and all those other things that people are supposed to say when they're upset but never do; and then twenty lines or so later they've pulled themselves together again and are saying that the Gods are just. Whereas, in my experience at any rate, I find that bad news takes at least a day to sink in properly, and it's only after people have stopped sympathising and are saying what a callous brute I am that I start going to pieces. Well, there you are; I felt no great urge to lament or tear my hair, only a sensation which I can best describe as a Godlike detachment, as the Gods must feel when they look down and see mortal men. After all, I had survived and everyone else in the whole world hadn't; this created a division between them and me as wide as that which separates the immortal Gods from mortal men. I couldn't feel any sorrow, or even any involvement, just as a human being can never feel involved when he pours boiling water on an ants' nest and so wipes out a city which in their terms might be as great as Athens or Troy. Perhaps, after all, I was too young to have feelings, or I was stunned by the sheer scale of the disaster. But I don't think so; I felt the same way when I was a grown man in the walled orchard, and that was just as great a disaster, or maybe even greater.

So there I was, standing by the rain-trough and thinking these deep thoughts, when I saw a man in armour hurrying up the street with his cloak round his face to keep the bad air out. I was just thinking that this was pretty foolish, since there is no special magic in a cloak that can counteract the effects of plague and death, and that was just another example of the folly of these puny mortals, when the man caught sight of me and nearly jumped out of his skin. Of course, I said to myself, he's frightened at seeing a God: I must reassure him; so I called out, 'Don't be afraid, I won't hurt you.'

27

'The hell with you,' said the man. 'You've got the plague, haven't you?'

'No,' I replied, 'I had it for a while but the God cured me. You're quite safe, I won't infect you.'

He didn't look at all convinced, so I started describing the symptoms and how I had recovered, and then he wasn't so frightened. It turned out that a fellow soldier of his had had the plague and survived, and so he knew I was telling the truth. He came over and sat down on the edge of the trough, with his cloak still up around his ears; but I could see his face. He was about twenty-two, with a long thin nose and sandy hair just starting to recede from his temples.

'What's your name?' I asked him.

'Callicrates,' he replied. 'I'm looking for the house of a man called Euthydemus son of Euxis, of Pallene.'

'The house is down there,' I said, 'just before you get to the corner; but if you're looking for Euthydemus himself, you'll find him right behind you.' For of course Euthydemus was my grandfather's name and Euxis was his father, and our village and deme was Pallene.

Callicrates looked round but could see nobody; then he caught sight of the body floating in the trough and started violently.

'For God's sake,' he said, 'what do you want to go playing tricks like that for? You nearly gave me a fit.'

'Honestly,' I said solemnly, 'that's Euthydemus there. I should know, because I'm his grandson, Eupolis. All the rest of us who were in the house are dead, except me. The God cured me, like I said.'

Callicrates stared at me, as if I had just told him that Babylon had fallen. 'Is that true?' he said, after a moment.

'Of course it's true,' I said. 'If you don't believe me, you can go and have a look for yourself, but I wouldn't advise it. They all had the plague, you see.'

He was silent for a very long time, staring at the knots on the thongs of his sandals as if he expected them to burst into flower. Then he turned his head and looked at me gravely.

28

'Eupolis,' he said, 'I am your cousin, the son of your mother's elder brother Philodemus. My father and I have been away at the war and we've only just come home. As soon as they told us about the plague my father went off to see if our house was all right, and he sent me to look for his sister.'

'I'm afraid she's dead,' I said gently, for I could tell that the shock of seeing my grandfather had unnerved him and I wanted to spare him any further pain; he was only a mortal and might be upset. 'But she died at her spinning-wheel and I'm sure the Ferryman will take her over for free, since she was Athenian on both sides. Have you got any water in your bottle? I'm really thirsty and I don't want to drink the water in the trough.'

He handed me the bottle and I'm afraid I drank it all, without thinking where we would get any more. But Callicrates didn't say anything, although I expect he was thirsty too. Then he opened his knapsack and handed me a piece of wheat bread, white and still quite soft, as good as cake.

Callicrates smiled when he saw how much I was enjoying it, and he said that where he had been they ate wheat bread as a matter of course and imported all their wine from Judaea.

I hope I haven't given you the impression that Callicrates was a coward, because he wasn't. He had made up his mind to go into the house, which not many men would have done, and the only reason he did it was for my sake. You see, he knew that if there was a lawsuit about property someone would have to give evidence about how everyone had died, and I was too young to take the oath. So he screwed his face even more tightly into his cloak, took a deep breath, and plunged in. He wouldn't let me come with him, and I was secretly relieved, since I no longer felt that the people in the house had anything to do with me. He was gone about five minutes and then came back, shivering all over as if he had been out in the snow in nothing but a tunic.

'Right,' he said, 'I've seen everything I need to see. Let's go to my father's house.'

That sounded like an excellent suggestion, since I liked Philodemus; you may remember that he was the one who arranged for me to meet Cratinus, and he knew a lot of people and was always quoting from plays. He was a small, jolly man and I thought it would be more fun living with him than with my grandfather, who had never really liked me very much.

'Callicrates,' I said, 'did you really have to go in there?'

'Yes,' he said, 'like I told you.'

'There won't really be a lawsuit, will there?' I said. 'I thought that was only when people did something wrong, like stealing.'

He grinned, and the cloak fell off his face. 'Don't you believe it,' he said. And he was right, too, as it turned out. There was the most almighty lawsuit, and if he hadn't gone into the house we would have lost, because of some legal presumption or other.

Whatever else I may forget, such as my name and where I live, I shall always remember that walk through the City. Everywhere we went, the streets were either totally deserted or frantic with activity; and where there were people, they all seemed to have bodies with them. There were bodies in handcarts, or on the backs of mules, or slung over men's shoulders like sacks, so that it looked for all the world like the grapes being brought down for the vintage. Some were taking them to be properly burnt (there was no space to bury anyone, not even the smallest child) but they had to hurry, because if anyone saw a pyre burning and no one watching he would pitch the body he was carrying on to it and go away as quickly as he could. Others were actually digging shallow trenches in the streets to bury their dead; in fact there was a lot of trouble about it later on, when people started scraping up these trenches to recover the coins that the relatives had left in the corpses' mouths for the Ferryman, and the whole plague nearly started all over again. Then there were many people who dumped dead bodies in the water-tanks and cisterns, partly because they reckoned that water would wash away the infection but mostly because by that stage they couldn't care less; and only a complete idiot left the door of his stable open, or even his house; because if he did he would be sure to find two or three corpses there when he came home, neatly stacked like faggots of wood. Really, it was like watching a gang of thieves desperately getting rid of stolen property when the Constables arrive.

Naturally I wanted to stop and watch, since I felt that if ever I wanted to try my hand at a Tragedy or a Poem this would make the most wonderful set piece; the plague in the Greek camp at Troy, for instance, or the pestilence at Thebes at the start of an Oedipus. But Callicrates just wanted to get away as quickly as he possibly could, and he virtually pulled my arms out of their sockets in his haste to get home.

'For God's sake, stop dawdling, can't you?' he said several times. 'You may be immune, but I'm not.'

And so I had to let all those marvellous details go to waste and scamper along at his heels, like a dog who can smell hares in the corn but has to keep up with his master. Eventually we reached Philodemus' house, which was mercifully clear of infection, and I was just able to eat a huge bowl of porridge with sausage sliced up in it and drink a cup of wine and honey before falling fast asleep.

Apparently I slept for the best part of a day and a night, and while I was asleep Philodemus and Callicrates took out the cart, fetched the bodies out of my grandfather's house, and cremated them honourably. Of course my grandfather himself was saturated with water from the trough and wouldn't burn, so they had to dry him in the sun like goat's meat for a journey; but they didn't tell me that until several years later. They performed all the proper rites, however, mixing the ashes with honey and wine and milk and burying them in an urn with all the right invocations, and I'm very grateful for that, since properly speaking it was my job. When they got back, both Philodemus and Callicrates washed themselves very thoroughly and even burnt the clothes they had been wearing when they handled the bodies; Philodemus had got it into his head that the plague was somehow directly connected with all the dirt and squalor that went with having the whole of Attica cooped up inside the City walls. But Philodemus always did have a thing about cleanliness, even to the extent of having all the household refuse put into jars and dumped in the next street.

So I came to live with Philodemus and Callicrates, which I suppose was the greatest benefit I derived from the plague. I say the greatest, since of course with so many of our family dead I was the heir to a considerable amount of property. It's true what they say, after all; men die, but land goes on for ever, and in those days people were only just starting to realise that land could be bought and sold. As a result of the heavy mortality among my kinsmen (most of whom, I confess, I had never even heard of) I stood to inherit a considerable holding.

Of course, there were endless lawsuits. About the only human activity not interrupted by the plague was litigation; indeed, with so many deaths the probate Courts were almost as busy as the political and treason Courts, and the litigants themselves never seemed to fall ill. Some of them were survivors like myself, laying claim to family estates, but even the others seemed to stay clear of the disease, at least while their case was being heard. Cratinus said that all the hot air and garlic fumes released in Court kept away the infection, and that Hades was in no hurry to crowd his nice orderly palace with noisy Athenian litigants, all shouting and calling each other names; he preferred to take quiet, honest men who would be a credit to his establishment. Cratinus, incidentally, went everywhere throughout the City visiting sick friends, helping them to laugh their way through the final agonising stages of the disease, and then burying them when even his jokes could keep them alive no longer. He claimed that his preservation was due to the prophylactic effects of cheap wine, but I prefer to think that Dionysus was looking after him too.

Philodemus conducted all my lawsuits for me, and although we lost some things we should have kept – I particularly regret five acres of vines down in the plains near Eleusis – I ended up with a personal estate of no less than sixty acres. Over half this land was hill-country and so no use for anything except scenic effect – although the land had been in our family since Theseus was a boy, apparently none of my ancestors had ever got around to removing the stones from the ground – and so my estate was in fact not nearly so impressive as it sounds; but it was easily enough to elevate me into the Cavalry class, 'and with a little bit over in case of bad harvests', as Philodemus put it. He was, for an Athenian, an almost divinely honest man, and apart from a few fields in Phyle and my grandfather's stake in the silver mines he handed all my property over to me when I was old enough to take charge of it, with a written account and record of the expenses of maintenance and repair to justify his use of the income. Yet he was no more than comfortably off himself, and paid for my keep while I was in his house entirely from his own resources, as if I had been his own son, so I never had the heart to sue him for the return of the stake in the mines.

The plague did not abate for two years, and learned men (like that little general) say that it killed one man in three. It spread from the City to our men in the army and the fleet, but somehow we never managed to pass it on to the Spartans; and it nearly brought the war to a premature end. But after a while the people in the City became resigned to it – it is quite remarkable what city dwellers will put up with, so long as they feel that everyone else is having just as horrible a time as they are – and carried on their lives as best they could. They redesigned the economy of the City slightly to accommodate their changed patterns of living, so that more people got out of agriculture altogether and started to specialise in the urban industries, like sitting on juries, metalwork and burglary. In fact, quite a substantial number of men caught the plague from breaking into infected houses, which caused considerable amusement to their neighbours.

One thing I must mention is the prophecy, because it

33

was the one great topic of discussion wherever people still met to talk. As soon as the plague became widespread, someone or other dug up an ancient oracle, which had actually been carved on stone in the time of the celebrated Solon. It went: *'The Spartans come bringing war, and hateful Death in the vanguard.'*

Most people took this as a reference to the plague, since in Solon's time the word Death was commonly used as a synonym for plague, particularly in poetry; but some grammarians and learned teachers disputed the reading for sound philological reasons which have slipped my memory, and amended the line as follows: *'The Spartans come bringing war, and hateful Dearth in the vanguard.'*

This, they said, meant that there would soon be a famine, compared to which the plague would be about as serious as a bad cold; and of course this caused great anxiety and panic-buying of food. Those who accepted the original reading replied by saying that the learned scholars were all in the pay of the corn-dealers, who were the ones who had started the plague by catching it themselves in the first place, and that something ought to be done about what was plainly a conspiracy. The City was soon divided into two rival camps, the Dearth-men and the Death-men (we were Death-men, I remember, except for a cousin of mine called Isocles who had a share in a grain ship) and these two factions took to going round the streets after dark burning each other's houses. This went on for a long time and ended up with a full-scale riot in the Market Square, during which several silversmiths' stalls and a butcher's shop were looted.

Chapter Three

Not so long ago I went to the Theatre – I think it was the second day of the Lenaea – after staying up late the night before with some friends. I was so tired that I fell asleep towards the end of the first of the three Tragedies and only woke up half-way through the second. I believe the first one was a play about Oedipus, and the second was some nonsense about Odysseus; I can't remember terribly well, to be honest with you. Anyway, when I woke up, to start with I thought we were still in the Oedipus play (it didn't seem to matter terribly much – it was that sort of play) and when I realised that it wasn't I was totally unable to work out what was going on. Eventually I came to the conclusion that it was something to do with Perseus and the Gorgon, and it was on that basis that I followed it through to the final exit of the Chorus. In fact it was several weeks before someone happened to mention what the second play that day had been about, and at first I didn't believe him.

Bearing this unfortunate experience in mind, I feel that I ought at this stage in my story to clarify exactly what is going on, just in case any of my readers has got it into his head that this book of mine is set in the middle of the Persian Wars or the dictatorship of Pisistratus. You see, I cannot in all conscience assume that you know the background to this story, even if you are an Athenian; after all, it is a well-known fact that we Athenians are not particularly good at history, and the only way we can be sure when something happened or who did what two or three generations ago is by asking a foreigner. I suppose this is because we Athenians make all the history in Greece, and just as you generally find that a weaver's own cloak is threadbare and worn and a potter's house is full of chipped and unglazed crockery, so we Athenians are most disdainful of our own principal export and take no great interest in it.

Now, of course, I am faced with the problem of where to start. For example, I would be perfectly happy to take you right back to the Heroic past, when the Gods walked undisguised among men and Athena competed with Poseidon as to who should be Athens' patron deity. After all, that sort of thing is extremely easy to do – I could fill a whole roll with it and never have to stop and think once – but I suspect that you would lose interest fairly quickly and start worrying about getting your winter barley in or manuring your vines. On balance, I think the best place for me to start would be just after the end of the Great Patriotic War, when all the Greeks were united against the Persian invaders and the world was a very different place.

Even before the war we Athenians had not been able to grow enough food in Attica to feed ourselves, and when the Persians broke into Attica, destroyed the City and dug up or burned all our vines and olive trees, we were all in a rather desperate situation. As you well know, it takes five years at the very least for a vine to become sufficiently established to yield harvestable grapes, while an olive tree can easily take twenty years or more to come to maturity. The Athenian economy was based on the export of wine and oil, in return for imported grain; our only other exportable commodity was silver, and the silver mines were all owned by the State and leased out to rich men, so there was no way that that source of income could be used to feed the people.

The one thing we did have was warships. You see, shortly before the Persians invaded, a man called Themistocles was put in charge of our long-running feud with the island of Aegina, and he had used the revenues from the silver mines to build and fit out the biggest and best fleet of warships in the whole of Greece. It was this fleet that we used to evacuate the City when the Persians came, and to defeat the Persians conclusively at the battle of Salamis.

The important thing to bear in mind about a warship is that it takes a considerable number of people to man it and make it work, and all these people have to be paid or they will get out of the warship and go away. In fact, a warship (or fleet of warships) is probably the most efficient way of providing gainful employment for men with no particular skills that has yet been devised by the human brain, and Themistocles realised this. On the one hand, he had a city full of people unable to make a living off their land, and on the other hand he had a harbour crammed with redundant battleships which had recently proved themselves capable of making mincemeat out of the most powerful navy in the world.

At the time, Athens was still part of the Anti-Persian League, the confederacy of Greek cities hastily formed to resist the invaders. By all accounts it was a wonderful thing while it lasted, for it was the first time in the history of the world when the Greeks had not all been at war with each other. Having driven the Great King out of Greece, the League was obviously redundant, and there was no reason why it should not be dissolved so that everyone could go back to cutting each other's throats, as their fathers and grandfathers had done. But for some reason the League continued to exist.

Now the best theory I have heard is that most of the cities of Greece were in roughly the same situation as Athens; their economies were in ruins because of the war, and nobody wanted to go home and face the mess. They greatly preferred drawing regular pay for fighting the Persians, and if the Persians had all gone back to Persia the only thing to be done was to follow them there. So they did; and for a while they had a perfectly splendid time sacking cities and looting treasuries. But then some of the Greeks, particularly those who lived on the islands in the Aegean and on the coast of Asia Minor, thought that it was high time they went home and started farming again, on the principle that sooner or later the supply of Persians would run out and they might as well get back to work before the soil had got completely out of hand.

By this stage, Themistocles had had his Great Idea, and so the Athenians pretended to be terribly upset at this defection by their allies, and spoke very eloquently at League meetings about avenging the fallen heroes and the desecrated temples of Athens. The islanders were profoundly embarrassed and didn't know what to say; and then the Athenians, with a great show of relenting and making concessions, said that they quite understood, and as a special favour they, the Athenians, would carry on the Great Crusade on behalf of all the Greeks, until the Persian menace had been wiped off the face of the earth and the anger of the Gods had been fully appeased. All the islanders had to do was contribute a small sum of money each year towards general expenses, as a gesture of solidarity; we would provide the ships and the men, and the loot would be shared out equally at the end of each campaigning season.

Naturally enough the islanders thought this was eminently reasonable; either the Athenians would wipe out the Persians or the Persians would wipe out the Athenians, and either way the world would be rid of a nuisance. So they swore a great many oaths and undertook to pay a small contribution each year into the League treasury. The hat was taken round, and the Athenians used the money to build more ships and fill them with Athenian crews, until nearly every adult Athenian who disliked the idea of hard work was adequately provided for. Shortly afterwards, however, when the islanders began to notice that the Athenians hadn't been near the Persians for some considerable time and the Great Crusade seemed to have lapsed, they stopped paying the small contribution and declared that the matter was closed.

The next thing that happened was that the Athenian navy turned up under the walls of their cities looking extremely hostile and demanding to know what had become of that year's gesture of solidarity. When the islanders tried to explain that the war was over, the Athenians were greatly amused and replied that on the contrary, unless the Tribute (as the small contribution was now called) was paid at once, plus the incidental expenses of besieging the island and a substantial Loyalty Premium, the war would begin immediately. Now an island, being entirely surrounded by water, is particularly vulnerable to overwhelming seapower, and the islanders realised that there was nothing for it but to pay or be killed. So they paid, and with the money so obtained the Athenians built more warships and hired yet more oarsmen.

Thus was formed the Great Athenian Empire, previously known as the Anti-Persian League, and for a while it seemed as if there was nothing that anyone could do about it. The Athenians were able to buy all the imported grain they needed, and there were no political difficulties since the City was a democracy and enough of the citizens were on the payroll to constitute a majority. In addition, the professional oarsmen mostly lived in or near the City, while those Athenians who had wanted nothing to do with the idea and were struggling to get their land back into cultivation tended to live out in the villages of Attica and were usually far too busy tilling the soil to spare a whole day every few weeks to attend Assembly. When there was no serious rowing to be done, the oarsmen were able to get on with the work of reclaiming and planting out their own land, which was not too difficult with their navy pay to tide them over while the vines and olives matured, and in this way the Athenian democracy took on its unique and unmistakable form. Power lay with the poorest and most numerous section of the population, who naturally enough voted for the system that provided for them. Anyone who wanted to succeed in politics had to make friends with the oarsmen and buy their favour with appropriate measures, entertain them with clever speeches, or both. Short of giving away free wheat on the steps of the Propylaea, the scope for buying favour was limited to a few well-tried and unsubtle methods which anyone could use, and so making and listening to political speeches became the national pastime and obsession of the Athenian people. The oarsmen had plenty of leisure when there was no naval action in hand, since most of them by definition had only small holdings of land to work (if they had more than a few acres they would qualify for the Heavy Infantry or Cavalry class, who are far too grand to live off the proceeds of State piracy) and there is no better way known to man of spending an idle afternoon than sitting in Assembly with a jar of dried figs listening to clever speeches and then voting to annex a few more cities.

This new style of politics called for a new breed of politicians. There was no longer much point in striving for the high offices of State now that the real power lay with Assembly. But in theory at least, any Athenian citizen was allowed to address Assembly and propose a measure, and it soon became obvious that the way to get on in politics was to make speeches and propose measures, as often and as loudly as possible. It was also open to any Athenian citizen to prosecute any other Athenian citizen in the lawcourts, and Athens has a great wealth of un-Athenian Activities legislation specifically designed to be useful to politicians. By this time we Athenians had already developed our wonderful judicial system, whereby all trials are heard by mass juries of several hundred citizens; all that remained to perfect the system was the introduction of a living wage for jury service. Thus was created the Athenian professional juryman, who gets up before dawn to stand in line for a place on the jury. If he gets there early enough he is assured of entertainment of the very highest quality from the speechmakers plus a day's wages at the end of the performance. This way of life is particularly attractive to older and less active men who can neither dig nor row, and they are extremely careful to convict anyone who threatens to destroy their livelihood by proposing political reforms. On the other hand, they are always grateful to people who do a lot of prosecuting, since for every prosecution there has to be a jury, and these people are very rarely convicted of anything, even if they are genuinely guilty.

And that, more or less, is how Athens came to have the most pure and perfect democracy the world has ever seen, in which every man had a right to be heard, the law was open to all, and nobody need go hungry if he was not too proud to play his part in the oppression of his fellow Greeks and the judicial murder of inconvenient statesmen. The by-products of the system included the perfection of oratory and a universal love among all classes of society of the spoken word in its most delicate and refined forms. No wonder we are a nation of aesthetes.

The only problem was Sparta. Ever since Zeus, whose sense of humour is not particularly attractive to us mortals, put Athens and Sparta on the same strip of land, there has been war between the two cities. Asking Athens and Sparta to live together without fighting is like expecting night to marry day, or winter to form an offensive and defensive alliance with summer. Having unquestionably the best land army in the world, the Spartans generally had the best of these wars; but since the population of Sparta was small and spent most of its time reminding its own empire in the south of Greece about the merits of absolute loyalty, it had never been able to take any lasting measures against Athens, such as burning it to the ground and sowing salt on the ashes.

Sparta had been the nominal leader of the League during the war, but as soon as it became clear that the Persians could only be defeated at sea the real leadership passed to Athens, and since the Spartans were busy with violent internal politics as soon as the war ended, there was nothing they could do to stop us building our empire in the way I have just described. As soon as they were clear of their local problems, however, they began to get seriously worried, for it was obvious that as soon as the Athenian Empire was strong enough, it would use every ounce of its new strength to stamp Sparta flat, liberate the subject races, and remove the one serious obstacle to Athenian supremacy in Greece. So, with a degree of hypocrisy remarkable even for them, the Spartans set themselves up as the champions of the oppressed and enslaved and demanded that we stop extorting tribute from our allies and disband the fleet.

And that is how Athens came to be at war with Sparta, eleven years after I was born. One of the first Athenians to be killed was my father, who went with the expeditionary force to Potidaea. By that stage, Themistocles had proved beyond question that he was the wisest and cleverest man in the whole of Athens, and had paid the inevitable penalty. As I recall, he escaped with his life and immediately went to the court of the Great King of Persia, who gave him a city to govern, and if he had managed to conceal his cleverness a little better he might have lived to be an old man. But he contrived to avoid being killed, for he took his own life by drinking bull's blood, stylish to the very end. A number of marginally less clever Athenians took his place in turn, in particular the glorious but profoundly stupid Cimon, who actually believed that the purpose of the League was to fight the Persians, until the celebrated Pericles came to power, just as the Spartan situation was beginning to come to a head.

In fact, it was this same Pericles who gave me my first set of armour. You see, in those days it was the law that when a man's father was killed on active service, the State provided his son with a suit of armour absolutely free, which is a very generous gesture in view of the price of bronze, if not exactly tactful. There is a touching little ceremony, and the General for the year makes a speech before handing each bewildered infant his breastplate, shield and helmet. Now in those days the General was elected, and Pericles' power depended on his being elected General every year – it was the one great office of State that still retained even vestiges of actual power – so it was natural enough that he should make as much as possible of this great speech of his, in front of the whole population of the City. Since I was already a budding dramatist I was extremely excited about the coming performance and looked forward to it with the greatest possible anticipation. For I would be placed right up close to the Great Man, in an ideal position to make mental notes of all his mannerisms and personal peculiarities, all of which I would lovingly reproduce in dramatic form.

You remember I told you about that little general who wrote that incredibly dull and pompous history of the war, the one who thought he'd had the plague? Well, I came across a copy of the first part of his book the other day; I had bought some cheese and someone had used the immortal work to wrap it in, which shows the degree of aesthetic judgement our Attic cheesemongers have. Before putting it on the fire I looked up a few things in it, and to my amazement I found that the little general had included the speech Pericles made that day. In fact, he had made a great fuss of it, using it as a convenient place to stuff in all the things he thought Pericles would have said if he had been half as clever as the little general, and by the time he'd finished with it the speech bore no relation at all to what I remembered Pericles saying; and I think I ought to know, since I was actually there, in the front row, studying the whole thing with the greatest possible care for the reasons I have just given you. But then again, my memory is not what it was. Still, I feel I ought to put down just a little bit of what I remember Pericles saying, just to set the record straight; and then if anyone else who was actually there reads it, he can either confirm that I am right or go around telling his friends that Eupolis of Pallene is a silly old fool, which may well be the truth.

I remember that we all walked out to the public cemetery, which actually lies outside the walls of the City, and that it was a remarkably warm day for the time of year. Now I had been dressed up in my smartest clothes and had some sort of foul sweet-smelling oil daubed all over my hair, and I was feeling distinctly uncomfortable – the oil on my head seemed to be frying my brains – and the whole thing seemed entirely unlike the way a funeral should be. On the one hand there were plenty of women howling away and gouging their cheeks with their nails until they bled, the way women do at funerals; but the men seemed to regard the whole thing as a party of some sort, for a lot of them had brought little flasks of wine and jars of olives and figs, and were chattering away as if it were market-day. There were sausage-sellers hovering around the edges of the crowd, and the very sight of them made me feel hungry (I love sausages) but of course I wasn't allowed to have one since I was supposed to be mourning my dead. As it happens, I didn't feel particularly grief-stricken, since I couldn't associate all this fuss and performance with my father's death, and the thought that his body was in one of the big cypresswood trunks trundling along on the carriers' carts seemed distinctly improbable. Still, I think I would have been able to make a reasonable job of looking solemn if it hadn't been for the flies. The smelly stuff on my hair seemed to have drawn out every fly in Greece, and I defy anyone to look serious and dignified if he can't see where he's going for a thick cloud of flies. I tried my best, but in the end I had to start swatting at them, and that was it as far as I was concerned.

It's a strange feeling being part of a huge crowd of moving people, and I don't suppose I had ever seen so many human beings congregated together in one place before. It wasn't the same as the Theatre, where the people don't all arrive at once. It was as if the whole world was crowded into one small space, with some of them feeling miserable and others feeling happy, and most of them feeling slightly bored and wishing they were doing something else, just as you'd expect. As we came near the cemetery it occurred to me that I was going to have to step out in front of all these people to collect a suit of armour, and I knew in my liver that I was bound to make a fool of myself – drop the helmet or send the shield rolling off on its rim into the crowd like a hoop – and for a while I was paralysed with fear in the way that only a small and self-conscious child can be.

At last it was time for Pericles to make his speech, and the crowd divided to let him through. It was the first time I had seen him close to, and it was rather a shock. I had been expecting a tall, important-looking man with plenty of presence and bearing, and sure enough that was what

I saw. I followed this figure with my eyes, dazzled by the dignity of the man; he was wearing a suit of burnished bronze armour that shone like gold and his back was as straight as a column. Trotting along beside him was a chubby little fellow with a strange-shaped head and rather thin legs, who I took to be his secretary, since he was carrying a scroll of paper. These two made their way to the side of the coffins, and the glorious fellow stopped. I held my breath, waiting for him to start speaking, but he just stood there, while the little chubby man climbed up on to the small wooden stage and cleared his throat, rather like a sheep in the early morning. Everyone immediately stopped wailing and chattering, and I realised that the man who I had taken to be the secretary was Pericles himself.

Once he started to speak, of course, there was no mistaking him, and when I began listening to that rich, elegant voice the man himself seemed to grow a head taller and lose about a stone in weight in front of my very eyes. It's extraordinary the difference a person's voice makes to the way you perceive him. I remember when I was in the army in Sicily there was a huge man with a head of hair like a lion's mane, but with the silliest little voice you've ever heard in your life. Before I heard him speak, I had always taken care to be near him in the line, since he looked like a useful person to be near in the event of fighting. As soon as he opened his mouth I revised this opinion and kept well clear of him, since it is well known that freaks tend to come to a bad end.

Where was I? Oh yes. Pericles cleared his throat and began to speak, and for the first few minutes everyone was spellbound. But after a while, I began to feel strangely uncomfortable with this wonderful speech. He was speaking tremendously well, even I could tell that; but he didn't actually seem to be saying anything. The words just sort of bubbled out of him, like one of those beautiful little springs you see in the mountains after the rain, and then soak away without leaving any trace of moisture behind. I particularly remember this bit, which doesn't appear anywhere in the little general's version. See what you make of it.

'Men of Athens,' said Pericles, 'when we say that these glorious heroes died for liberty, what exactly do we mean by liberty? Is it the liberty of the individual, to do what he pleases when he pleases? Can this be the sort of liberty for which brave men would selflessly lay down their lives? Is that rather not a form of lawlessness and self-indulgence? No, surely we mean the liberty of our great and imperishable City, which will still be here, in one form or another, when we are all long since dead and buried. For no man can be free while his fellow citizen is in chains, and no one man can claim to live in a free city when his brother Athenian is not every bit as free as he is. It is precisely this, men of Athens, which these comrades of ours shed their priceless blood for, and that same liberty shall be their memorial when all the temples of the Gods have fallen into dust and the statues of famous men are buried by the sands of Time.'

I wanted to interrupt at this point, for the celebrated Pericles had just said that the City would always be here, and now he was saying that the temples would one day fall down and the statues in the Market Square would get covered up with sand. In short, I was feeling terribly confused and I didn't think much of a public speaker who allowed his audience to lose the thread of what he was saying. But everyone else in the audience was standing there with his mouth open, as if this was some message from the Gods, and I remember thinking how stupid I must be to have missed the point of it all.

Then the great speech came to a splendid but largely obscure end, and it was time for the presentation of the armour. We children were formed up in an orderly queue, with me somewhere towards the end, and a large cart full of trussed-up breastplates, shields, helmets and leg-guards was backed carefully into the space by the rostrum. A couple of men let down the tail-gate and started unloading suits of armour and reading off the names, and the recipients walked forwards, were embraced by Pericles (who seemed to have shrunk back

46

into a chubby little fellow once again) and clanked off into the crowd to be fussed over by their mothers. After what seemed like years I heard my name, and so I took a deep breath, prayed to Dionysus for luck, and plodded across to the rostrum. By this stage the two men who were unloading the armour were feeling tired and thirsty, and they bundled the great mass of metalwork into my arms and virtually shoved me at Pericles, who tried to embrace me and nearly lacerated his arm on the sharp rim of the brand-new shield. Without altering the expression of dignified grandeur on his face he whispered, 'Watch out, you clumsy little toad, you nearly had my arm off,' then he dragged me towards him, gave me a token squeeze, and pushed me away. I was so intent on keeping hold of all that armour that I bumped into the next child on his way up to the rostrum and knocked him clean off his feet. After a journey that seemed longer than all the wanderings of Odysseus put together I found my way back to my place in the crowd, breathed a deep sigh of relief, and let go of the armour. Of course it all fell to the ground with the most almighty clang, and everyone in the crowd seemed to turn round and stare at me. I hated that suit of armour from that day forward, and it didn't bring me a great deal of good luck, as you will see in due course.

Well, a year or so later Pericles was dead, as I have told you. I suppose as a Historian I should consider myself lucky to have met such an important and significant man, but I don't. I think it would have been much better if my father hadn't been killed and I had never received a suit of public armour. My excuse for this deplorable attitude is that although I am a Historian now, I wasn't one at the time – in fact, I'm not sure that the writing of History had been invented then – and so my impression of the whole business was formed without the benefit of the Historian's instinct. As for Pericles himself, I have managed in a quite extraordinary way not to let my meeting with him influence the vaguely superhuman image of him that I have to this day. The dumpy little man with the funny head, I argue, can't have been the glorious leader who led the

City in the days before the war, and neither can he have been the spectacular monster of depravity that springs to mind whenever I hear one of my contemporaries singing a passage from a play by Cratinus after a good night out. Those two beings had, and still have, a life of their own, and it's enough to make you believe in all that nonsense you hear these days from the men who hang around talking in the Gymnasium about the Immortality of the Soul and the Existence of the Essential Forms.

In fact, all this remembering the past has got me confused, and I find it difficult sometimes to come to terms with the fact that I was there in those days and mixed up in all those great events which are now thought worthy of being recorded. There's a bit in the *Odyssey* that's quite like this strange sensation; Odysseus has been shipwrecked on some benighted island miles from anywhere, with all his ships lost and his men drowned, and nobody has the faintest idea who he is. But he's sitting there in the King's hall, eating his porridge and minding his own business, and the minstrel starts singing a tale of ancient valour, all about the legendary hero Odysseus and the fall of Troy. For a moment our hero thinks of standing up and saying 'That's me', but he doesn't bother; after all, it's a hero they're singing about and not him at all, and he never did the wonderful deeds that are being attributed to him.

Come now, Eupolis, return to your story while you are still within a long bowshot of coherence. Pericles' policy for fighting the Great War was nothing if not simple; he reckoned that since any major land battle between Athens and Sparta would be bound to result in a decisive Spartan victory, it would be a shrewd move on his part to delete major land battles from his programme of events. Instead, he crowded the population of Attica into the City whenever so much as the toe of a Spartan sandal crossed the border, and sent out the fleet to cause legitimised mayhem up and down the coast of the Spartan possessions in the Peloponnese. The Spartan army came bounding into Attica like a dog after a cat, only to find that the cat climbed up a tree and refused to come down to fight. So the Spartans amused themselves as best they could by chopping down our newly matured olive trees and rooting up our vines like a lot of wild pigs, and then went home again, having achieved nothing that a really good thunderstorm couldn't have done twice as thoroughly in half the time. With the tribute-money pouring in and the grain ships jostling each other for space in the Piraeus we were none the worse off for the annual burning of our crops – indeed, some of the people who think that agriculture is a science and not a lottery declared that the annual destructions prevented us from overworking the soil as we have been doing for generations and would result in bumper harvests once the war was over. Now this was an exaggeration, needless to say, and it stands to reason that the plague would have been far less serious had the City not been crammed to bursting-point with human beings. But by and large the policy of Pericles would have worked if we had had the patience to persevere with it, and if Pericles had survived.

Which is much the same as saying that we could grow far more to the acre if only it rained more often. One of the hallmarks of an Athenian is his impatience and his restlessness, and when you coop all the Athenians in the world up inside a walled city, this characteristic becomes more marked than ever. Another thing that happens is that all these Athenians will go to Assembly and vote for things just to pass the time. For the first time in history, the ideal on which our democracy is based was being put into action; all the citizens of Athens did go to Assembly and listen to the speeches, and of course the result was absolute chaos. Simple-minded straightforward men from the back end of Attica suddenly found out how their State was being run, and of course they wanted to play too. Even Pericles couldn't have kept control of fifty-odd thousand thinking Athenians for very long.

By God, though, it made the City an interesting place to live in (though decidedly squalid), having all those people hanging around with nothing at all to do except talk. It may just be the exaggeration of childhood memory, but I'll swear the City hummed just like a beehive, so that wherever you went you weren't far from the sound of human voices. With no work to do and not much money to spend, the only available pleasure was the pleasure of words. If ever there was a time and a place to be an aspiring Comic poet, that was it; because, with a few minor exceptions, the one topic of conversation was politics and the war, which of course is what all Comedy has to be about.

When the Spartans had had enough of smashing up our crops and went away again, and the fleet came back from doing roughly similar things in Messenia and Laconia, we all trooped off home to see what had been burnt or chopped down this year and plant out our winter barley. It's an extraordinary thing, but we always did plough and plant out vine-cuttings, in the hope that there would be no invasion next year. I think it goes to show that none of us ever dreamed that we could possibly lose the war, and that the worst that could happen is that we would all meet up in the City next year to continue our conversations and discussions. But in those days, we Athenians knew that there was nothing that we could not achieve and no limit to our realisable ambitions; not only were we bound to conquer all the nations of the earth sooner or later, but we were all on the point of pinning down the answers to every question that anyone could ask, and that anything could be solved or explained if you thought and talked about it for long enough. In short, there was always something to be busy with and something new and wonderful to look forward to, and the fact that in the meantime we all had to get on with the business of scratching a living from the same little scraps of land that our fathers had worked themselves to death over before us tended to be overlooked in the general excitement. I remember once an exile from the court of some Scythian chieftain came to Athens at a time when the City was full of people – and this was many years before the war, on just an ordinary market-day – and he couldn't believe all the things that he heard people saying. He heard them talking about how once the Persians had been dealt with we would be able to get on with conquering Egypt, and how it should be perfectly easy to work out whether the Soul survived the moment of death by making comparisons with things like fire and the attunement of musical instruments, and finally he could restrain himself no longer and burst out laughing in the middle of the Market Square. Of course his hosts were terribly embarrassed and didn't know where to look, and the barbarian at once apologised for his extraordinary behaviour.

'I'm sorry,' he said, 'but I just can't help laughing. You Athenians are all so incredibly perverse.'

'Why?' said his hosts, puzzled. 'What do you find so peculiar about us?'

'Well,' said the Scythian, 'here you all are busily dividing up the world between you and neatly explaining the heavens and making excuses for the immortal Gods, and yet you still empty your chamber-pots on to each other's heads first thing in the morning. So while you're walking about with your heads in the air and your undying Souls are flying through the ether, your feet are up to their ankles in someone else's shit, and all it takes is a shower of rain to make this glorious city of yours utterly intolerable. In my country we may have no intention whatever of annexing the valley next to ours, and none of us has the faintest idea about whether rain is caused by the action of the sun on the ocean or not, but at least we carry all our excrement to a place outside the camp and dump it there where it isn't a nuisance to anybody.'

I used to know what the Athenians replied; I expect it was very brilliant, because the whole point of the story is to show that we are superior to all other races on earth. But there's a sequel to the story which verges on relevance, and since I feel in the mood for telling stories you will have to bear with me a little longer.

This same Scythian, while he was in Athens, had an affair with the wife of a citizen. Her name was Myrrhine, and her husband was a man called Euergetes; he was a very upright, pious sort of man and probably quite unbearable at home, so it's not too hard to forgive his wife for seeking a little fleeting entertainment.

Anyway, one day the Scythian came to call, confident that Euergetes would be out at Assembly until well into the afternoon. He brought a little jar of expensive Syrian perfume with him as a present, and had just got his cloak and tunic off and was struggling with the laces of his sandals when Euergetes pushed open the front door and walked in. Assembly had been cancelled because of a bad omen – something to do with a polecat giving birth under the altar in the Temple of Hephaestus – and he had hurried home to make propitiatory sacrifices.

He was rather startled to see a large, naked stranger standing in his house, and probably expressed himself rather forcefully. But the Scythian was a quick-witted man and had heard all about Euergetes' piety from Myrrhine. So he drew himself up to his full height (these Scythians are often quite tall, and this one was taller than most by all accounts), scowled hideously and shouted, 'How dare you come bursting in like this?'

Euergetes was puzzled, and for a moment he wondered whether he had come to the right house. But the next moment he saw his wife standing beside the stranger and trying to do up her brooch, and so he knew he was right.

'I like that,' he said. 'Just who do you think you are, God Almighty?'

The Scythian was just scrabbling about in the back of his mind for something to say when these words of his antagonist provided the necessary inspiration. 'Yes,' he replied.

Euergetes blinked. 'What was that?' he said.

'Are you blind as well as impious?' said the Scythian. 'Can't you see that I am Zeus?'

It took Euergetes a moment to come to terms with this, but as soon as his mind had managed to choke the concept down he believed it implicitly. After all, in the legends Zeus is always slipping in between some human's sheets, with such results as Sarpedon, Perseus and the glorious Heracles. To a naïve and trusting man like Euergetes it must have seemed far more probable that his lifetime of piety was being rewarded by a visit from the

52

Great Adulterer than that his wife could possibly think so little of him as to have taken a lover. He hesitated for about a seventy-fifth of a second and fell on his knees in a stupor of religious awe.

Now Myrrhine was a sensible girl and she knew that this fortunate state couldn't last. After all, if the God was a God he would now perform some miracle, such as filling the room with flowers or making a spring rise from the floor, and he certainly wouldn't put on his tunic and cloak and just walk out into the street. Then she happened to notice the little jar of perfume. While her husband was busily praying to the Scythian, she crept up behind him and hit him on the head with the jar as hard as she could. Of course Euergetes went out like a lamp in a gale, and the Scythian flung his clothes on and fled. A few minutes later, Euergetes came round and sat up, holding his head and moaning. There was blood, mixed with expensive Syrian perfume, all over his face and he was distinctly disorientated.

'What happened?' he asked.

'You idiot,' said his wife, 'you got struck by lightning.'

'Did I?' asked Euergetes. Then he remembered. 'Was the God really here, then?'

'He was,' said Myrrhine. 'And you insulted him, so he hit you with a thunderbolt. I was terrified.'

Euergetes drew in a deep breath and of course he smelt the perfume. 'What's that funny smell?' he said.

'A God has been in our house and you ask me that,' replied Myrrhine.

At once Euergetes staggered off to make preparations for a sacrifice, and to his dying day he swore that he had seen the God. And when, nine months later, his wife bore a son, there was no prouder man in the whole of Athens. He named the boy Diogenes (which means 'Son of Zeus') and had a mural of Leda and the Swan painted on the wall of the inner room, with Leda looking just like Myrrhine. Unfortunately the blow on his head did some sort of lasting damage and he died not long afterwards, but that was probably no bad thing; for his son turned out most unZeuslike, and the family fortunes declined from that moment on, so that Diogenes' children had been reduced to rowing in the fleet and sitting on juries by the time that I made the acquaintance of one of them. Nevertheless, parts of the commemorative shrine that Euergetes built on his land just outside Pallene can still be seen to this day; indeed, it was quite a well-known landmark when I was a boy. But the roof blew off in a storm a few years ago and then people started taking the stones to build walls and barns with, and all that's left now is the sacred enclosure and the altar itself.

Chapter Four

There are some people, I know, who can't enjoy a poem or a story unless they're told what the hero looks like. I suppose this is due to some deficiency in their imaginative powers that I ought really not to encourage; but I can sympathise, since I was exactly the same when I was a boy and attending that miserable little establishment, the School of Stratocles.

The professed purpose of this organisation was to teach the sons of gentlemen to recite Homer – in my day, it was universally believed that the only skill a young man needed to acquire before he was launched into the world was the ability to recite the *Iliad* and *Odyssey* off by heart, like one of those rather sad-looking old men who make their living that way on the edges of fairs – and for all my aspirations to being a literary man and an aesthete I couldn't be doing with it. For a start I don't like Homer (I know this is like saying that I don't like sunlight, but I can't help that) and at that age my patience with things I didn't hold with was far shorter than it is now. However, the schoolmasters at the School of Stratocles were all bigger than me (I think it was probably the only quali-fication Stratocles looked for when buying staff at the slave-market) and so I was compelled to find some way of tricking my mind into accepting the endless passages of galumphing hexameters that I had to commit to memory each day. I eventually hit on the idea of identifying each of the protagonists in the epics with someone I knew; I could thus picture a familiar figure doing and saying the absurd things they got up to in the Heroic age, and my task became marginally easier.

For instance, Achilles, who I have always heartily despised, became Menesicrates the sausage-seller, a strikingly handsome man with a violent temper who sold rather gristly sausages outside the Archon's Court. Agamemnon, being boastful, cruel, cowardly and stupid, merged seamlessly with Stratocles himself, while Agamemnon's fatuous brother Menelaus will now always remind me of the young slave Lysicles, who was one of my teachers. The school's clerk Typhon suited the part of the slimy and scheming Odysseus perfectly – that's Odysseus in the *Iliad*, of course; Odysseus in the *Odyssey* is a different proposition, and I must confess that I rather liked him. So he came more and more to look like my father, which inevitably made me Odysseus' son, the handsome but intellectually negligible Prince Telemachus, who waits for his glorious sire to return from the war. As for Hector – well, I reckon that all the small boys of Attica had the same picture of Hector in those days: a man in early middle age, but looking rather younger, with a careworn face forced into an encouraging smile and a strangely shaped head that Homer somehow forgets to mention; in other words, Pericles. In fact, this Hector-Pericles even survived my friendship with Cratinus and my meeting with the man himself, and has lasted to this day.

All this gratuitous reminiscence is simply an excuse for putting off for a little longer the unpleasant task of describing myself. I have justified this omission thus far in my story on the grounds that there would be no point in describing what I looked like as a boy – all children under the age of ten are exactly identical, and don't let anyone ever tell you otherwise – besides which, the plague altered my appearance drastically.

The loss of a finger wasn't the only scar that I was left with. Something unpleasant and permanent happened to the muscles in the left side of my face; I think they must have withered, or at least stopped developing. Ever since, I have gone around with a permanent grin on my face, which is appropriate for a Comic poet but profoundly irritating to everyone I have ever met. My hair, which was formerly thick and very curly, started falling out in handfuls like a punctured cushion, so that by the time I reached thirteen I was as bald as marble. Also, I never grew to full stature, so that now I am a full head shorter than most men. My arms, chest and shoulders never filled out or became round and attractive, and I look much weaker and feebler than I actually am. In fact, I can do a full day's work as well as the next man, even if I do have arms like a girl; but I have never been what you might call handsome, and so I never had the swarm of admirers that most boys acquire when they are on the verge of maturity. Nobody gave me little presents of apples or pears on my way home from school or ogled me at the baths, and no vases with *'Eupolis is beautiful'* painted on them ever came my way. Nor, for that matter, did anyone ever sing songs outside my window at night or scratch obscene compliments on our doorposts – except once, and that, I do believe, was my dear cousin Callicrates, who didn't want me to feel utterly left out.

Now the invariable rule is that all Athenians are beautiful, and only beautiful people can be good or well born or clever or anything at all. This is why we call the upper classes, the Cavalry and the Heavy Infantry, 'the beautiful and good', while the oarsmen and landless classes are described as 'the ugly men' and 'the snub-noses'. There is, of course, a degree of logic behind this, since in order to be good-looking you have to be healthy and have plenty to eat, while unsightly complaints such as rickets and eczema are largely caused by malnutrition.

Since I was palpably not beautiful, it stood to reason that for all my acres I must have the soul of a slave, and not many people were prepared to waste time on me. But I soon learned that human beings can be induced to disregard even ugliness if they can be made to laugh. Naturally, you will never have so many true friends as you would if you looked right, but it's better than nothing, and

I made the best of the talent that Dionysus had given me. I soon came to realise that when two people meet together they will sooner or later start criticising a third; and if a fourth joins them who can make himself unbearably amusing at the absent party's expense, they will accept him into their fellowship, if only temporarily, and may even invite him to a relevant dinner party.

After the plague had subsided, there was a remarkable feeling of euphoria in Athens, and indeed the whole of Attica. If the war was not going well for us, it was not going particularly badly, and although the Spartans continued to visit us once a year, we had come to tolerate them as just another of the hazards of agriculture. For my part, I hardly thought about them at all; I had wonderful things to see and do.

It seemed as if there was no limit to my domains, or to the number of men and women who called me master (at least to my face). I expect that if I had been born to it I wouldn't have taken very much notice; I'd have been far too busy eating my heart out with envy whenever I saw anyone who had two more acres or a better plough. It's a curious thing, but I've always found that the wealthier a man becomes, the more obsessed he is with the idea of wealth, until he gets to thinking that nobody but he should be allowed to own anything at all. Then of course he goes into politics, and ends up crawling on his belly to the oarsmen in Assembly, licking their sandal-straps and pretending to take an interest in food distribution and rural poverty. I suppose it's Zeus' way of keeping the extremely fortunate under control.

One such man, indeed, was Pericles' successor as Leader of Athens; a man called Cleon. Oddly enough, I can justify including a few words about him at this point since this Cleon's wealth was in part derived from a tanner's yard which should by rights have belonged to me. I won't bore you with the details; my grandfather had taken a share in it many years before, and had promptly forgotten all about it, and when my grandfather died my uncle Philodemus briefly considered going to law to get the share back for me. But, quite understandably, he didn't bother, since at the time Cleon was not the sort of man you took to law for any reason whatsoever, unless you wanted an excuse for travelling the world for the next ten years.

It was Cleon's father who owned the other share in the tanner's yard, and despite (or because of) his partner's lack of interest in the business it did tremendously well. At the time there was a great demand for quality leather for making shields and other military necessities, and since Cleon's father didn't fool about with the running of the thing but left it to a competent manager the yard got its fair share of business. But when his father handed over the yard to him as part of his marriage settlement, Cleon took a great interest in the leather industry – he was the sort of person who just can't leave well alone – and had soon made it twice or three times as profitable as it had been before, so that it represented the most valuable part of his possessions and the stench of tanning could be smelt from the Propylaea to the Pnyx.

Now had he stuck to tanning and the management of his land, I doubt whether Cleon would have had a single enemy in the world, apart from the people who happened to live next to the yard. He was a quiet, sensitive man by nature, who liked nothing more than a couch in a friendly house, a cup or two of good wine, and a few friends to join him in singing the Harmodius. But he had this restless streak in him that drove him to try and improve things; he couldn't bear the sight of inefficiency, muddle or wasted opportunities. In addition, the Gods had cursed him with a very loud voice and an innate ability with words, and at some stage some idiot must have told him that if he could run a tanner's yard so well he could probably run Athens. So Cleon goes ahead and takes up politics; and since he has this terrible need to make a success of everything he does (typically Athenian, you see) he sets about politics as he set about the leather trade, by cutting out the middleman and selling direct to the mass market. He doesn't waste his time standing for election to any of the great offices of State, as Pericles had done; he simply stands up and speaks (or shouts) his mind at Assembly.

Now it turns out that his mind is perpetually filled with new and more exciting ways of enriching the voters, or else defending them by way of prosecutions in the Courts from the largely undefined but extremely threatening and dangerous activities of his rival politicians. As a result, he quickly becomes the most powerful man in Athens.

Shame on me for a sentimental, soft-hearted old democrat, but I find it hard to be savage about Cleon, for he was a much-maligned man. I'm not saying that he was a good man, or even a well-meaning one; on the contrary, he was a self-centred megalomaniac who did untold damage to Athens. But the same can be said for all the great statesmen in our long and glorious history, so that after a while one takes it for granted. Cleon at least brought a touch of style to an otherwise sordid and unedifying spectacle, and if he hadn't done it someone less entertaining undoubtedly would. What I cannot forgive Cleon for was more of a crime against the God than against the City; he prosecuted a Comic poet.

When I say Comic poet I mean Aristophanes, the most talentless man ever to be granted a Chorus by an overindulgent nation; and Cleon was undoubtedly provoked beyond endurance. I don't mean by what Aristophanes said about him in the Theatre; he could appreciate a joke, even a bad and endlessly reiterated joke about the size and appearance of his reproductive organs, as well as the next man. Indeed, I watched him in the audience during a play of Aristophanes' which was entirely devoted to personal attacks on him, and I believe he enjoyed it much more than I did. No, what aggravated Cleon so much was what Aristophanes said about him behind his back, at parties and sacrifices and in the Market Square. For some reason which I have never been able to understand, people believe things that Aristophanes tells them, although anyone who knows him half as well as I do wouldn't believe him if he told them they had two ears.

Nevertheless, the fact remains that Cleon prosecuted Aristophanes the poet on a charge of slandering the City in the presence of foreigners. This is a terrible crime to be accused of, although nobody has yet got around to defining it, and Aristophanes was duly tried and convicted. He escaped with his life but was very heavily fined, and from that day onwards not only Aristophanes but every other Comic poet in Athens marked Cleon down as a prime target. Not only did they attack him (which was only to be expected and therefore quite innocuous); they also refrained from attacking his enemies, which is a rather more serious matter. You see, nobody had ever before thought of challenging the Comic poet's right to say exactly what he wanted about who he wanted, from the Generals and the Gods down to the street-corner birdseller who sells him a diseased hoopoe and refuses to give him his money back when it dies. It is a matter of principle, and although I would be hard put to it to name a Comic poet who wouldn't spend the next week celebrating if he heard that one of his fellow poets had just been sentenced to death, a threat to the freedom of the poet is a threat to all poets. It was just like the Persian invasions, in fact; we all stopped fighting each other and united against a common enemy.

Naturally, Cleon never tried anything so stupid ever again, and next year it was business as usual. The only difference was that whereas before his conviction Aristophanes was just another hack Comic poet, for ever afterwards he was the man Cleon tried to muzzle, and accordingly anything by Aristophanes had to be good. This is the only explanation, apart from a total lack of taste and discrimination on the part of the Athenian public, for Aristophanes' brilliant record of winning prizes in the Festivals.

Now, about Aristophanes. He's seven or eight years older than me, and he started young. His first play, *The Banqueters*, was put on years before he was legally old enough to be given a Chorus, and so he had to go through the charade of pretending that his uncle had written it; although as soon as the Chorus had been allotted he wasted no time in setting the record straight. But by then it was too late to stop him having his Chorus, since the Committee on Plays and Warships had already appointed him a producer, and in those days nobody would even have considered trying to back out of their duty to finance a Chorus. It was a splendid system, all told; the Committee assessed the means of all the citizens and drew up a list of those wealthy enough to equip a trireme warship for the fleet and to pay the production expenses of a play. Rich men were actually proud to be appointed (it was a sure way of letting the whole world know how rich they were) and by and large the system worked. It was a good way of doing these things, and considerably better than the way we do it now.

I suppose that if I had met Aristophanes in the Market Square or at some literary gathering I might conceivably have got on well with him, and the whole course of my life would have been different. But I first set eyes on him among the goats above Pallene, although then, of course, I hadn't the faintest idea who he was. I was eight at the time, so he must have been about fifteen or sixteen, and probably writing his first play. His father had a strip of maybe two and a half acres in our part of Pallene; most of their land was over in the south-east of Attica, and they had various properties on Aegina. Anyway, Aristophanes occasionally had to tear himself away from the City to do a little half-hearted agriculture, and to relieve the tedium of this he would play tricks on his neighbours.

One day, then, I was on Hymettus with my goats, sheltering from the sun under a stunted little fig tree, which was all that was left of some desperate individual's attempt to farm in that miserable region. In fact, there's a story attached to that attempt, and since it's a Pisistratus story I think I'm justified in putting it in here under the general heading of Athenian history. Pisistratus, as you know, was the dictator of Athens well over a hundred years ago; he was the first man to coin silver money, and he used State revenues to set up many poor landless people in small farms. In his day, every cultivable acre was pioneered and reclaimed, and he carried on his programme of subsidy long after there was nothing left but bare rock. He has a bad reputation these days because he ruled without the People and imposed taxes

62

on citizens; but I have taken the trouble to find out about him over the years and my belief is that without him Athens would now be a little village surrounded by a wooden fence.

Be that entirely as it may, one day, Pisistratus came up to this steading on Hymettus, and saw the crazy fool who was trying to turn it into a farm. He was ploughing, but all he succeeded in doing was turning over a few of the smaller boulders. Pisistratus was impressed, for this was a man after his own heart, and so he strolled over and started talking with the man.

'That looks like hard work,' said the dictator, amiably.

'Yes,' said the man, 'it is.'

'So you're taking advantage of this new scheme, are you?' said Pisistratus encouragingly. 'What sort of thing do you grow up here?'

'Blisters, mostly,' said the man, 'together with a little pain and suffering, of which that bastard Pisistratus takes five per cent. Well, all I can say is that he's welcome to it.'

As soon as he got back to Athens, Pisistratus abated the tax on the pioneers, and that was the beginning of his downfall. In order to cover the shortfall, he increased the tax on everyone else to ten per cent, and everyone who mattered was so livid with him that he met with nothing but obstruction and bad feeling until the day he died.

It was on this historic spot, then, that I met Aristophanes the son of Philip for the first time. I was lying on my back with my eyes closed, thinking how nice it would be if only I didn't have to herd goats, when I was woken by a sharp kick on my collar-bone. I woke up and reached for my staff, and there was this tall man standing over me.

'Right then,' he said, 'on your feet.' He had a City voice, high-pitched and sharp, and I took against him at once. 'Who's your father and what's his deme?'

'Euchorus,' I replied, rubbing my collar-bone, 'of Pallene. Who wants to know?'

'Shut up,' replied the stranger. 'I'm charging Euchorus of Pallene with goat-rustling.'

Now I started to feel suspicious of the stranger, since I knew my father would never do a thing like that. He knew every animal he owned by sight and had names for them all, and even when someone else's stray got into his flock he would go out of his way to try and find out who it belonged to, and if he couldn't he would sacrifice it to the Gods and hold a party for the neighbours.

'Are you sure about that?' I said. 'Name your witnesses.'

This shook him, I think, since he hadn't expected a child to be so well up on criminal procedure. Not that I was, of course; it just so happened that the words were a catch-phrase in our family, and I think they must have slipped out without my thinking. Anyway, the stranger looked around, as if seeking inspiration, and he happened to catch sight of the old white billy-goat, who was destined one day to be my chairman of judges.

'For a start,' he said, 'I hereby cite as chief witness for the prosecution Goat son of Goat, of the steading of Pisistratus. That goat there, which belongs to me.'

'No, you're wrong,' I said. 'It belongs to my father.'

'Be quiet, you little heathen,' said the stranger, 'or I'll have you for receiving.' Then he seemed to be torn by some inner conflict, which made him want to relent. 'Tell you what I'll do,' he said. 'I don't want to go to all the trouble of a lawsuit; they can drag on for days and they cause bad feeling between neighbours. I'll just take back what's mine and you can tell your father what a narrow escape he's had. How does that sound?'

'I think that's really nice and Athenian of you,' I said humbly. 'And since he's your goat you'll know all about his habits.'

'Habits?' said the stranger. 'Yes, of course I do. I reared this goat from a kid, and I've rescued it from wolves more than once with my own hands.'

So he advanced on that old white goat, shooing it with his hands and the hem of his cloak. Now I knew he would do that, just as surely as I knew that that was one thing our old white billy couldn't abide; after all, it was a Goat King and had rights. It lowered its head, made a noise like a disappointed audience, and charged straight at the stranger, butting him in the pit of his stomach and knocking him over. He fell awkwardly, bumped his head on a stone, and swore. The goat gave him a look of pure contempt, nodded his beard like a councillor, and trotted off to join his flock.

'To the charge of goat-rustling,' said the stranger, dabbing the blood elegantly from the side of his head with the hem of his cloak, 'I shall add a charge of witchcraft tending to cause a breach of the peace. Your father, who has evidently been to Persia and is almost certainly a collaborator, has cast a Babylonian spell on my poor goat and turned him into a savage, man-slaying monster. It is my sacred duty as a Greek to kill that goat and appease the anger of the Gods.' He rose painfully to his feet, wrapped his cloak around his left arm and drew his sword with his right. As he did so I saw that he was wearing a little Hecate charm round his neck to ward off evil spirits, and that told me that he was superstitious. That was all I needed to know.

'You're clever as well as brave, stranger,' I said. 'Not many people would have noticed that. What gave it away? Was it the split hoof on the offside front leg?'

The stranger paused for a moment, and his hand may instinctively have moved towards that charm I was telling you about just now.

'Split hoof,' he repeated.

'It's not a Median spell, though,' I continued brightly. 'I think it's Thessalian, or something like that. It's been really dreadful, ever since Father came back from Thessaly. None of the neighbours will talk to us any more, and I think they've put a dead cat down our well.'

'Your father's been to Thessaly, has he?' said the stranger.

'Oh yes,' I said, trying to sound miserable. 'That's where he brought that *thing* back from. It's really horrible, making those awful noises all night. And we haven't had a fresh drop of milk in the house since it came.'

'What thing?' said the stranger.

'That goat over there,' I said, pointing to a big black goat with a twisted horn, which had raised its head and

65

was staring at the stranger, the way goats do sometimes. 'Eurymenes in our village says it's a witch and they tried to burn it the other day, but it wouldn't burn, even when they poured pitch all over it. Then it went trotting through their houses setting all the hangings alight. They were going to take Father to Court but they were too frightened.' I stopped and gazed at the stranger as if he were a Hero come to deliver us. 'Will you really prosecute my father for witchcraft?' I said. 'We'd be ever so grateful.'

'Of course,' said the stranger, backing away, with his eyes fixed on the black goat. 'In fact, I'll go straight to the Archon this very day.'

Then he turned round and walked away terribly quickly. I managed to keep myself from laughing until he was out of sight, and told my father the whole story as soon as I got home. Of course he thought I was making the whole thing up and made me learn fifty lines of Hesiod as a punishment.

Well, that was the first time I met Aristophanes. The second time was over seven years later; but I recognised him at once and he recognised me.

My cousin Callicrates and I were returning from a quiet dinner party with some boring friends of his, where we had drunk very abstemiously and discussed the nature of Justice. It was as dark as a bag in the streets, and Callicrates and I had our hands on our sword-hilts all the way. We were nearly home and safe when we rounded a corner and saw the one sight that the traveller by night fears above all others; a Serenade.

Perhaps you have never been to Athens, and the young men in your city are rather better behaved; so I will tell you what a Serenade involves. A group of young men, probably Cavalry class, meet at a party which they find uninspiring. So they appropriate what's left of the wine and the better-looking of the flute-girls, light torches and set off to find a better party. In their search for the Perfect Party they spare no pains and leave no flat stone unturned; they surge out into the Market Square and run in and out of the Painted Cloister, then they throw up outside the Cloister of the Herms, cross the Square, and work their devastating way uphill from house to house like a Spartan army, to the sound of flutes and singing. There are, of course, the inevitable casualties by the way; some of them fall over and go to sleep, and others who find themselves passing under their girlfriends' windows stop to sing a Locked-Out song until they get the slops in their faces. Generally, however, they stick closely together, like heavy infantry in enemy territory, for while the Serenade itself is vaguely sacred to Aphrodite and Dionysus, any straggler can be picked up by the Constables or charged with assault by a citizen. The general objective of most Serenades is to capture the Acropolis and overthrow the Democracy; but since in the history of the City no Serenade has ever managed to stay together long enough to get much further than the Mint, little substantial political change has ever come out of one of these affairs.

This particular Serenade was a truly terrifying spectacle. There were at least forty young men, armed with swords and torches, wreathed in myrtle and singing the Harmodius. The ten or so girls with them looked scared out of their wits, and I noticed that one of them was a free-born girl, whom they had presumably confiscated from one of the houses they had visited.

It was round her neck that Aristophanes was hanging, and he was clearly one of the leaders of this Serenade. He was yelling at the top of his voice – I think he was shouting orders, like a taxiarch – and his companions replied by cheering loudly and occasionally being sick. Callicrates and I stood very still and pretended to be doorposts, but they noticed us and stopped in their tracks.

'Line halt!' called out Aristophanes. 'Spartans to your left front. No prisoners.'

Callicrates, who had been on Serenades himself when he was younger, knew better than to run, for they would have been sure to chase after us and beat us up or kill us if they caught us. Instead he stood his ground and said nothing, in the hope that they would go away. This usually works, but not always; and this was one such occasion.

'Look, gentlemen,' said Aristophanes, 'there's a Spartan over there who isn't afraid of us. What'll we do to him?'

His co-Serenaders made several excellent suggestions, and I could tell that Callicrates was beginning to get worried. Now I am not a brave man, as you will discover in due course, but I was too young to understand the real danger I was in, and besides, fear brings out the cleverness in me like nothing else. Also, some malicious God was urging me to rescue the poor free-born girl that Aristophanes was holding, since if he got her to himself for any length of time later on, her chances of a good or even reasonable marriage would be gone for good. Remember, I was then at an age where girls have that sort of effect, although now I regard them as an intolerable nuisance.

Anyway, I filled my lungs with air and called out, 'Are you so drunk that you don't recognise the Goatherd of Hymettus, from the Steading of Pisistratus?'

Then I raised the torch I was carrying so that he could see my face. Of course, there was no guarantee that he would recognise me after so many years, not to mention the effects of the plague; on the other hand, I was so ugly, particularly by torchlight, that recollection on his part might not be necessary to achieve the desired effect. But he recognised me all right, and nearly dropped his torch.

'Have you still got that little Hecate?' I asked. 'Because if you have, you'll need it. Remember the Thessalian spell, and the goat who broke your head, and my father who learned magic?'

Here I raised the torch over Callicrates' head, and he, although he hadn't the faintest idea what I was on about, did his best to look sorcerer-like and evil. Aristophanes turned his head to spit in his cloak for luck, and that gave the girl the chance she needed. She bit Aristophanes' hand, he let go, and she ran over to us and hid behind Callicrates' shoulder. At the time I took that rather hard, since it was me who saved her.

'Tell you what I'll do,' I went on. 'I can't be bothered to put a spell on you, seeing as how it's late and tomorrow is the Feast of All Witches. I'll just take this goat of yours, in full and final settlement, and you can tell yourself what a narrow escape you've had.'

Aristophanes may have been terribly superstitious, but he wasn't a complete fool and he realised that he'd been had. His companions seemed to tumble to it as well, although of course they didn't know the joke, and they started sniggering. At any rate, their interest in killing us seemed to have evaporated, and I imagine they were starting to feel thirsty again. They started jeering at Aristophanes, who gave me a scowl that would curdle mustard. Then a thought seemed to strike him and he suddenly smiled warmly.

'I think that's very good and Athenian of you,' he called back, 'and since she's your goat, of course, you'll know all about her habits. You can keep her, mate, and welcome. Her name is Phaedra, daughter of Theocrates, and she lives just behind the Fountain House.'

At this, all the Serenaders burst out laughing, though I couldn't imagine why, and the procession moved on, singing the Leipsydrion at the tops of their voices, leaving me, Callicrates and the girl standing there feeling greatly relieved.

We recognised Phaedra's house from the way its door had been kicked in, and restored her to her parents, who had given her up for lost. In fact they were in floods of tears and were kneeling by the hearth pouring ashes on their heads when we walked in, and when they learned from Phaedra herself that she had been rescued before anything drastic had happened to her they were beside themselves with joy. Callicrates nobly ascribed the entire rescue to my quick thinking and they hugged me and washed my feet in perfumed water, which made me feel like Hercules restoring Alcestis from the dead.

'Don't mention it, please,' I kept saying, 'it was the least I could do, really it was.' But of course I wasn't looking at them but at the girl, who was blushing and glancing at me from under her eyelashes in the way girls do – I think they must learn the trick from their mothers at an early age. She was, on close inspection, rather a pretty girl, and I expect you can guess what was going on inside my idiotic little soul.

'It's positively the last time that man comes into our house,' the girl's mother was saying, 'and I don't care how much money he's got, or who his rich friends may be. And he's married already, so if he'd . . . why, we'd *never* have got Phaedra off our—'

At which her husband kicked her under the table and offered us some wine and honey in a loud voice. I should have taken notice of that 'never', but I was far too preoccupied to notice.

'Our Phaedra is the best girl in the whole of Attica,' said Theocrates. 'She's got all the accomplishments, she can cook and she can sing, she even knows her Hesiod, don't you, pet?' He scowled at her till she nodded, and then gave me a long, meaningful look that nearly took the top of my head off; the sort of look that fathers usually only give young bachelors just before they get down to working out dowry figures. 'And there's ten acres down by the coast with her. Oh yes, the young man who gets our little girl will be very lucky indeed.'

I remember once I was out shopping and I saw this really handsome horse in the market. I stood there for a while and I couldn't see anything at all wrong with it, and so I walked over and asked the dealer how much. Instead of answering my question he started off into a long and noisy encomium of the animal's virtues, half-way through which the horse arched its neck across and bit me painfully on the arm for no apparent reason. In other words, when a salesman starts praising wares that look good enough without further description, put your hands over your ears and walk away. I didn't know that, then. I think Callicrates did, because he started getting restive, but it was my moment, and I guess he hadn't the heart to interfere. He just suggested that it was time we were getting along, and of course I ignored him. For Phaedra had brought the wine and honey, with grated cheese on it, and when I took the cup my fingers brushed against hers and seemed to burn as if I had inadvertently leaned on a hot tripod.

'So who exactly was our noble assailant?' Callicrates was saying. 'Eupolis seemed to know him but he won't let me in on the secret.'

Theocrates spat ostentatiously into the fire and replied, 'That was Aristophanes son of Philip of Cydathene, the Comic poet. First thing in the morning, I'm going to see the Archon about a kidnapping suit.'

For a moment, I forgot even about Phaedra. 'Aristophanes?' I squeaked. '*The* Aristophanes, who brought on a Chorus of our allies dressed as Babylonian slaves and turning a treadmill?'

Theocrates sniffed disdainfully. 'That's an old gimmick,' he said. 'Cratinus did it in *The Sardines*, only you're too young to remember.'

Then, of course, we started talking Comedy, and after that Tragedy, until it was dawn and time to go home. I remember walking through the streets in the pale red light and thinking that I must have died and been born again as a God, the way the Pythagoreans say, since how else could I account for the fact that I had met the great Aristophanes and overcome him in battle, recited the *parabasis* of the play I was composing (which had seemed to amuse old Theocrates greatly) and above all, been given permission to call again whenever I liked, all in the space of one brief night? The last point could mean only one thing; that, if suitable terms could be worked out between our two families, I could become Phaedra's suitor, since we were both the right age and unpromised and our families were compatible. It was only when I got home and climbed into bed that Aristophanes' words about her habits flashed momentarily across my mind, and before I could consider them I was fast asleep.

Although many people have competed for the honour over the years, I still maintain that I am my own worst enemy.

Chapter Five

This book is rather like a cousin of mine called Amyclaeus, who has a truly appalling sense of direction. He's bad enough in the country, but if you put him in the City he has no more idea of where he is than a blind man. To make matters worse, he himself firmly believes that he's a born navigator and is always insisting that he knows a little short cut here or a back way there, which of course he doesn't. But, because the Gods look after fools, he has this uncanny knack of eventually ending up where he meant to go, even though he has no right to end up there at all.

It's the same with me and writing prose. I start off meaning to tell you a story, and then I get sidetracked with something that interests me, and I go wandering off all over the place; yet here we are, nicely on schedule, at the point where I have just met Phaedra and am just starting off on the long process of getting betrothed to her. In fact, we are here rather ahead of time; so, while we are waiting for the main stream of my narrative to catch up with us, I shall tell you about my first meeting with the Spartans.

As I was about to tell you before I started on about Cleon, I had inherited rather a lot of land as a result of the plague, and as soon as I came to understand what this actually meant, nothing would satisfy me but to go and inspect all this property myself. Philodemus and Callicrates approved of this notion by and large, since it's right and proper that a man should take an interest in his possessions and not just leave them to a steward or a slave to look after, and so we set off for a tour.

Nowadays, of course, what with the amalgamation of holdings and the buying and selling of land for commercial motives, things are very different; in my day, virtually the only way land changed hands was by inheritance, and so most people with more than two or three acres to their names had little snippets of land here and there all over Attica, and I was no exception. Quite apart from my father's lands in Pallene and Phyle (which were good properties, if a touch on the mountainous side) I had bits and pieces all over Attica, from Prasiae to Eleutherae and Oropus. Admittedly, none of these parcels of land was large, and with some of them you couldn't put down a cloth to spread out a picnic without trespassing on the land of at least two neighbours, but that was more or less beside the point as far as I was concerned.

Well, my uncle and my cousin humoured me as far as Eleutherae, but their patience was worn down almost to the lettering, as the saying goes, and I can't say I blame them; I must have been a quite insufferable companion, with my perpetual boasting and self-preening. For I would insist on examining every last inch, and it was getting on towards the time of year when sensible people were moving back towards the City. We had seen virtually everything there was to see except for a tiny patch of land on the very slopes of Cithaeron – half an acre if that – which had been thrown in as a makeweight in a marriage-settlement about four generations back, and where there had been a few stringy old olive trees the last time anybody had bothered to look.

We were staying at an inn at Eleutherae, and reports were already coming in of the approach of the Spartan army on their annual holiday. As soon as Philodemus heard about this, he paid the bill and gave orders for our mules to be loaded up.

'We aren't leaving yet, are we?' I asked. 'We haven't seen the property on Cithaeron.'

'Don't be a fool,' said Philodemus, 'you heard what

the shepherds said. The Spartans will be up here soon.'

'I don't care,' I said. 'I'm going to see my land.'

'Eupolis,' said Philodemus patiently, 'one of the great things about land as opposed to Spartans is that it stays put. There's a good chance that it'll still be there in the summer when the Spartans have all gone home. If you insist we can come back then. Now, we are going home.'

'You can if you like,' I said. 'I'm going to look at my land.'

'Eupolis,' replied Philodemus, not so patiently, 'you can do what you like. Callicrates and I are going home while we still can. If you want to stay here and get killed, that's a matter between you and your soul.'

What with seeing all that land I had become exceptionally arrogant, and I replied to the effect that neither I nor my soul were going to be kept from taking possession of what was ours by a load of Spartan garlic-eaters. Then Callicrates tried to reason with me – he always had more patience with idiots than his father – and that just made me more stubborn than ever, since when he explained it I could see I was in the wrong. Then Philodemus flew into a temper and stormed out. Callicrates stayed where he was.

'Aren't you going too?' I said grandly.

'Don't make things worse,' said Callicrates angrily. 'I can't leave you here on your own, there's no knowing what stupid things you might do.'

'You suit yourself then,' I said. 'First thing in the morning, we're going to take a look at my property.'

And we did. Callicrates said that if we were going to do this stupid thing, we might as well do it in the least stupid way possible, so he woke me up about two hours before dawn, bundled me into my sandals and hat, and led the way off up the mountain.

I don't know if you've ever been to Cithaeron, but if you haven't I can assure you that you haven't missed anything. It is an indescribably miserable place, even when dawn breaks over it, and the thought that he was risking his life just to give an idiot a guided tour of half an acre of it did little to improve Callicrates' temper. He wasn't talking to me and I was damned if I was talking to him, so we stomped along in silence like an old married couple who have quarrelled on the way to market. After what seemed like a hundred years of difficult walking we came to a rocky outcrop with three tree stumps on it, and Callicrates stopped in his tracks, flung his arms wide and said, 'This is it.'

'Is it?' I said.

'Yes,' replied Callicrates.

'How do you know?' I replied. 'It looks just the same as everything else.'

'I recognise that mortgage-stone over there,' said Callicrates, pointing to a lump of rock sticking out of the earth. 'It's one of the few they never got around to pulling up in Solon's time. It's the only interesting thing on the whole of Cithaeron, and I came up here when I was a boy to see it. Can we go now?'

'Hold on,' I said. 'I want to have a look at this ancient monument of yours.'

'Oh all right then,' said Callicrates. 'But for God's sake hurry. You realise anyone for miles around can see us up here.'

I wandered over and had a look at the stone. It was nothing but a pillar of rock with some very old writing on it which said something like *Mnesarchides to Polemarchus; one sixth*.

'Satisfied?' Callicrates asked. 'Or do you want to take measurements?'

Of course I wasn't the slightest bit interested in a slab of old rock, but just to irritate Callicrates I made a great show of examining the thing minutely, as if I was carried away by the historical significance of it. While I was doing this, I noticed the smoke.

The first thing that struck me about this smoke was that it wasn't like chimney smoke at all; it was coming up in a big cloud, and it was black. I had seen smoke like that once before, when our neighbour's barn caught fire when I was a boy.

'Callicrates,' I said, 'come and look at this.'

'Don't fool around, Eupolis,' said Callicrates. 'I've had just about enough of you for one day.'

'There's smoke coming from over there,' I said. 'What do you think it could be?'

Callicrates followed where I was pointing and his mouth dropped open. 'There's a little farm over there,' he said, 'I went there once. One of those little places. Belongs to a man called Thrasydemus.'

We looked at each other for a moment. For my part, I admit I was terrified, the way I had never been before in my whole life. Far away in the distance, I could hear the sound of flutes, and everyone knows that the Spartans march to war to flute music. Either that, or it was the God Pan; and I would be hard put to it to say which I would least like to encounter.

'Let's go home,' I said. 'I don't like it here any more.'

Callicrates nodded. 'That's right,' he said, 'you go home, quickly. Keep your head down and don't show yourself above the skyline if you can help it. Head for the village; you'll be safe there until midday at least if I know the Spartans.'

'What are you going to do?' I said, feeling quite weak with fear. 'I'm not going back on my own.'

'Don't be stupid,' said Callicrates. 'Just so long as you take care you'll be all right.'

'Stuff that,' I said, 'I'm coming with you.'

Callicrates thought for a moment and then nodded. 'Maybe that would be best,' he said. 'That way I can at least keep an eye on you. But I've got to take a look at that farm over there.'

'Why?' I said. 'You can't fight a Spartan army on your own.'

'Of course not,' said Callicrates irritably. 'But there may be people down there who need help.'

'Oh, for God's sake,' I shouted, 'what about me? I want to go home.'

Callicrates was angry now. 'Go ahead,' he said, 'I'm not stopping you. You got us into this, so you might as well clear out now before you cause any more disasters.'

We both knew that I wasn't going anywhere on my own

76

by this point, since I was far too scared and Callicrates was far too conscientious. So I nodded wretchedly and followed on.

The nearer we came, the more obvious it became that the fire was coming from a house of some description. I think we had both been hoping that it was just a field of barley or a rick; but it was definitely the sort of smoke that comes off burning thatch. Eventually we came to the edge of a sharp ridge, and Callicrates stooped down to avoid making himself visible to anyone watching below. I did the same and we peeped over.

Down below us was one of those small farms that used to be scattered about the remoter areas of Attica then, before they were finally abandoned after the war. It consisted of a long, thatched house and a storage tower, all enclosed by a little courtyard. From where we were, we could see that the whole place was on fire, and that in the courtyard there were a lot of men in red cloaks, apparently enjoying the spectacle.

'Do you think they got away?' I whispered.

'I hope so,' replied Callicrates. 'But if we didn't notice them coming out on the hill, I don't suppose they did down here. This place wasn't built as a lookout station, it was built as a farm.'

Then I saw two of the red cloaks coming out of an outhouse that hadn't been set alight yet, and they were bundling along an old woman and an old man. They made these two kneel down beside the brick wall of the well. A third red cloak walked up and seemed to inspect them; then he reached for an axe that was lying beside a pile of logs ready for splitting. He pulled out one of the logs and the red cloaks put the old woman's neck across the log. The old man didn't want to watch, but the red cloaks made him. The third red cloak threw his cloak over his shoulder so that it wouldn't get in the way, and cut the old woman's head off; it took him three or four strokes. Then the red cloaks threw her body and head down the well, and dragged the old man up. He didn't seem to struggle as much as the old woman had done. The third red cloak managed rather better this time; he

77

had the head off the old man in two strokes and a bit. I was glad we weren't closer.

Then they threw his body down the well too, and set light to the outhouse. As soon as it started to burn, a little old grey dog dashed out and they killed that too. Just then a small child came running out – I suppose he had been hiding in there hoping to escape notice – and at first they didn't see him. I held my breath, but then one of the red cloaks must have caught sight of him out of the corner of his eye, because he pointed and two or three of the others went off after him like dogs after a hare. They caught up with him as he was trying to scramble over the courtyard wall – it was just too high for him to get over – and brought him back. The third red cloak had lifted his axe up again, but then he seemed to change his mind, and he pointed to the burning outhouse. The red cloaks who had caught the child lifted him off the ground by the arms, the way parents do when they're walking a child round the market, and pitched him in through the window. I heard a very small, faint scream.

Then the red cloaks had a good look round to make sure they hadn't missed anything, and formed up into a column. The third red cloak went along the column counting them to make sure they were all there, and he stopped at one point and relieved one of them of a chicken he was trying to hide behind his shield. He hit the offender behind the head with the flat of his sword and threw the chicken into the fire, and then they moved off, marching extremely quickly. There were three boys playing flutes marching along beside them. I shall remember that tune till the day I die; in fact, I sometimes find myself whistling it when I'm not thinking.

We watched until they were out of sight over the brow of the slope, and then went scrambling down the hillside as quickly as we could go. But we had to take a long way round even then, because the hillside overlooking the farm where we had been watching was more cliff than hill, and by the time we got there the thatch was almost burnt away and there was nothing left but bare rafters, like the branches of an oak in winter.

Callicrates wound his cloak round his face to keep out the smoke and went into the house; I didn't try to stop him. He came out again a moment later coughing dreadfully, and shortly after that there was a crashing sound as the house started to fall in. He shook his head to signify that there was nothing he could have done anyway.

Round the back of the house, by the cowshed, we found the farmer Thrasydemus. He had tried to defend himself with a pruning-hook. There were four deep holes in his chest and he was quite obviously dead. We couldn't find any trace of his wife or any other of the children; they must have been in the house, or perhaps they hadn't been there at the time, although somehow we couldn't bring ourselves to believe that. But when I was looking at the farmer's dead body, I saw something shining under a small fig tree and went to investigate. It was a small jar full of silver money, which someone had smashed. I wondered why the Spartans hadn't taken it; then I remembered that they don't use silver for money, they use iron bars like roasting-spits, so of course it wouldn't have been any use to them. Probably one of the Spartans had found it and the captain had made him throw it away, just like the chicken. The Spartans are very honourable and don't hold with looting.

'Right,' said Callicrates, 'there's nothing we can do here. We might as well get back to the village and make sure they know what's going on.'

I was delighted to leave the place, and we walked very quickly away. Obviously we couldn't go back by the road, since that would be courting disaster, so we picked our way along just under the line of the hill, where we could see but, with luck, not be seen. After about half an hour, we cut across the top of the mountain, following a little goat-track that Callicrates remembered, which he reckoned would bring us down a few hundred yards from the village itself. That way, we ought to outrun the Spartans comfortably and maybe in time to raise the alarm, if it hadn't been raised already. As we walked we saw another column of smoke coming up from a sheltered little combe below us, but this time we didn't try and interfere.

'Callicrates,' I said as we hurried along. 'Do the Spartans always do things like that? I haven't heard any stories about it.'

'Only the last year or so,' Callicrates said, 'ever since we started doing that sort of thing in Messenia when we go raiding there.'

I was horrified. 'You mean we started it,' I said. 'We're in the wrong.'

'What do you mean, in the wrong?' Callicrates replied. 'It's a war, things like that happen. And they only happen when people are stupid enough to hang around when the enemy are approaching.'

I couldn't believe what I was hearing. 'Are you trying to say it was their fault they got killed?' I asked.

Callicrates stopped walking and looked at me. 'Don't you understand anything?' he said. 'It's nobody's fault. It's just the way things are. Why does everything have to be somebody's fault all the time?'

I wanted to argue but suddenly I couldn't think of anything to say – a most unusual state for an Athenian to be in, whatever the circumstances. Then Callicrates started walking again, faster than ever, and his legs were much longer than mine.

That walk seemed to go on for a very long time. The closer we got to the village, the more scared I became, and I made myself dizzy staring at the horizon looking for more columns of smoke. But we didn't see any and Callicrates seemed to cheer up, hoping that we had managed to steal a march on the Spartans.

'I reckon that what we saw back there was just a raiding party,' he said. 'If they're going to have a go at the village they'll concentrate their forces and surround the place. They don't want any more trouble than they can help – I expect they're as fed up with it all as we are, and they certainly won't want to risk getting themselves killed by taking on a populated place without proper forces. All they're really interested in is doing as much damage to crops and livestock as they can; they'll want to give the bigger places plenty of time to evacuate.'

'It didn't look that way back there,' I said, but more out of general argumentativeness than for any other reason. I wanted nothing more than to find the village undisturbed; even the prospect of getting the better of Callicrates in an argument (which was something I had never managed to do) was not particularly inviting at that moment.

We were getting down on to much more level ground now, among the vineyards and olive groves, and we couldn't see any sign that the Spartans had been through before us. Callicrates told me that he had done much the same sort of thing in his military service, and that after a while it turns into a very boring sort of a job, with no one displaying any sort of enthusiasm for it or wanting to find ways of doing it better or quicker. I didn't ask him if he had killed any farmers himself; I didn't really want to know.

Callicrates had a splendid natural sense of direction, and we came out more or less exactly where he had said we would, on the top of the ridge above the village. We looked down and to our immense delight saw a column of mules, ox-carts and men with parcels on their shoulders streaming out of the place as fast as they could go. The Spartans hadn't arrived yet, and this was the village evacuating itself, in a proper and organised fashion, according to the proper custom of war.

I was just about to go plunging down the hill to join up with this column when Callicrates put his hand on my shoulder and pulled me down. I couldn't understand what he was doing and struggled, but he clapped a hand over my mouth and pointed. Just behind the village there was a cloud of dust.

'Sit still,' he said. 'Perhaps it's nothing, but we'd better just stay here for a moment.'

I pulled his hand away. 'Don't be stupid,' I said. 'If they haven't seen it, we've got to warn them.'

'Shut up and stay here,' Callicrates said furiously. 'Do what you're told, just this once.'

So I crouched down beside him in the shade of a boulder, while the cloud of dust came nearer. The people in the column had seen it too, and they didn't like the look of it any more than I had. Some of them dumped their loads in the roadway and started running, along the road or up the hill. Others turned back towards the village; others just stood where they were.

The cloud of dust suddenly turned into a column of horsemen, riding very fast. I couldn't see the colour of their cloaks, but they had helmets that flashed in the sun and they carried two javelins each. They didn't look anything like any of the cavalry units that I had seen in Athens; they were far too businesslike and organised. Under different circumstances, it would have been a pleasure to watch them.

Callicrates pulled me further behind the rock, and then we peeped out. The cavalry had caught up with what was left of the column, and they were throwing javelins. It was rather like a high-class boar-hunt, such as you get in the hills when a lot of rich young men go out for a day's sport – except that there weren't any dogs or nets, and the quarry were rather less inspiring in their resistance than the average wild boar. When the cavalrymen had thrown their spears they drew their sabres and closed in, and since I had had quite enough of that sort of entertainment for one day, I didn't bother watching too much after that. I had this strange feeling that I was at the Theatre – probably because I was sitting a long way back and watching what was going on – and that some tasteless God was laying all this on for my benefit. I wanted to stand up and tell him that I was a Comedian not a Tragedian and so all this was wasted on me; and besides, it was against all the conventions of the Theatre to have the actual killing on stage. Besides, I wanted to say, I've seen this play before not two hours ago and I didn't reckon much to it then.

I don't suppose it lasted more than ten minutes. I remember Callicrates saying, 'It's all right, they've gone now,' and me thinking that that was exactly what my father used to say when my cousins from Thria came to visit and I used to hide in the stables because the woman had a hare lip and frightened me, and then looking out and seeing the mess.

Mess is the only word to describe it. I don't know if you've ever been in the City the morning after the Festival of Pitchers and wandered down to the Market Square; but it was just like that, I promise you – exactly that same sort of sorry-looking, depressing mess that comes of people trying to enjoy themselves just a little bit too much. Except that instead of smashed wine jars and abandoned sandals and little pools of vomit at the feet of the statues of the Heroes of Athenian History, there were dead bodies and shattered carts and puddles of blood; and even they were the same colour as spilt wine, until you looked closely at them. The way I account for it is that the human soul can't really cope with strange and horrible things, and so it tries to pretend that what it's seeing is something everyday and normal; I guess that's why similes work so well in poems. If I tell you that the roadway was littered with severed arms and legs you can't really picture that in your mind since, unless you've seen a few battlefields, your soul doesn't know what that looks like and probably doesn't want to imagine it. But if I say that there were arms and legs scattered about like bits of driftwood on the beach after there's been a storm at sea, you'll be able to identify with that; and, if you know your Homer, you'll be able to say exactly which passage from *The Cypria* I've just lifted that simile from. But there we are.

Callicrates and I wandered down the hill – there didn't seem to be much point in hurrying – and did our best to make ourselves useful, but there was nothing much we could do. The other villagers who had had the wit to run away when they saw the cavalry coming had crept back and were seeing to such of their relatives and friends who weren't completely past helping and sprinkling dust on those who were, and Callicrates and I just got in the way for most of the time. I remember we saw one man lying on his side, and he didn't look particularly dead; but when we lifted him up to see if he was still alive, his head rolled right back and dangled from his neck by a strip of skin, and the expression on his face was frankly ludicrous, so we scooped a little dust over him and walked away quickly, the way you do when you're shopping in the Market Square and you accidentally bump into one of those neatly piled pyramids of melons or oranges and knock them over.

Just as we were despairing of being able to do any good, we found an old man who apparently didn't have any family, because he was just squatting there all over blood and nobody was taking any notice of him. Anyway, he was calling out for water in a horribly wheezy voice, and so I sprinted off and found a helmet which one of the cavalrymen had dropped, and I filled it with water from a stream that ran down the hill and brought it back, feeling like the God of Healing. The old man grabbed it from me and poured its contents into his face; but none of us, not even he, had noticed that he had a great big hole in his throat from a sabre-cut, and of course most of the water just poured out of this on to the ground. A moment later the man made a sort of rattling noise, like someone gargling with salt water when they've just had a tooth pulled, and rolled over and died, so that was a complete waste of time. Now I come to think of it, that was the first time I ever saw anyone die when I was close enough to see the expression on their face.

And then there was a little girl – she couldn't have been more than eight or nine – who had had an arm cut off at the shoulder, and what with the fear and the pain she had wet herself, and this seemed to be causing her more unhappiness than her injury. She wasn't weeping or screaming, just grizzling like any other small child, and her mother had finished doing the best she could to stop the bleeding and was trying to change her wet clothes, and was swearing at her for not keeping still. Really, it made me want to burst out laughing to see them, but maybe I was just getting hysterical. Now perhaps you're thinking that that sounds a little strange coming from someone who had seen Athens in the plague, but I assure you that it was all very different. You see, there had been no blood and no wounds in the plague, just a lot of dead bodies, and besides I was very much younger then. But it was like the plague in one respect, because however unhappy and sick it all made me feel I nevertheless couldn't help noticing the little details, not because they were heartrending or disgusting but because they were interesting, as being curious specimens of human behaviour.

I'd better stop talking like this before you start getting the idea that I'm some sort of ghoul, like that terrible fellow Chaerophon the scientist who goes around watching people having their gallstones cut out. Please don't think I was enjoying any of this; I was absolutely terrified, since I was firmly convinced that the Spartan infantry were going to arrive at any minute and finish off the job. I think Callicrates had much the same idea, for all his good intentions about helping the wounded, because he kept looking over his shoulder in a worried sort of a way. But for all my fear, I don't think it ever seriously entered my head that anything was going to happen to me; I was rather more interested in not witnessing yet another massacre. I seemed to have the idea that I wasn't really part of what was going on, as if I was a tourist from one of the islands, or a God who could make himself invisible.

I think we were both nerving ourselves to get out of there when I felt this incredibly sharp pain in my foot and found that I had stepped on a broken sabre-blade and lacerated my right heel. I communicated this fact to Callicrates, who sagged as if someone had just melted his spine with a candle.

'You *idiot*,' he said miserably, 'what the hell did you want to go and do that for?'

I explained that it wasn't intentional, and that I must have lost my sandal somewhere; I felt terribly guilty for some reason and very conscious of having picked quite the wrong moment. Callicrates cut a strip off his cloak and bandaged my foot as best he could; but for all the inventiveness of mankind, there is no known way of bandaging a heel effectively, because it's such a difficult shape and so there's nothing to tie the bandage to. So we glanced round to see that nobody was looking, and tugged a right sandal off the body of a dead man lying close by, and tied that firmly to my foot with the strip of cloak. It was better than nothing, but it was profoundly uncomfortable.

'That settles it,' said Callicrates, as if he was secretly glad of the excuse, 'we'd better get going.'

'Where?' I asked, like a fool. 'We're surely not going to try and get back to Athens.'

'Well, we aren't going to Sparta,' Callicrates snapped, 'and we'd better not stay here. Look around and see if you can find something to use as a walking stick.'

I found a javelin – I won't mention where – and Callicrates chopped the head off with his sword. With this to lean on, I was able to hobble along reasonably well, but I won't pretend that I was relishing the prospect of a ten-hour hike back to the City across the mountains. Callicrates could see that I was worried and even offered to carry me on his back – he would have done it, too, if I'd let him – but that was obviously a stupid idea. What we needed was a horse or a mule or something like that.

'You're off your head,' said Callicrates when I suggested it. 'I'm not wasting time combing through the village looking for our mules. And anyway, Philodemus may have taken them back to the City with him.'

'All right then,' I said, 'we'll buy one.'

Callicrates blinked. 'In the middle of a massacre you want to stop and buy a mule.'

'Yes,' I replied.

'Oh, for God's sake.' Callicrates scratched the back of his head, and I could see he was lost for words. 'Have you got any money on you?' he asked after a while.

I turned out my purse into my hand. 'Yes,' I said. 'Thirty-two drachmas.'

'You won't get much of a mule for thirty-two drachmas.'

I didn't bother to reply to that. Instead I hoisted myself up on the javelin-shaft and hobbled over to where I could see an old woman standing beside a cart. The cart itself had been smashed – the axle was broken – but there were two mules standing beside it with their harness still on. I looked them over for a while and then said, 'How much for the little grey one.'

'You what?' said the old woman.

'I want to buy the grey mule,' I said. 'How much are you asking?'

The old woman frowned. 'I don't know,' she said. 'I'll have to ask my husband.'

Then she seemed to remember something, and she looked down at the cart. What had broken it was being turned over by the cavalry, and under a big clay jar, obviously crushed to death, was an old man's body.

'Well,' said the old woman, pulling herself together, 'it's no good asking him, is it? How much are you offering?'

'Twenty-eight drachmas,' I replied.

'Thirty,' she said.

'Done with you,' I answered, and tipped the eight coins into her hand.

'Hold it,' she said, 'you've given me too much. There's thirty-two here.'

I was busily stripping the harness off the mule. 'Oh,' I said. 'I haven't got anything smaller, I'm afraid.'

She frowned. 'I might have some change,' she said, and she opened her mouth and picked out two half-drachmas and an obol. 'That's still five obols short,' she said.

'Never mind,' I said, 'that'll do.' I pulled the harness clear and tried to get up on the mule's back, but I couldn't make it. Instinctively, I stood on the cart as a mounting-block and there was a sort of creaking noise where the running-board was resting on the dead man's head. I didn't look to see the expression on the woman's face; I just kicked the mule with my good foot and trotted it over to where Callicrates was standing.

'Ready?' I said.

'Yes,' he replied. 'I reckon if we go back the way we came we can go overland to Thria and then on to the City from there without crossing too many roads.'

That sounded eminently sensible to me, and so off we

went. We made good time, what with me riding along like a gentleman and Callicrates striding along beside me, and it was comforting to see Parnes away in the distance on our right. After about two hours and a bit we were in country that I knew reasonably well; in fact, we weren't far from a bit of land that we had been looking at only a day or so before which belonged to me.

'Callicrates,' I said, 'why don't we go to the house at Phyle instead of making for Athens? We'd be safe there.'

'Why?' said Callicrates.

I thought. 'I don't know why,' I said. 'Except the Spartans have been raiding for all these years and they've never burnt it yet.'

'They've never attacked Eleutherae yet,' Callicrates replied. 'Haven't you had enough of visiting your estates for the time being?'

'My foot is hurting and I want to go to Phyle,' I replied.

So we went to Phyle, getting there just before nightfall. They were all most surprised to see us, but not half as surprised as we were to see them. They had no idea the Spartans had arrived; they were just considering packing up to go.

'So they've come early this year, have they?' said the steward. He made the Spartans sound like the frost or locusts.

'I think we ought to move on tonight,' Callicrates replied. 'I don't imagine the Spartans will be too active in the dark.'

Of course, I protested like anything, but I don't think my views on matters were being taken too seriously by that stage. The steward hurried off to see to the last of the packing, while Callicrates eased the dead man's sandal off my foot and put on a new bandage.

Well, there's nothing to tell about our journey back to the City, except that it seemed very long and unpleasant and that as soon as we got home I tumbled on to a couch by the hearth and went straight to sleep, leaving Callicrates to take the news of the massacre at Eleutherae to the Council. My foot healed up quickly enough, since it was a clean wound and I was young, and a week or so later I was virtually back to normal and playing at being a landlord again. I didn't even have nightmares, which was a great relief to me, as I need my sleep; but I remember that I got rid of that mule as quickly as I could. In fact, I got forty-five drachmas three obols for it in the Market Square, and I felt dreadful about making a profit on the deal. It wasn't even a particularly good mule; but the man who bought it from me seemed happy enough. He was probably an idiot too.

It was at about this time that I composed the bulk of what was to be my first Comedy, although it wasn't presented for some time, as you'll hear in due course. In fact, between composing it and presenting it to the Archon I changed most of the jokes and completely rethought two of the characters, since the political situation changed and even I couldn't salvage material that was so hopelessly out of date. Nothing, except possibly fish, goes stale so quickly as topical jokes, and if I hadn't lost all my hair as a result of the plague I'd probably have torn it all out in exasperation at seeing my funniest jokes floating hopelessly out of my reach just because some fool of a politician fails to get re-elected.

You see, I can't abide wasting good material, and this is a serious handicap for a Comedian. I think the root of the trouble lies in the way I started off as a Comic dramatist, composing things on Hymettus among the goats. What I did then was to work up little set pieces and then fit them together to make up a play; which is rather like trying to build one pot from the smashed fragments of six different pots. I know I shouldn't do it. A proper poet starts off with an idea or a theme and creates characters and situations to illustrate and dramatise his idea. But if you're a bodger like me, you start with some clever little scene, like a fight between two pastrycooks or a Big Speech, or even just a single very funny joke, and you make up a story to go round it. Mind you, I'm not the only one who does it this way; and at least I don't repeat myself endlessly, like Aristophanes does.

The idea for this first play of mine was a single joke, and as it happens the joke was cut out as being no longer topical long before the play was produced and I can't remember it any more (which shows that it can't have been all that funny). Once I had the Joke, I knew who two of the characters in the play had to be, and after that it just seemed to flow. The next thing I had to think of was a new and startlingly funny costume for the Chorus; if you can do that, then you stand a chance of winning the prize however dreadful the dialogue is. And there's nothing quite like that tension you get in the Theatre when the audience all lean forward in their seats to catch the first glimpse of the Chorus as it makes its entry. I've heard it said that it's physically impossible for ten thousand people to be absolutely quiet all at the same time, and I suppose that's right; but the audience in the Theatre come pretty close to dead silence in that crucial moment. And then they either burst out into furious applause or they start muttering, and one way or another the tension is broken.

Well, my Chorus was original, if nothing else, since they were all dressed as trireme warships. So as not to give this away, I called the play simply *The General* – I don't hold with the school of thought that says that you ought to whet their appetites by calling the play *The Four-Toed Camels* or *The Two-Headed Satyrs*, because all that happens then is that the audience expects too much and will be disappointed when they see what the costume designer has actually managed to come up with.

I started off with a good safe opening scene; two slaves sitting outside their master's house at sunrise, listening to some peculiar and unexplained noise going on inside. This is scarcely original but it's the best way to start a play off unless you're going for a really high-powered opening, since it doesn't commit you to anything and it doesn't let the audience know too much about what's going to happen next. Anyway, the slaves sit there exchanging wisecracks about the domestic problems of prominent statesmen, and meanwhile the noises get louder and more inexplicable. The trick with this, of course, is to know exactly how long you can keep it up without the audience seeing that you're just doing it to be clever (which is fatal). At last one of the slaves catches sight of the audience out of the corner of his eye and condescends to let them in on the secret.

Their master, he says (like countless Comic slaves before him), is a lunatic. A complete and utter lunatic. What sort of a lunatic? Well, he's got this idea for ending the war at a stroke and providing for the People for ever, not to mention making himself General for life. He's going to take the fleet and sail up Olympus, to make the Gods into allies. Since the Athenian fleet has never been defeated, and an oracle has just said that it never will be, even the Gods themselves won't be able to stop him. Then he'll confiscate Zeus' thunderbolt, flatten Sparta, wipe out the Great King, and set himself up as King of Heaven with all the citizens of Athens as his new Pantheon. There is then a short digression about which prominent public figures of the time will replace which Gods, which was probably very funny in its day but which wouldn't mean a thing to you and doesn't mean much more to me, after all these years.

The only problem, the slave continues, is that Olympus is quite some way inland. That worried his master for a bit, but he's found a way round it. He's going to fit little wheels to each of the ships, like the platform in the Theatre, so that they can be propelled along the ground.

This doesn't explain the funny noises off-stage, of course, because they aren't hammering and wheel-fitting noises at all. Oh well, says the slave, we thought you'd be able to work that one out for yourselves, since you're Athenians and so damned clever about everything. You can't? Honest? Well, then, you'd better see for yourselves.

Then the stage-hands wheel out the platform with the interior set on it, to show what's going on inside the house. There we see the hero – originally Pericles; eventually, after many changes, Cleon – being sliced up like bacon by two sorcerers armed with whopping great knives. The sorcerers are in fact the City's two leading teachers of public speaking – I can't remember their names any more, I'm afraid – and they're chopping Cleon up and boiling him in a tanning solution, just as Medea chopped up Aegeus and boiled him to make him young again. But the purpose of this experiment is not to make Cleon young but to transform him from a reasonably honest man into a politician capable of getting his motion passed by Assembly. You can imagine what this scene was like, with the two sorcerers flinging in little turns of phrase and figures of speech like herbs and potions, until Cleon is well and truly tanned.

When they've finished and said the magic words *Three Obols a Day for Life*, out jumps Cleon, in the most grotesque portrait-mask you've ever seen, and indicts the two sorcerers for conspiracy to overthrow the democracy by helping him to succeed in justifying the conquest of Heaven. Then he stomps off to the Pnyx, and we have the big debate scene, with his speech. And still the Chorus haven't come on – the voters in Assembly haven't said a thing, since they're just the stage-hands without masks on. Then, as soon as his bill is passed, Cleon claps his hands and out comes the fleet, complete with little wheels, hats shaped like battering-rams and little banks of oars instead of sleeves.

The upshot of all this is that the fleet goes off to Olympus and besieges the Gods, just as we besieged the people of Samos, until they surrender and are sold as slaves to the Savages. Zeus, for instance, is sold to an Egyptian who wants him to make rain, and Aphrodite is bought by a Syrian pimp, while the celebrated poet Euripides turns up to buy some of the strange meta-physical concepts he keeps putting into his Tragedies, only of course they don't exist anywhere outside his needled brain. Eventually he buys Hermes, since as God of Thieves and the Dead he'll be able to help Euripides steal even more ideas from his predecessors on the Tragic stage. The play ends with Cleon taking his place on Zeus' throne, while the fleet is wheeled off to be broken up and sold to the Spartans (in whose pocket Cleon has been all along) for firewood.

From all that, you can see that it was a dialogue-play rather than a chorus-play, and that's my personal preference. But I was particularly pleased with the Address to the Audience, when the Chorus-leader takes off his mask and comes to the front of the stage and addresses the audience as if he were the author. In it, I begged the citizens of Athens not to allow the campaigns in Sicily (which, as you've already guessed, was what the play was all about) to get out of hand; they were simply State piracy, I said; and although there's nothing wrong with that *per se*, it was plain stupidity to embark on any ambitious scheme of that sort when we hadn't dealt with the Spartans on a permanent basis. There would be plenty of time for conquering the universe when Sparta was a heap of rubble, I said; in the meantime, we should get on with the job in hand. I reminded everyone of the great disaster in the days of the celebrated Cimon, when we sent our whole army and fleet off gallivanting round Egypt when we should have been consolidating our gains against the Persians in Ionia, and most of them were wiped out in the marshes. If that happened now, I said, we would inevitably lose the war and the empire, and the Spartans would pull down the Long Walls and leave us an open city.

When I showed the play to Cratinus (for I was still young and naïve) he was quite sullen and bad-tempered, which meant that he thought it was good. Never believe what they say about truly great poets always being ready to encourage talented young newcomers; in my experience, the better a poet is the more paranoid he is about competitors. Anyway, I pressed him for a comment of some sort, and he finally admitted that it might conceivably stand a chance of coming second, in a bad year, if everyone else presented farces.

'Only for God's sake,' he said, 'fix that *parabasis*. That Sicilian stuff is a load of crap. When you advise against something, make it something that's likely to be proposed, or you're wasting your time. Nobody in their right mind would ever seriously consider trying to conquer Sicily.'

I think the Gods must hate sensible people.

Chapter Six

Do you remember Diogenes the offspring of Zeus, who was the son of the Scythian who had an affair with Myrrhine, wife of the pious Euergetes? Well, his eldest son was named Diogenides ('*son* of the offspring of Zeus') who was born on the same day of the same year as me. Everyone knew the true story of his parentage, of course, and so he acquired the nickname of Little Zeus.

I met this remarkable person when I first harvested my own olives at Phyle; he was one of the itinerant day-labourers who came looking for work. You may be surprised that the scion of such a noble line should be reduced to being another man's employee, which is the worst degradation (barring actual slavery) that a human being can endure; think of what Achilles says in the *Iliad*, when he renounces glory –

> I'd rather be alive and a farm labourer,
> Working for a poor man with only a few acres,
> Than be King and Kaiser of the glorious Dead.

But Little Zeus had been the victim of one of those family disasters that can ruin the noblest of houses. His father had had seven children, all sons, and none of them had died in childhood.

Diogenes had done his best to reduce this formidable total. He had brought them up to love boar-hunting and horse-racing and other aristocratic but dangerous sports; but they had all proved naturally talented, and all survived. He set them, while still young, to watch the sheep on wolf-infested hillsides; but they killed all the wolves with their slingshots and became heroes. Finally, during the plague, he moved house to the middle of the Ceramicus; but the only member of his family to die was Diogenes himself.

The result was that his thirty acres of vines, which produced enough wealth to keep him in the Cavalry class, was split up into seven plots of just over four acres, one for each son. This would have been bad enough, but since the Spartans chose that year to devastate Acharnae, the seven heirs of the Offspring of Zeus each inherited nothing but vine-stalks and smashed trellises.

The brothers paid for Diogenes' funeral by selling his Infantry armour, registered for service as oarsmen, and set out to make the best living they could. The other six stayed in the City and were soon regular jurymen, loyal members of what we used to call the Order of the Three Obols; but Little Zeus (who was, by the way, the tallest and biggest man I ever met) felt that such a life was too demeaning for a descendant of a family who had been in Athens before Theseus was ever born, and became a hired hand, hoping to save enough money to buy vine-shoots when the war was over and replant his four acres.

He told me this tragic story as we harvested the olives – me up in the tree knocking them down with a stick, and Little Zeus underneath catching them in a basket – and I am not ashamed to say that I wept (with laughter, naturally). However, since his four acres shared a short boundary with some land held by my mother's uncle Philodemus, he was effectively a neighbour, and since I was young and full of my new Cavalry status, I decided to help him.

Descending from the olive tree like Prometheus the Saviour from heaven, I said, 'Your troubles are at an end, Little Zeus. I will buy your four acres as a present for my uncle, and with the money you can set up as a trader or a craftsman, which is a better life than day-labouring.'

But Little Zeus shook his head vigorously. 'I wouldn't dream of it,' he said. 'That land is our land. We've lived there since before the Dorians came, and my forefathers are buried there. Do you want their Furies to haunt me?'

I was rather taken aback by this. 'All right then,' I said, 'I'll enter into a bond of hectemorage with you, and plant out your land for you in return for a sixth of your produce until you've paid off the debt.'

Again he shook his head, and spat into his gown to avert evil. 'My great-great-great-great-uncle was related by marriage to the sons of Solon, who tore up the mortgage-stones,' he replied. 'Do you think he would rest easy in his grave if one of his seed became a hectemore?' He lifted the basket of olives on to his shoulder with all the resignation of Niobe, and carried it over to where the donkey was tethered.

'Tell you what I'll do, then,' I said, struggling to keep a straight face, 'I'll plant out your four acres for you as a gift between neighbours, in memory of your immortal ancestor Solon.'

'He wasn't actually an ancestor, just a relative by marriage,' Little Zeus started to say; then he dropped the basket of olives. 'You'll do what?'

'And if,' I continued blithely, 'when your vines are yielding fifteen jars to the furrow, you would care to share your good fortune with a neighbour, I'm sure the great Solon would approve, from whichever mansion he shares in the Isles of the Blessed with Harmodius and Cleisthenes the Liberator.'

'As it happens,' said Little Zeus, 'I am indirectly descended from the glorious Cleisthenes.' And he told me all about it as he shovelled the spilt olives back into the basket.

From that day onwards, I found it hard to turn round without finding Little Zeus there, all six and a half feet of him, watching me intently like a dog at feeding-time. He was forever warning me to take care lest I slip when the street was muddy, and warning me of the approach of fast-moving wagons; and if he thought the water I was about to drink was in any way tainted, he would snatch the cup from my hand, pour the water out, and sprint off to refill it from the nearest reliable well. At first I put this down to natural gratitude and was deeply touched. It was only later that I realised that he was determined not to let any harm come to me until his four acres were safely planted and producing. Twice he was nearly arrested and brought to trial for striking citizens, because they dared come near me when Little Zeus thought they might have the plague; and when I went to visit Phaedra once, he killed her father's dog because he imagined it was about to bite me.

Apart from this obsession, however, and his total lack of a sense of humour, Little Zeus had many sterling qualities. He was totally fearless – which is understandable given his immense size – and a tireless worker, once he had got it into his head that he was not so much a hired hand but a sort of dispossessed prince at the court of a royal benefactor who would one day restore him to his possessions. As befitted a man in this Homeric position, he strove to act as a hero should, 'always being the best' as the poet says, and excelling all around him in whatever the task of the moment happened to be. He would stay at the plough when the rest of us had long since given up and collapsed under a handy fig tree; and when he stood guard over the vines with a slingshot, not a single bird dared show the tip of its beak for miles around. He swung his mattock as if he were Ajax and the clods of earth were Trojan warriors, so that the rest of us were showered with flying stones and fragments of root; and when the harvest or the vintage was carried in, he would bear almost his own weight in produce, all the way from the barns to the City, watching me every step of the way like a hawk to make sure I didn't slip or fall on the mountain-tracks.

In the City, too, his zeal to please and excel was unabatable. Whenever there was wine or company he would sing the Harmodius until the roof shook; he had a fine voice but rather too much of it. As befitted a gentleman, he knew all the aristocratic poets – Theognis and Archilochus and every word ever written by Pindar – which was a great help to me when I needed a quotation for parody in a play. His greatest aesthetic

97

accomplishment, however, was his ability to give a one-man performance of Aeschylus' *Persians*; his great-grandfather, needless to say, had been in the same rank of the phalanx as the great poet at Marathon, so the play was virtually family property. First he would be the Chorus of Persian nobles – with occasional interpolations such as 'This is the authentic mourning posture of the Persian aristocracy; my great-grandfather saw them in the battle, you know' – and then he would be each of the actors, turning round to indicate a change of speakers during the dialogues and raising his voice to a squeak for the female roles, until his audience had to stuff their gowns into their mouths to keep themselves from laughing. Once my dear Callicrates was too slow and a snigger eluded him, at which Little Zeus stopped in mid-verse and looked round to see who had cracked a joke.

By and large, then, Little Zeus was an asset to me as I started to go about in Cavalry society. For I had outgrown, in a very short time, the Infantry friends of Callicrates and Philodemus, and I wanted to get to know the men I was insulting in my Comedy; the politicians like Cleon and Hyperbolus, and their henchmen Theorus and Cleonymus; the Tragic poets Agathon and Euripides, and the wicked and corrupt scientists, men like Socrates and Chaerophon, who was reputed to be a vampire.

Of course I knew all these people by sight and had greeted them by name in the Fish Market or the Propylaea, but that was not the same thing as drinking out of the same cup or joining them in the songs. It is essential for a Comic poet when he brings on a real person that he should be able to reproduce exactly the way that person speaks, and teach his actor precisely how each man makes his characteristic gestures. There is no substitute for close observation in this respect; anyone can make Cleon shout or Alcibiades talk with a lisp, but what makes the audience laugh is the way Cleon always brushes away the dust with his hand before he sits down, and Alcibiades' habit of sneezing elegantly over his shoulder.

I remember as if it was yesterday the first really

prestigious party I went to. It was given by Aristophanes to celebrate his victory with *The Acharnians* – a truly awful play and well worth avoiding if you ever come across a revival of it in one of those theatres-cum-cattle-pens in the outlying parts of Attica where they still occasionally produce old plays for people who can't get to the City – and I was in two minds whether to go or not, bearing in mind my previous encounters with that gentleman. However, a houseboy had appeared at our front door that morning, bidding Eupolis of Pallene to bring food and himself to the house of Aristophanes son of Philip at nightfall, and I could not resist the invitation, especially when I heard who else the boy had been told to summon.

'I've already called on Theorus, and he's coming,' he said, 'and Socrates the scientist, who's promised to come, and next I'm going to call on Euripides the poet, who's bound to come after what my master made him say in the play; and Cleisthenes the Pervert will probably accept, because he likes being put in plays and wants to be in the next one.'

'Why me?' I asked, and added, pouring out a cup of wine, 'Go on, you can tell me.'

'My master said invite you so I did,' said the boy, draining the cup quickly. 'And now I've got to get on. Good health!'

So that evening, with Callicrates and Little Zeus as my supporters, I set off for Aristophanes' house, carrying with me two fine sea bass in a rich cream sauce, a basket of wheat bread and twelve roast thrushes which Little Zeus had snared the day before. I had not the faintest idea what to expect, and my heart was beating like a drum.

You could hear the singing half-way down the street:

'We call upon our local Muse,
Our wonderfuel goddess Coal;
The radiant heat thy chips produce
Shines in the embers of our soul . . . '

Which was the Invocation from *The Acharnians*, of course, and the loud and rather tuneless voice leading it was unmistakably that of the poet himself, as I had heard him singing the Harmodius in the Serenade. One day, I thought, they'll be singing something of mine to celebrate a victory, with Little Zeus bawling out the words so loud they'll hear them in Corinth. I set my jaw as firmly as I could, and hammered on the door with my stick.

'You heat the pan,' they sang, 'that fries the fish,

> That turns the sprats a golden brown,
> (Golden BROWN!)
> Come, Anthracite, and grant a wish,
> To all who love Acharnae town!'

Pathetic, I murmured under my breath, and the houseboy opened the door.

'You're late,' he said, shouting to make himself heard, 'so they've started without you. Don't you know how to behave in good society?'

This scarcely encouraged me, but Callicrates grinned, and we made our way through to join the party.

Let me first describe the house. It was most sumptuously furnished, with hangings on the walls that had obviously been liberated from the Theatre; I recognised the front of Chremylus' house from *The Banqueters*, and the treadmill from *The Babylonians*. The floor was newly strewn, there were couches *and* chairs for everyone – never had I seen so many chairs together in one place – and the mixing-bowl for the wine was not earthenware but bronze. All the storage jars were painted, the flitch of bacon hung over the hearth by a brass chain, and the clothes chest was richly carved cedarwood, almost certainly imported. Up in the rafters I could see Aristophanes' shield; the rim was embossed with figures, and on its face, where usually there is a painted Gorgon to strike terror into the enemy, was a grotesque portrait of Cleon, his jaws open in the middle of a thundering tirade. The shield was also totally unmarked, which showed how much soldiering the fearless young poet had actually done. The rest of his armour was draped over an old-fashioned statue of Hermes in the corner of the room, with a sword-belt hanging from its upraised phallus, and three Victor's Wreaths encircling its brows under the (virtually unworn) helmet.

If the house made Philodemus' establishment look like a hovel, the company was enough to make me feel as if I had lived my life among grooms and fishmongers. Not only had all the guests that I had been told about turned up; there was also Philonides, the best Chorus-trainer in Athens, and Moschus the flute-player (specially hired, would you believe, just to entertain the guests), and, reclining next to the host and looking thoroughly bored, the most notorious man in Athens, Alcibiades.

Imagine what effect this had on me, already petrified and hardly able to speak. But my soul inside me told me to be strong, as if I were facing a squadron of cavalry or a ravenous bear, and I stepped forward, presenting the food I had brought with a modest smile. Cleisthenes the Pervert must have heard the words 'roast thrush', for without turning his head he leaned back, grabbed one of the birds from the tray, popped it into his mouth, crunched it up, and spat out the bones, and never once interrupted the highly dramatic story he was telling. Obviously the art of being a gentleman didn't just consist of being able to recite Archilochus.

Aristophanes rose languidly to his feet and embraced me, whispering in my ear as he did so, 'Say one word about that damned goat and I'll kill you.' Then he banged on the table with a jug for silence and introduced me, declaring, 'This is Eupolis son of Euchorus of Pallene', which seemed to be all he could find to say about me.

There was a mortifying silence, as all the guests looked at me. I did my best to smile, and Alcibiades sniggered.

'And this is Euripides the poet,' Aristophanes went on, 'and Theorus the politician, and here we have Socrates son of Cleverness,' naming each guest to me in turn as if I were an idiot or a foreigner, who had never been in the City before and thought the Acropolis was a public granary. Not for the first or the last time, I could cheerfully have murdered Aristophanes.

I took my place on the end couch and hid behind my

neighbour, Theorus, whom I knew very slightly. He had been made to look a fool in *The Acharnians*, and was ever so faintly resentful, so I decided he might be an ally. As he passed the cup to me, therefore, I whispered to him, 'Noble Theorus, why in God's name have I been invited to this? All these exotic people . . . I've never been in company like this in all my life.'

Theorus laughed; he was a fat man, and seemed to tremble all over. 'In a way it's a compliment,' he said, taking back the cup and spilling wine over his gown. 'Our host has heard of you.'

'Me?' I said, astonished.

'What do you expect,' Theorus yawned, 'if you go about reciting your choruses and dialogue to anyone who'll listen? The son of Philip has heard most of your *General* from one source or another, and I believe you have him worried. So for God's sake, whatever you do; get drunk, smash up the tables, set fire to Socrates' beard, anything you like; but don't go reciting any speeches, or you'll find that when your *General* is brought on, the audience will have heard that speech before, only slightly modified.'

I was stunned. 'You think he'd steal it?' I said.

'If you're lucky, yes,' said Theorus, 'and then let it be known that you stole it from him at this very party, abusing his hospitality like a Theban. If you're unlucky, of course, he'll write a parody of it. Then you'll get laughs all right, but not the sort you want. I think he's already nobbled your joke about the eels.'

I was uncertain whether to be furiously angry or deeply flattered, but my soul within me advised being flattered, so I laughed. It was obviously the right thing to do, for Theorus drew a little closer to me and went on:

'If you want to get your own back on the son of Philip, see if you can't find some excuse to tell the story about the goats on Hymettus, which we're all simply dying to hear.' Then a thought seemed to strike him, and he said quickly, 'No, don't do that. Just tell me now, quietly.'

I told him, and he laughed again, and by then all the food was finished. Little Zeus and Callicrates (who was pretending to be my servant so that he could stay and watch the party) rescued my plates and trays, and the flute-girls came out and started playing. The party was about to begin.

I don't know if you go to that sort of party very often; if you do, you'll know what the talk is like before the wine starts to take hold. At first, it's all very aristocratic stuff – 'When I was on an embassy to Mytilene', and 'The largest boar we ever bagged when I hunted in Crete', or 'That was the year Alexicacus won the chariot-race at Delphi; I shall never forget.' This was where Theorus and Cleisthenes the Pervert were in their element, although of course Alcibiades had the last word on everything. Then Aristophanes made a sign to the houseboy to increase the ratio of wine to water in the mixing-bowl, and after a while everyone was talking frantically about the Gods and the nature of Justice. Socrates the scientist and Euripides started a private two-handed battle here, and gradually everyone else stopped talking and listened. As for me, I had both my ears open, since this was the sort of thing I so urgently needed for my play. For a while, the issue hung in the balance, for Euripides was able to speak very quickly. Eventually, however, he began to tire, and Socrates managed to seize the reins.

'I take your point, Euripides,' he said, unfairly taking advantage of his opponent's fit of coughing, 'but I'm still not sure what you mean by *attending to*.'

'Well . . .'

'I presume,' Socrates continued blithely, 'that you don't mean attending to the Gods in the way we use the word . . . Well, to take an example at random, we say that not everyone knows how to attend to horses, but only the horse-trainer. Correct?'

'Well, yes, but . . .'

'Because horse-training is attending to horses?'

'Yes, but . . .'

'And in the same way, not everyone knows how to tend dogs . . .'

'Quite, but . . .'

'But only,' Socrates went on, raising his voice ever so slightly, 'the dog-trainer?'

'Absolutely, yes, But . . . '

'And cattle-farming is attending to cattle?'

'Undoubtedly. But . . . '

'Then piety must be attending to the Gods, mustn't it, Euripides? Is that what you're getting at?'

'Well . . . '

Socrates grinned and went on, 'Yes, of course. But isn't the effect of attendance always the same?'

A pause, for Euripides has lost his train of thought entirely. 'Yes,' he says lamely. 'But . . . '

'What I mean is, it's for the good of the thing attended to, so that, to use your example, horses are benefited by horse-training.'

'Actually, it was your . . . '

'And so (I presume) are dogs by dog-training, and cattle by cattle-farming, and so on.'

'But . . . '

'Or do you think,' said Socrates, narrowing his formidable brows, 'that attendance aims to hurt the thing attended?'

'Obviously not,' replied Euripides. 'But . . . '

'It aims at the benefit of it?'

'Yes, yes, of course. What . . . '

'Then if piety is *attending on* the Gods, as you said, is it a benefit to the Gods?' A little gesture here; a shrug of the shoulders and a raising of one eyebrow. 'Does it help them in some way to become better Gods, or somehow more Godlike?'

'No, of course not. But . . . '

'I didn't think you meant that, Euripides,' replied Socrates, sitting back in his couch. 'Now, what were you saying?'

Of course, by this stage Euripides had entirely forgotten what he had been trying to say, and just sat there with his mouth open. Before he could marshal his thoughts, Socrates started off again, and soon had him tied up in little knots over the meaning of the word 'service', until Aristophanes restored order by banging on the table again.

Then the mix of wine and water was strengthened again, and we began to talk about Poetry. Especially Comic Poetry, with particular regard to the excellence of *The Acharnians*. This went on for quite some time, as you can imagine, what with Euripides trying to be ever so polite about the extended personal attack on him in the play, and Philonides the Chorus-trainer telling a long and pointless anecdote about a Chorus-member who always kicked left when he should have kicked right. All this talk – even the boring anecdote – was extremely exciting for me, and I think Aristophanes must have noticed how enthralled I was, for he sent his boy over to me with the wine, and said, 'Friend Eupolis here is going to be a Comic poet.' He didn't add 'when he grows up', but he certainly implied it. 'I think we should hear a little of this *Colonel* of his, don't you?'

Theorus dug me in the ribs with his elbow, and I had an inspiration.

'Surely not,' I replied, mumbling slightly. 'I'd be ashamed to repeat my rubbish under the roof of a master. Can't we have the big speech from *The Acharnians* instead? I know that by heart.'

'Later perhaps,' Aristophanes said. 'But now we'd like something by the immortal Eupolis. Wouldn't we?'

'Well, if you insist,' I replied modestly. 'Let me see,' I mused, 'I could give you the Goatherds' dialogue from *The Steading of Pisistratus*.'

Aristophanes turned bright red. 'Not a dialogue scene,' he said. 'They're so hard for one speaker to do properly. Let's have something from this *Brigadier* of yours.'

'There's a good scene at the end,' I replied. 'A drunken party, with a Thessalian witch in it.'

Some of the others had got an idea what was going on by now. 'That sounds good,' they said. 'Let's have the Thessalian witch.'

'Dreadfully *passé*, those witch scenes,' Aristophanes muttered, 'don't you think? What about your *parabasis*? That would be worth hearing, wouldn't it?'

It was a nasty moment, but I kept my head. You may remember that I told you that my mother used to say that I spoke verse before I spoke prose. Well, when really pushed, I can extemporise verse – not very good verse, granted, but verse that scans. I took a deep breath, cleared my throat, and began to recite anapaests.

It took several lines before Aristophanes realised what I was doing, and then, of course, it was too late to stop me. The theme of this extempore *parabasis* of mine was that hardy perennial, scurrilous abuse of one's rival competitors. I started off with the hackneyed attack on Cratinus – his drinking and repellent habits and so on – then did a couple of lines on Pherecrates before launching into my main target Aristophanes, basing myself on his own attacks on Cleon for the more virulent compound epithets.

Not only (I said) does the son of Philip steal goats; he also lifts jokes and scenes and whole choruses from better and cleverer poets, which he overhears in wine shops and the public baths and copies down in the little pocket tablet he carries inside the sleeve of his gown. Of course he writes so quickly that he often gets a word wrong here or there, and since he's too thick to understand really clever writing, he doesn't notice the mistakes and reproduces them in the text he gives up to the Committee. His motive for this wholesale plagiarism is not, as you might suppose, envy; rather, it's partly to eke out his own bald and unimaginative texts, and partly because he doesn't have much time for writing, what with all his little trips to Sparta to tell his friend Brasidas about our naval tactics – what, didn't you know about that? Why else do you suppose he's always urging the City to accept the peace offers from Sparta, when it's obvious that they're woefully inadequate. You ask for proof? Well, you know how the Spartans don't use coins for money like normal people, but instead use great big iron bars, like spits. If you'd ever been to Aristophanes' house, you'd see a brand new iron spit in his hearth, with '*Made in Sparta*' stamped on it in Doric letters.

At which, everyone's eyes turn to the hearth, and see a beautiful iron spit inscribed in Doric letters ('*Made in Plataea*', actually, but I was the only person close enough to read it), and a great shout of laughter goes up from the company. Euripides in particular seems highly amused.

'Encore!' he shouts. 'And *now* let's have the Thessalian witch.'

'No, really,' I said, holding up my hand for silence, 'off with the flute-players and on with the actors, as I believe you poets say. Let's have the big speech from *The Acharnians*, like you promised.'

Of course, the big speech from *The Acharnians* is a plea for peace with Sparta, saying that the outbreak of the war was as much our fault as theirs – which was exactly why I'd made him promise to recite it. In short, I did to him what Theorus said he intended to do to me, and although the audience laughed at his great speech, they laughed for quite the wrong reason.

After that, we sang Harmodius and played riddles, and Moschus played the Orthian; but I was too exhausted to take much of a part in the proceedings. I ended up sitting next to Philonides the Chorus-trainer; and while Theorus (who by now was completely drunk) was singing a Hymn to Dionysus, he leant over to me and said, 'When you're old enough to bring on your *General*, you'll need a Chorus-trainer.'

'Certainly,' I replied.

'I like to see a play as soon as it's written, so that I can start blocking out the moves. My house is near the Temple of Hephaestus – anyone round there will point it out to you.'

I thanked him as best I could, but he grinned and turned away. In those days, for a Chorus-trainer like Philonides to approach a poet was almost unheard of; rather like a captain of a warship asking the crew's advice on when to start rowing.

Not wishing to push my luck, I left the party shortly afterwards. This, of course, was a mistake – you should never leave a party until either all your enemies have gone or everyone is too drunk to be dangerous. I later heard that after I had left my name was linked with a number of very unsavoury characters. For some reason, when someone spreads a rumour at a party, people always believe him; and one of the guests who heard that rumour was Alcibiades . . .

But I was so full of myself for days afterwards that there was no living with me, and even Philodemus and my dear Callicrates began to regard me as insufferable. I naturally put this down to jealousy; but it started me thinking that when quite soon I came of age, I would be leaving Philodemus' house and becoming a householder in my own right. In which case, obviously, I would need a wife.

I had been visiting Phaedra and her family ever since the night of the Serenade, so that my intentions by now were plainly obvious. Her family seemed to welcome the idea of me as a son-in-law, which I put down to my wealth and, I fear, my wit and magnetic personality. In fact, they seemed quite happy to do without some of the required stages of courtship and get straight on to a betrothal.

But Philodemus, who was conducting the negotiations for me, seemed unwilling to press on so quickly, and insisted on formal discussions about the dowry, even though they seemed quite happy to pay what we asked. I found this infuriating, and we quarrelled about it.

'But don't you see, you young idiot?' he told me. 'If they're so keen to offload the girl on you, there must be some reason . . .'

'Offload?' I replied angrily. 'What do you mean offload? She's beautiful and accomplished, they're offering ten acres . . .'

'Exactly,' said my uncle. 'And still, at nearly sixteen, the girl is unpromised. What's your explanation?'

'Simple,' I replied, trying desperately to think of one. 'She was promised to a man who suddenly lost all his wealth or was killed in the war.'

'Don't you think they'd have mentioned something like that?' he persisted.

'Since the subject has never come up,' I replied grandly, 'no.'

'If the subject has never come up,' said my uncle

despairingly, 'all that proves is that you're a bigger idiot than I thought.'

I decided to attack. 'All right, then,' I said, 'what do you think the reason is? Like I said, she's beautiful and accomplished, and the dowry is marvellous, and I'm absolutely sure she doesn't have any deformities or diseases. That doesn't leave much, does it?'

Philodemus shook his head. 'I don't know either,' he said, 'and neither does anyone else. But all the people I know are Infantry; they don't mix in Cavalry circles. And Callicrates says he thinks his army friends know something but won't say.'

'You've been asking?' I said furiously.

'Of course I have,' said Philodemus. 'It's my duty to ask, or why do you think marriages are arranged this way? It's so that young idiots like you with stars instead of eyes don't end up marrying girls with Thracian grandmothers or only one leg.'

I decided to be reasonable. 'Look,' I said, 'I know you're doing what you think is for the best and I appreciate it, really I do. But there's nothing wrong with Phaedra. I swear there isn't.'

'Then why,' said Philodemus, 'don't you ask some of your new Cavalry friends we hear so much about in this house, and see if they know anything.'

This made me very angry. 'So that's what it's all about, is it?' I shouted. 'You think I should be marrying some Infantry girl with red hands and a few goats on Parnes. Got someone in mind, have you, with a nice little commission in it for yourself from her grateful father?'

For a moment I thought Philodemus was going to hit me, and I backed away. He turned bright red in the face and grabbed his walking-stick; then with a visible effort he calmed down and became as cold as ice.

'If that's the way you feel,' he said, 'I shall conclude the negotiations on the terms as offered, and then you can go to the crows for all I care. And I hope your damned Phaedra turns out to have two club feet and leprosy.'

I tried to apologise but he was offended, so I made

my excuses and left. As I walked up to the Market Square I thought over what he had said, and it occurred to me that the only person I knew who seemed to know something about Phaedra was Aristophanes. Hadn't he said something about her 'habits' on the night of the Serenade? But how could I go and ask him for help, when I had made him look a fool in front of his guests? True, I had only been paying him back in advance, so to speak, for what he was going to do to me; but I doubted whether he would see it in that light. And then a horrible thought struck me. What if Theorus, who had a grudge against him, had lied to me about Aristophanes' motive in inviting me? What if he had invited me so that I could meet Philonides the Chorus-trainer and all those other important people? My blood seemed to freeze in my veins. Supposing the great Comic poet had been extending the hand of friendship, as one craftsman to another, and I had repaid him by wrecking his Victory celebrations? The more I thought about it, the more convinced I became that Theorus had been lying – he was not, after all, the sort of man you would believe if he told you your name – and that I had made the most terrible mistake.

As I wandered through the anchovy stalls, feeling as if I had just murdered my host, who should I bump into but Aristophanes himself? He was arguing heatedly with a fishmonger about an eel he had bought the day before, and which he swore blind was off. The fishmonger was adamant that a real Copaic eel, smuggled through enemy lines at the risk of the courier's life, was bound to smell a bit hooky, that that was what gave them their flavour, and a proper gentleman would know Copaic eel when he tasted it. Aristophanes replied that he knew perfectly well what Copaic eels tasted like, that he had eaten them in the company of the richest men in Athens, and that a proper Copaic eel doesn't make you throw up like Mount Aetna half an hour later. The fishmonger, who obviously never went to the Theatre and so didn't know the risk he was taking, replied that even the best-behaved Copaic eel is likely to get a bit frisky when a man of dubious citizenship like Aristophanes son of Philip gobbled it up like a starving dog, instead of chewing it like a gentleman, and then washed it down with half a jar of unmixed wine.

Aristophanes gave up the unequal struggle and retired to a neighbouring stall to buy a crab. I came up behind him and tapped him on the shoulder. He jumped.

'What in God's name did you do that for?' he snapped. 'I nearly swallowed my change.'

I apologised, feeling that I had not begun this vital interview in the best possible way. Aristophanes fished an obol out of his mouth, paid for the crab and started to walk away.

'Please, Aristophanes,' I said humbly, 'I want to apologise for spoiling your party.'

'So I should think,' he said cautiously. 'That's the last time I try to help a young poet.'

'Someone told me a dreadful lie about you,' I explained, 'and I got so drunk that I believed it.'

'You didn't seem very drunk when you were spewing up those anapaests,' he said. 'Honestly, I didn't know where to look. And can you think of a worse omen than that for a Victory party? I'll be lucky if I get a Chorus at all next year.'

I had forgotten how superstitious he was, and I blushed. 'I really am sorry,' I mumbled. 'It really was a stupid thing to do.'

'Never mind,' he said, forcing himself to smile. 'After all what could be a better omen than to be mentioned in a *parabasis*? Means I'm bound to get a Chorus, or why am I being mentioned at all? Forget it, Eupolis. Set it off against that confounded goat.'

He slapped me, hard, on the back and I smiled. 'I'm glad we've got that sorted out, then,' I said, 'because I want your advice.'

'Certainly,' he said warmly. 'Got a scene you're having trouble with?'

'No, it's not that.'

'Oh.' He looked disappointed, and I saw that he really was taking an interest in my career.

'No, it's about my marriage. You remember that girl you . . . '

'At the Serenade?'

'Yes.'

'Phaedra. Nice girl. What about her?'

'That's what I wanted to ask you, actually. I've been wondering why a girl like that, with everything going for her, is still unpromised.'

A smile crossed Aristophanes' face, and he put an arm around my shoulders. 'I thought you might wonder that,' he said.

'Do you know something then?'

'As it happens, I know the whole story. Buy me a drink and I'll tell you all about it.'

We went across to a wine shop and I bought a jar of the finest Pramnian. We exchanged healths, and he told me the story. It was just as I had guessed. Phaedra had indeed been promised, and to a truly marvellous man called Amyntas. I had heard of him, vaguely.

'Wasn't he killed in the war?' I asked.

'It was a tragedy,' said Aristophanes sadly. 'Friend of mine, actually. Died defending a wounded comrade. Phaedra was heartbroken.'

'I can imagine,' I said.

'Of course, the family hadn't announced a formal betrothal – there was some problem with the dowry; apparently Amyntas' family were asking seven acres, when the girl would be a bargain without any dowry at all. What are they offering you, by the way?'

'Ten acres,' I said. Aristophanes whistled, and went on:

'I imagine they haven't mentioned it because of the bargain they had to strike with Phaedra after she heard the news. Apparently she was so upset that she was all for running away and becoming a priestess of Demeter. They only stopped her by promising never to mention his name again. You know what girls are like.'

'Of course, I see,' I said. 'Well, thank you, you've taken a great weight off my mind.'

'If I were you,' said Aristophanes, drinking off the rest of the wine and wiping his chin daintily, 'I'd get the betrothal all sealed and concluded as quickly as possible, before she starts thinking about her lost love and changes her mind. You may have noticed that her parents are a bit anxious to get her married off; you can see their point, can't you?'

'Absolutely. Thank you.'

'Not at all, not at all,' said Aristophanes. 'After all, considering how I insulted the poor girl that night, the least I can do is make sure she gets a suitable husband.'

'And what you said about her habits. . . .?'

'I forgot to mention that,' said Aristophanes. 'She's a lovely child, but she's a terror for accidentally knocking over vases. It's the only thing that can be said against her, so far as I know. Is that the time? I've got to rush.'

I thanked him again, and set off for home to make my peace with Philodemus. Not only, I reflected, had I found out the truth about my beloved Phaedra; I had also made a good and worthwhile friend.

Chapter Seven

In Tragedy, of course, there is a convention that the action – the battles and the murders and so on – always happen off-stage. Orestes drags Clytemnestra off into the wings and we hear horrible screams, while the Chorus turn to face the audience and make their breathtakingly profound comments, like 'All is not well within the house'; then the playwright treats us to five minutes of metrical lamentation and the proceedings are adjourned. When I was young I always felt cheated by this squeamishness, and I remember one year slipping out of my seat (I think it was an Agamemnon of some description) and sprinting round to the wings to see if I could see the King getting his skull split. I found a little tear in the painted backcloth and looked through, but all I saw was the actor frantically pulling his mask and gown off to change into the Messenger costume.

So now I am tempted to follow the Tragic convention, and let my wedding take place behind the curtain. Flutes. The torchlight procession winds its way round the orchestra and in through the left-hand door, the door closes, all is not well within the house. But there; any fool can be a Tragedian. It takes courage to compose Comedy.

Actually, I remember very little of the wedding itself. It was a mild evening, not too warm, and I had the sort of headache that makes everything else seem entirely irrelevant. It was obvious from the start that the whole thing was going to be a complete and utter disaster, but

114

that was only to be expected, considering that I had seen my name posted in the Market Square that morning on the Three Days' Rations list.

'Where are we going?' I asked the man standing next to me.

'Samos,' he said, 'just for a change.' He spat out a mouthful of chickpeas. 'You ever been there?'

I said no, I hadn't.

'Samos,' he said gravely, 'is the armpit of the Aegean. The goats are all gristle and the people pee in the wells. The west coast is all right if you're not prone to catching fever, but we're probably going to be over on the east. This time of year, of course, it's worse than usual . . . '

'I'm getting married this evening.'

He scowled at me and spat into the fold of his tunic. 'Get away from me,' he said. 'I don't want anything to do with you if you're unlucky.'

That, I think, is when my headache started. I spent the rest of the morning cleaning my armour, which had gone green up in the rafters, and putting a new plume in my helmet. Little Zeus tried to help, but his contribution consisted of putting his foot through my shield. I sent him out to get it mended, and poured myself a large cup of neat wine, which was a mistake.

'Cheer up,' Callicrates said, as we tried to force the plume into the socket. 'After all, you've got your wedding to look forward to, don't forget.'

My hand slipped and came down hard on the sharp bronze of the socket, splashing blood on to the white horsehair. 'I'm not likely to forget,' I replied. 'Have you seen my sword-belt anywhere?'

'Borrow mine,' he said, 'it's about your size. It's just a tax-collecting expedition, apparently. I was talking to a man who'd heard the debate. You'll be back in a month or so, I expect.'

I shrugged. 'I couldn't care less,' I said.

'The important thing to remember about Samos,' he went on, 'is not to eat the sausages. A friend of mine – you know, Porphyrion who has that dog with the stunted tail – he was in Samos a year or so ago when there was that trouble, and he says they don't boil the blood properly before pouring it into the skins. Otherwise it's not a bad place, except that the women throw stones a lot.'

'Why?'

'They don't like Athenians, I guess. Has anyone been across to tell Phaedra?'

'No,' I replied. 'Will you go?'

He shrugged his shoulders. 'If you want,' he said. 'I promised to take the cooks round some time this morning.'

I had forgotten about the cooks. We had hired five of them for the wedding, but one had gone down with dysentery. It made me wonder about the other four.

In the afternoon, I went to the baths and had my hair cut and scented. The barber talked about nothing but the war, and how it was not going well, and how someone had seen a really horrible omen.

'What I heard,' he shouted over his shoulder, 'was that when the watch were handing over the keys last night, this great big snake appeared out of nowhere – thick as your wrist and a sort of olive green was what they told me – and curled all round the key. Now if you ask me . . .'

'Bollocks,' said a man at the back of the shop. 'Now if the key had curled all round the snake, that would be an omen.'

The barber ignored him. 'The key's obviously this lot they're sending off to Samos. Stands to reason.'

'Why's that?'

'Don't show your ignorance,' said the barber, picking a spot of verdigris off the blade of his razor. 'The top man in Samos these days is called Draco – "The Snake" – right? This Draco's going to surround our boys and squash them flat.'

'There's an oracle about that,' said someone else. 'The snake is going to bite the feet of the owl, and the wedding-torches will light a hundred funerals.'

'What wedding-torches?' said the barber. 'I think they just put in any old thing to make it scan.'

When I got home, the torch-bearers were having a

fight with the flute-girls and Little Zeus was back with my shield. It had a great big plate of new bronze riveted over the tear, which was apparently the best they could do at such short notice.

'It's all for the best, if you ask me,' he said cryptically. 'Do you want your sword sharpening, or can I get on with my packing?'

'Where are you going?' I asked.

'With you, of course. Shield-bearer. You're entitled to a shield-bearer, being Cavalry class. I asked about it down at the smithy.'

For a split second I was touched; then I remembered the five acres. 'Get the rations packed,' I said wearily, 'and put in plenty of cheese.'

About an hour before sunset I started to shiver, and I drank another cupful of neat wine. I had discovered that my left greave was too tight, and in trying to open it up I buckled the clips. While I was wrestling with it, Philodemus came in and asked me if I had made a will.

Not long after, I heard the flutes in the street; they were bringing in the bride. Suddenly I felt a sort of blind terror. They were singing the wedding-hymn, but for some reason it sounded flat and mournful, and I remember hoping that they would pass on to the next house.

Callicrates put his head round the door. 'For God's sake,' he said, 'aren't you ready yet? I'd better tell them to slow down. Get your garland on, will you? And try to look interested.'

I pulled on my new sandals, fumbling with the straps. There were little Cyclopes forging thunderbolts in my head, and I felt sick. The thought of dancing made my blood run cold. I could hear Philodemus arguing with the women in the inner room, something about some idiot sprinkling the wrong flower-petals on the marriage-bed, and whose brilliant idea was it to put out the coverlet with Pentheus and the Bacchae on it? I stood up and splashed cold water on my face. 'Get that fool of a nephew of mine out here this instant,' Philodemus was shouting. 'I wish to God I'd stayed in bed this morning.'

The smell of burning resin from the torches made my stomach lurch, and I wanted to hit somebody, but there is a time and a place for everything. I made my way to the front door and jammed a smile on to my face. It didn't fit. I think my teeth were in the way.

> 'With just such a song hymenaean
> Aforetime the Destinies led
> The Master of Thrones empyrean
> The King of the Gods, to the bed
> Of Hera, his beautiful bride . . . '

I had made a point of asking them not to sing that particular wedding-ode; but perhaps it was the only one they knew. Something with a bit of a *tune* to it, they must have said to themselves, something that everyone can join in . . .

> 'And Love, with his pinions of gold,
> Came driving, all blooming and spruce,
> As groomsman and squire, to behold
> The wedding of Hera and Zeus . . . '

Which, as any child will tell you, has never exactly been a success, what with Zeus turning himself into swans and showers of gold, and Hera sending plagues of sores down on all her husband's favourite cities. I adjusted my garland; but I felt more like a sacrifice than a bridegroom. Who gives this lamb to be slaughtered? And why, in God's name, was I feeling like this?

Then I saw Phaedra being led along by her father, and she looked like that painting of Galatea by Scythines in the Temple of Hephaestus, on the left as you go in. You know how she's just turning her head to look at Pygmalion, who's standing there with his mouth open, obviously feeling a complete fool; and her head is just slightly tilted, as if she's just noticed him, but she knows who he is; and she's just about to say something, and you stand there for minutes at a time in case she opens her lips. I've been in love with that painting as long as I can remember, and that was how Phaedra looked; and my head was hurting so badly I could hardly stand up straight. Perhaps it was the way she seemed so still, with all the wedding-guests lolloping about around her; or perhaps it was the glow of the torches, which seemed to make an unofficial sunset, with her as the setting sun. Certainly she looked very young indeed in the torchlight, but not a bit nervous, wrapped up like a parcel in all her wedding finery; and I thought of the old story of how the dictator Pisistratus got back into Athens after his exile by dressing up a woman as Athena, with gold dust sprinkled in her hair, and sending her in front of him in a golden chariot, so that all the City guards threw away their spears and fell flat on their faces, thinking that the Lady was bringing Pisistratus home.

The flutes stopped, and I stepped forward, feeling rather as I used to feel when it was my turn to recite at school and I couldn't remember beyond the third line. I reached out and made a grab for her hand. I think I got about three fingers. Her father was saying his lines, and I smiled idiotically. I couldn't remember mine to save my life. In fact, I believe we would all be there still if Callicrates hadn't whispered them in my ear.

Phaedra raised her head and looked into my eyes. Her face seemed as bright as the sun, and I suddenly felt much better. I drew her towards me into the house. She stumbled.

'Oh my God,' someone said, 'she's touched the threshold.' That is, of course, the worst possible omen.

'Shut up,' hissed someone else. 'For God's sake, somebody, sneeze.'

'It's a bit late for that, isn't it?' said the first voice. There was a trumpeting noise, which I took to be somebody feigning a sneeze.

'Oh well,' said Phaedra's father, 'it can't be helped now, I suppose.'

'Now,' she said archly, 'we're alone at last.'

The thong of my left sandal had resolved itself into an impenetrable knot, and the little miners inside my head had found a new lode. I mumbled something like 'How nice', and sat down on the floor. Things were not going well. My armour, spear and three days' rations were propped up against the wall, all ready for the morning, and I knew that two or three of the Thracian housemaid's children were listening at the door, for I had heard them sniggering about a quarter of an hour ago. Phaedra, apparently, had gone deaf.

'How's your poor head?' she cooed. 'Does it hurt awfully?'

'No,' I said sullenly. The sandal-thong broke, and I kicked it away.

'Would you mind putting something over *that*,' she pointed to the pile of armour with the helmet perched on top of it. 'It looks like somebody watching us.'

She had a point. I looped my cloak over it, and sat down on the bed.

'Shall I put the light out?' she whispered. I nodded and pulled my tunic off over my head. She licked her fingers and there was a tiny hiss as she pinched out the lamp. For some reason, I felt utterly miserable. 'Come on,' she said.

I crawled in beside her. She smelt, very faintly, of sweat.

'My cousin Archestratus went to Samos once,' she said.

'Oh yes?'

'He got bitten by something. They had to cut his foot off in the end.'

I took a deep breath and moved my arm, with the general idea of putting it round her shoulders. 'Ouch,' she said.

'Sorry.'

'That was my ear.'

I moved my arm and put it down on the pillow. 'Now you're pulling my hair,' she said. 'You really know how to get a girl in the mood, don't you?'

'Perhaps we'd better light the lamp,' I suggested.

'No,' she said firmly. 'Better not.'

'All right.'

'There are rose-petals all over this bed,' she said after a while.

'That's traditional, isn't it?'

She sniffed. 'It might be in your family,' she said. 'Can't you brush them out or something?'

'I'll light the lamp.'

'Please yourself.'

I always have been a fool with flints and tinder, and by the time I had the lamp going I could sense a distinct atmosphere of hostility in the room. 'Now,' I said, 'let's see about these rose-petals.'

'Forget it,' she said, and she threw her arms around me, like a swimmer nerving himself to dive into cold water. I had my mouth open at the time, and I felt her chin connect with my teeth. She unravelled herself and said, 'God, you're so clumsy. What do you think you're doing?'

'I'm sorry,' I mumbled. My lip hurt where she had banged it against my lower teeth, and when she kissed me, I winced.

'That does it,' she said, and she folded her arms across her breast.

'Don't be like that,' I said; but for some reason I felt rather relieved, just as I used to feel when the schoolmaster said, 'You obviously don't know it, do you? Sit down and let's hear from someone who does.' There was something not exactly inviting about Phaedra, just then.

'I've met some cack-handed people in my time,' she went on, 'but you're just about the worst, do you know that? This is supposed to be the happiest day of my life, you realise. That's a joke.'

'I'm sorry.'

'You're pathetic.' She blew her breath out through her teeth. 'And for God's sake shut your mouth. You look like a dead tuna.'

'Oh.'

She closed her eyes. 'And what did you think you were playing at, dragging me through the door like

121

that? Anyone with any sense would have realised I was bound to catch my feet on the threshold, especially in those ridiculous sandals they made me wear. And now I'll have everybody saying I'm unlucky, and the maids blaming me if the milk goes sour.'

'I don't believe in all that stuff,' I said soothingly.

'I do,' she replied sharply. 'I suppose you don't believe in the Gods, either.'

'Yes I do.'

'That's not what I heard,' she muttered. 'I heard that you go around with that Euripides, who thinks that the Gods are all states of mind or something, and Helen of Troy was spirited away to Egypt before the Trojan War. Absolute rubbish.'

I felt I had missed something somewhere. 'What's Helen of Troy got to do with anything?' I asked.

'Do you believe in the Gods or don't you?'

'Of course I believe in the Gods. Phaedra, this is our wedding-night.'

'You've realised that, have you? Oh *good*.'

I put my hand on her shoulder. She removed it with her finger and thumb, as if it was a spider.

'And what sort of man,' she went on, 'gets called up for military service on his wedding-day? When they told me I couldn't believe it. I thought they were being funny, honestly I did.'

'That's not my fault, is it?' I said. I felt as if I was arguing with five different people at once, all about different things.

'Well let's just get one thing straight, shall we?' she said. 'There'll be none of that nonsense till you get back, and that's final.'

'What?'

'You heard me. If you think you're going to get me pregnant and then wander off and get yourself killed fooling about in Samos, and leave me to bring up your horrible little child on my own—'

'Phaedra—'

'I am a free-born Athenian woman, not a breeding heifer. Have you made a will?'

122

'What did you say?'

'Deaf as well as feckless,' she confided to the pillow. 'I said, have you made a will?'

'No.'

'Well, don't you think you should?'

I blinked. 'What, now?'

'For God's sake,' she snapped, 'you're going off to war in the morning. Have you no sense of responsibility?'

I took a deep breath, closed my mouth firmly, and tried to draw her towards me. 'No,' she said, 'not till you—'

I think that must have been the last straw for the housemaid's children, for there was a shriek of childish laughter, and Phaedra's face went bright red. She hopped out of bed, grabbed the chamber-pot, opened the door and let fly. Unfortunately there was nothing in it.

'Go away!' she shouted – I hadn't realised how loud her voice was – and slammed the door. 'You buffoon,' she said.

'What have I done?'

'How could I marry someone so unlucky?' She flopped back into bed and pulled the coverlet over herself, right up to her chin. 'You realise this'll be all over Athens in the morning?'

I shook my head feebly. 'Phaedra—'

'What makes it worse,' she said, 'is those stupid plays of yours.'

'What?'

'You'll never live it down,' she sighed, 'once Aristophanes and those other idiots hear about it. And people will point to me in the street, and say—'

'Shut up, will you?' My head was just about to split. I could feel it pulling apart, like a log full of wedges.

'Don't you talk to me like that,' she yapped, 'or you can sleep on the floor.'

'I might just do that anyway,' I replied.

'Good.' She made a snuffling noise which was presumably meant to be weeping, but I suddenly realised I couldn't be bothered. I leaned over her, pinched out the lamp, and banged my head down hard on the pillow.

'Now what are you doing?' she said.

'Going to sleep,' I said through the pillow. 'You can do what you like.'

She said quite a lot after that, and I found it strangely soothing, for I actually fell into a sort of a doze. When I came round from it, my headache had gone completely and she was fast asleep, with her nose pressed against the back of my neck. Very gingerly, so as not to wake her, I turned and looked down at her.

One of my father's neighbours used to tell the story of the creation of woman; how the Good Gods moulded woman's body out of clay, making it more lovely than anything else in the world, and left it to dry in the sun, and how while they were away, the Bad Gods came and put woman's soul into it, so that mortal men should never know quiet and happiness. I will never forget how beautiful Phaedra looked just then. A strand of hair had fallen over one of her eyes, and I stroked it back over her forehead; then I tried to kiss her, but her lips were half-buried in the pillow, and I only managed to make contact with the corner of her mouth. I slid a finger down under her chin to lift her face, but she woke up, said, 'Get off,' and rolled over on to her other side.

'No,' I said. 'Come back here.'

'Go to hell,' she yawned. 'You snore, too. I hope the Samians get you.'

'What's that supposed to mean?'

'It means that, right now, given a choice between you and no husband at all . . .'

'Look . . .'

She wriggled away on to the edge of the bed. 'Given a choice . . .' she repeated; then she was suddenly quiet. My soul was whispering something to me, and then everything seemed to fall into place, like a wheel fitting on to an axle before the pin is driven home. 'So that's what's wrong with you,' I said.

'Look who's talking.'

I sat up and rubbed my eyes. 'Seriously, though,' I said. 'What is it now?'

'Whenever I asked people about you,' I said, 'I always

124

got the impression that there was something I ought to know, but I could never find out what it was.'

She made a despairing face, as if I were a troublesome child who could not be bribed, not even with a slice of honeycomb. 'Go to sleep,' she said wearily.

'But I never thought . . .' At that moment, I hated the sound of my own voice, high and infantile in the dark and nothing to do with me, 'I honestly never thought it could be as simple as . . .'

'As what?'

'As a really filthy temper,' I said, driving the words through the gate of my teeth like unwilling sheep. 'That's what it is, isn't it? Do you throw things as well, or do you just shout?'

'I have not got a filthy temper,' she shouted. Just for a moment, I sensed that I had the advantage, and I was glad.

'And that's what everybody else knew, and I didn't,' I continued, raising my voice and not caring what it sounded like. 'That's what your father managed to keep from me. That's what Aristophanes meant when he said . . .'

'That's absolutely typical, isn't it,' she hissed. 'It's all right for men to yell and throw things about, oh yes. They're allowed to be as loud-mouthed and disgusting as they like, especially when they're going about in packs like dogs. I suppose when you come home in the middle of the night with vomit all down your cloak and some pretty boy you've picked up in the Shoemakers' Quarter—'

'I might have known,' I went on, leading my picked troops out against the enemy cavalry. 'It's like the fishmonger's, just like that—'

'And you start howling the place down and upsetting all the jars, and wanting fried whitebait and cream sauce double quick, and why hasn't this floor been swept—'

'Anybody's got any rotten fish to sell, it's all right, lads, here comes Eupolis, we can sell it to him. Eupolis will buy anything, everyone knows that—'

'What are you talking about?'

'You know perfectly well,' I said furiously. 'And you knew all along, didn't you?'

She snorted, just like a horse. 'For God's sake, Eupolis,' she said, 'exactly what is it you want out of life? You didn't expect me to sidle up to you and say, "You'd better not marry me, I throw plates", did you? And even you couldn't have been so utterly stupid as to think we agreed to the match because we *liked* you.' She shook her head vigorously. 'I mean, look at you. I've seen better-looking men in the silver mines.'

I stared at her open-mouthed. Just then, I could have strangled her.

'That's it,' I said. 'First thing in the morning, you go back to your father.'

She stared at me with such hatred that I was sure I could feel the skin on my face starting to peel. 'You wouldn't dare,' she said.

'And if you think you're getting back a lead obol of your dowry,' I went on, 'you're more stupid than you look, because I know the law and—'

Then she jumped at me. I put my arm up to cover my eyes, but that wasn't what she had in mind. She went for my mouth with her tongue like a thrush with a snail, and by the time I realised what she was doing it was far too late to do anything about it, although I tried my best. My mouth was full of blood from where she had bitten into my upper lip, and I felt sick.

'Right,' she said, pulling herself off me, 'now try and divorce me.' She pulled the coverlet towards her with a jerk. 'And if you do, I'll make sure that every Comic poet in Athens hears the full story. In fact, I might just do that anyway, because you make me want to throw up. And another thing; that's the first and last time, so far as I'm concerned. You're pathetic, do you understand?'

Just then, I was in no mood to argue. I was thinking, this must be how Agamemnon felt, when his wife split his head with an axe as he lay back in his bath, and the water turned royal purple all round him. I felt bad luck buzzing round me like flies in summer; you can't catch them and they climb all over you, into your ears and down under

126

your tunic. I crawled out to the extreme edge of the bed and sucked the blood from my cut lip.

But then again, said my soul inside me, think how lucky you are, Eupolis of the deme of Pallene, to have dog-headed Comedy as your most intimate companion. There will be laughter in this before your nails next need cutting – not for you perhaps, but for others certainly. When they have tired of Heracles and the pot of soup, when the capture of the Cercopes is met with stony silence, and even Cleon and the thirty talents cannot move them, someone will say, 'Come on Eupolis, let's have the story of your wedding-night, and don't forget the bit about . . . ' Remember, whatever happens to you, they can only hurt your body; but your mind is the mind of a Comic poet, and everything ridiculous, grotesque or absurd is more valuable to you than coined silver. Pull yourself together, my soul shouted inside me, it's time to pull off Agamemnon's mask and put on the Messenger's.

'Well, say something,' said Phaedra. 'Or are you dumb too?'

I smiled, lay back on the pillow and closed my eyes.

'Alas, dear wife,' I said, more to myself than to her, 'I fear that all is not well within the house. And the hell with you, too.'

Chapter Eight

For most of the first day out of Piraeus, I slept peacefully; but after that I felt horribly sick. Not all Athenians are more at home on ships than on dry land, whatever we try and make you believe in the Comedies, and the thought that I was on my way to a distinctly unfriendly part of the Athenian empire did little to settle my stomach.

To get from Athens to Samos on a troop-ship, you have to cross a lot of open water; first, Euboea to Andros and Tenos, then straight across to Icaria (where they threw stones at us when we went to get water) and eventually to Samos, which is unquestionably the most miserable place I have ever been in my life.

True, parts of it are quite remarkably rich and fertile – much more so than anything we have in Attica – and a large proportion of the rest of it is perfectly good for vines. But the generosity of Zeus has done nothing to sweeten the people, who have a generally bad attitude towards the rest of the world, and Athens in particular. The key to understanding Samos is their hatred of their neighbours the Milesians, which has lasted ever since time began. You may think you hate your neighbour (that is, after all, the natural condition of mankind) but you occasionally think of something else; whether the vines will get blight again this year, and is the King of Persia going to invade Bactria? Not so the Samians and the Milesians. It was fear of the Milesians, not the Persians, that made the Samians join the Athenian alliance in the first place, and when we sided with the Milesians over some local squabble at the beginning of the war, they broke away from the empire and sent for ambassadors from Sparta. As a result, Pericles had to go over and sort them out, which he managed only after a long and bloody siege. Since then, they have not liked us at all; but fortunately, they have the Milesians to keep them busy. I am told that a Samian's idea of a good time is to invite his friends and neighbours round, open a jar or two of wine (Samian wine tastes like tanning-fluid, incidentally) and stick knives in a woollen cloak, since wool is the principal export of Miletus.

Our job in Samos was to get in the taxes, and nobody knew whether this was going to be easy or not. According to our taxiarch, it would be like picking apples off a low tree; all Samians are fat, on account of their eating too much ewes-milk cheese, and since the democrats and the oligarchs are perpetually at each other's throats about the latest plan for a surprise attack on Miletus, one side is bound to betray the other, open the gates of the city, and cut the General's throat as he sleeps. On the other hand, a couple of men who had been to Samos with Pericles told a very different story. According to them, incessant war with Miletus has made the entire citizen body as hard as shield-leather, and once they get inside their city walls, nothing short of actual starvation will get them out again. Also, they are very good at defending fortified towns and cities (the Milesians again), and have an unpleasant habit of pouring boiling lead on the heads of anyone who comes close enough to make it worth their while. The Samians have plenty of lead, the veterans added, which they get from the Carians in exchange for olive-curd and decorated pottery.

In fact, we didn't see a single Samian during the whole of our first week on the island. Instead, we built a wall. Nobody knew what it was for, where it was supposed to come from or go to, how high it should be, or which side of it we were eventually to defend. It started in the middle of a vineyard, and finally petered out on the gentle slopes of a hill, either for sound strategic reasons or because we ran out of stones. Speculation as to its purpose and exactly why both ends had been left open kept us reasonably well entertained for the first two days, and after that it rained; by all accounts, for the first time in that particular month since the days of the dictator Polycrates. I had done a little gentle wall-building once or twice before, but there seemed to be a general feeling among our taxiarchs that this wall, although inexplicable, was going to be needed very soon: and when a large section of it fell down during our third night in Samos, redoubled efforts were called for, and my attitude towards soldiering took a turn for the worse.

Eventually, however, the job was finished, and no sooner was the last stone triumphantly in position than our unit got orders to fill our water-skins and march up into the mountains, which in Samos are very high and crawling with political dissidents (which is Samian for bandits) to collect the taxes from the outlying villages. We waved goodbye to our wall, which we never saw again, and set off to die for our country, should the need to do so arise.

When we did meet some Samians, they didn't try and kill us; they were only about twelve years old, and small for their age. Instead they tried to sell us local pottery and the company of their sisters, who were (they assured us) very nice girls. We marched on until we came to a large village, I think it was called Astypylaea, where we were due to collect the first payment of taxes.

Astypylaea was just like any other substantial hill village, with a sprawl of houses, a small thatched temple and a market square marked off with weather-beaten boundary stones; it could have been anywhere up the mountain from Pallene, or out towards the back of Phyle. There were rather more sheep and rather fewer goats than we're used to in Attica, and some of the people had a rather unGreek look to them, which my companions attributed to interbreeding with the Persians when Samos was part of the Persian satrapy of Ionia. But if they weren't exactly friendly they didn't throw stones, and there was no shield-wall in the main street as some of us had been expecting. Instead, there was an old man who we took to be the village spokesman, and a couple of bored-looking boys of about fifteen holding some very thin sheep on short reins. These, it appeared, were a gift to their beloved Athenian guests, hand-chosen by Polychresus himself to grace our tables when we dined together. Our taxiarch indicated dignified thanks and made tactful enquiries about the tax money.

At this the old man looked truly sad, as if we had reminded him of something he had been trying to forget about.

'To our lasting shame, Athenian brothers,' he said, 'we no longer have the tribute-money. I say "no longer"; had you been here this time yesterday, there would have been no problem. But,' he bowed his head, 'honoured friends, these mountains are wild and lawless. Up there,' and he waved his stick vaguely at the encircling rocks, 'live a band of fierce and wicked men, oligarchs who were made outlaws when they tried to seize the temple of Hera by night two years ago. This morning, my house was broken into and the tribute – ten minas of fine silver, just as you commanded – was stolen. My boy Cleagenes here,' he said, and shoved one of the boys, who was staring at his sandal-straps, 'tried to resist them, and look what they did to him!' The old man pointed vigorously at a minute cut just above the boy's left eye. 'We are poor men,' he went on. 'All our silver went to make up that ten minas. We have nothing more to give you. So if you want the tribute, you must go and get it from those thieves and bandits.' He shook his fist at a different sector of the horizon, and leaned heavily on his staff.

Several of my companions made rude noises, but our taxiarch, who was new to this sort of work, ordered us to be quiet and assured the old man that we would have the silver back by nightfall if he would provide us with a guide.

'The best in Astypylaea,' said the old man, 'my boy Demetrius here' – he gave the other boy a shove – 'he knows the hills like a mountain goat, and is entirely without fear. You may follow him to the ends of the earth.'

131

Somehow we soldiers had the feeling that the ends of the earth would probably be a reasonable guess in the circumstances, but we had been ordered to keep quiet, so we said nothing. The taxiarch called out, 'Be ready to march in five minutes,' and went into one of the houses to be briefed on the bandits. I sent Little Zeus off to get fresh water and some bread, if there was any to be had, and sat down on a mounting-block to rest my feet. My head was sodden wet under my helmet, and I wanted to be left alone.

'This is going to be interesting,' said a voice beside me. I looked round and saw Artemidorus, one of the men who had been in Samos before. He was a demesman of mine and we had met at festivals, although I could remember very little about him.

'So how do you like soldiering, young Eupolis?' he said cheerfully. 'A bit different from prancing round the Market with Cleon and Alcibiades, isn't it?'

I made some feeble joke or other and he laughed loudly. 'That's good,' he said when he had managed to regain control of himself. 'Man with a sense of humour's always welcome in the wars. You'll find that out before you're much older, I reckon.'

'Why's that?' I asked. Artemidorus chuckled.

'You could put it in one of your plays,' he said, and a thought struck him. 'Are we all going to be in your next play, then? That'd be good, wouldn't it?'

'Marvellous,' I said. 'Do you know what's going on?'

He grinned. 'Like I told you, I've been here before, I know these sheep-shaggers like Homer. What's happening is, they've got these bandits up in the hills they want shifting, and they're too chicken to do it themselves. Also they don't want to pay any taxes, which is fair enough if you ask me. I'm a democrat, I don't hold with taxes, except for the empire of course, because when it comes down to it they're foreigners, they're used to it. Anyway, they put up this load of old cock about bandits, we go up into the hills and either we get lost and die of exposure, or the bandits get us, which saves them paying any taxes, or else we get the bandits, which suits the villagers, and they still don't pay any taxes, because they say the bandits have got it stashed somewhere and they don't know where. So we give up and go away, and everyone is happy.'

I stared at him. 'For God's sake, man,' I said, 'why don't you tell the taxiarch? We could get killed up there.'

Artemidorus shook his head. 'Son,' he said, 'you'll learn this about the army. You don't go telling things to the officers because one, they don't believe you; two, it gets you noticed; three, if it isn't here it's somewhere else.'

'What's that supposed to mean?' I asked.

'It means that we're here, and there's nothing we can do about it, so we might as well get on with it. When you're in the army you don't try and change things; you wait till you get home and you vote to have the General executed. That's democracy. Don't knock it.'

'But this is stupid,' I burst out. 'Are you sure about this? I mean, it's not just some rumour, like the women in Andros having three breasts, because Epinices saw one washing in the river, and . . .'

Artemidorus smiled, displaying his remaining teeth. 'It's true all right,' he said, 'solid silver all the way through, you could cut it with a chisel. For God's sake, my brother Callides told me. Are you calling him a liar, or what?'

'No, no,' I reassured him. 'Look, can't we just *suggest* it to the taxiarch?'

'Forget it,' Artemidorus said, and just then Little Zeus came back with the water-bottles and a huge black loaf, which he said had cost him a quarter-stater. We smashed the loaf up with a stone (it was hard and brittle, like pumice), soaked it in water, and ate it. By the time we had finished, the taxiarch was back and yelling orders.

It was a long way up the mountain, even with Little Zeus carrying my shield and pack for me, and the sun was unbearably hot. Even our guide seemed to be feeling the strain, for he kept stopping and looking round for no apparent reason. By midday we were high above the cultivable zones, and there were only a few emaciated sheep to be seen, scattered about like little white thorn trees. The taxiarch had set off at a parade-ground pace, singing some military chorus to set the tempo; but that had soon given way to a festival hymn, which was replaced in turn by a sort of dirge, all about the death of Theseus. Nobody knew the words, and his voice eventually dwindled away into a sort of semi-private hum.

Then the rocks started coming down on us. The first one bounced just in front of our guide, who decided that it was probably time he went home. The taxiarch tried to grab him, but a couple of small rocks hit him on the backplate and he fell over. Someone yelled something, but none of us could understand him – we had our helmets on, and of course you can't hear a thing inside a helmet, something that your average taxiarch (or general, for that matter) finds hard to remember. But I saw Artemidorus kneel down and put his shield over his head, and so I snatched my shield from Little Zeus and did the same. Something banged on the shield, like a gatecrasher at a party, and I remember thinking, 'Oh God, I bet it's hit that new bronze patch'; then I felt a sharp blow on my head, and my helmet-plume, which Callicrates and I had spent so long wrestling into place, was lying on the ground beside me. I let go of my spear to pick it up, and of course the spear rolled away down the side of the mountain. I stayed where I was; but Little Zeus, who had been trying to fit his enormous body under a small ledge of rock, jumped up and dashed after it, like a three-year-old dog chasing a hare. I almost expected him to bring it back in his mouth.

Someone shoved me from behind, and I saw that we were moving on. The taxiarch was on his feet again, dusting off his cloak, and no one seemed to be seriously hurt. I fell in beside Artemidorus, and pushed my helmet up on to the back of my head. He did the same, and we were able to talk.

'What was all that about?' I asked nervously.

'Could be the bandits,' he said gravely, as if he were Miltiades himself, sizing up an enemy formation, 'or it could just have been a couple of startled sheep or something, I don't know. I don't think the taxiarch's too happy.'

I wiped the sweat out of my eyes, and my arm felt very weak. 'What are we going to do now?' I asked. 'I mean, are we going on, or what?'

'We're going on, of course,' said Artemidorus. 'You wait till you've been in a couple of real battles. First time I was in a battle, we saw some horsemen coming up – great big cloud of dust, we were terrified. I pissed all down my legs and never knew it. Turned out to be our own men, actually. When we got to see the enemy we were all so knackered with marching up and down in the heat that we weren't frightened at all, just glad to get it over with. This sort of thing is just routine.'

As we marched on I began to feel unbearably tired – my legs were weak, and I had to lean heavily on Little Zeus' shoulder. Apparently, that was normal too, because of the sudden shock, but that didn't make it any easier. I asked Artemidorus if there was likely to be any more trouble; he drew on his vast military experience and replied, No, probably not.

We had come round the side of a spur into a narrow defile, with the main bulk of the mountain on our right and a sort of rampart of bare rock to the left. I had known just such a place on Parnes when I was a boy, and had often lain there under a bent old fig tree, imagining that I was an Athenian general and a Spartan army had been foolish enough to march straight into this naturally perfect mantrap. The final deployment I had decided on, after a year or so of intermittent speculation, was to put my heavy infantry at both ends (like Leonidas at Thermopylae) and my light infantry on the heights on either side, shooting and throwing javelins.

Perhaps I should have been a general. I was just about to tell the story to Little Zeus when I felt a tap on my shield, like the first drop of rain on a roof. There were other taps up and down the line, and we started looking round. Then someone went down on his knee, lifting his shield in front of his face, and we realised what was going on; we were being shot at by slingers, positioned on the

135

side of the mountain. This time, I wasn't nearly so startled; in fact, it was almost a pleasant relief after the tension of the past couple of hours. What I wasn't prepared for was sling-bolts coming from the other side of the defile. I braced myself as best I could, tucking my head into the hollow of my shield. But nothing came, although I could hear sling-bolts pattering down on either side of me.

'Put your helmet down, you idiot,' someone hissed in my ear, and I remembered that it was still perched on the back of my head. I put up my hand, and something smacked against my forearm. I swore, calling on all the Gods I could think of; then it occurred to me that the blow had not been particularly fierce; I could still move my fingers and everything.

Hold on a moment, said my soul inside me, they're out of range.

I thought about it for a moment, then looked up to my left. Sure enough, I could make out a figure against the skyline; a boy, maybe thirteen years old, loading his sling-shot. He was at least sixty yards away, much too far away to do any serious damage, especially to a man in armour. I suddenly felt extremely foolish; an Athenian heavy-armed infantryman, the terror of the Greek world, cowering under his shield against the blood-chilling but entirely ineffectual onslaught of a thirteen-year-old goat-herd.

My fellow soldiers were slowly coming to the same conclusion; one man in particular. I can't remember his name, but I think he was a shipwright by trade, and certainly not used to being made a fool of. He got up, laid his shield down carefully beside him, and turned to face the foe, for all the world like Ajax in the *Iliad*.

'All right,' he shouted up the mountainside, 'pack it in.'

There was no immediate effect; but after a while the pattering started to die away, and the Athenian expeditionary force resumed its formidable order. It was then that we noticed the enemy infantry, leaning on their spears at the mouth of the defile.

When I say spears, I am exaggerating slightly. Most of them had sharpened vine-props, and some of them had nothing at all. There were four men sharing a suit of armour between them – one had the helmet, another had the breastplate, and the other two had one greave each; the rest of them had nothing but home-made wicker shields and tunics, and their feet were bare.

The taxiarch let out a great shout, and we charged, shouting *Io Paian!* at the tops of our voices. The Samians threw their spears and bolted, scrambling away over the rocks like sheep. Their volley fell well short, and we drew up, breathless but happy, our honour totally restored, to find that two of the Samians were still there. Just two, no more.

I heard the story later. One man, who was the son of an Infantry farmer, had slipped and twisted his ankle, and his lover had stayed with him to defend him to the death if need be. As a result he was extremely excitable, and he also had one of the few genuine spears in the whole band. I can picture him now, jabbing his spear in the general direction of the taxiarch and calling on some obscure local Hero.

Nothing would have happened if the taxiarch hadn't still believed in the existence of the tax money. As it was, he wanted a prisoner to interrogate, and he sent two men forward to grab the Samians. The man with the twisted ankle made a remarkable recovery and rolled off down the hill as fast as he could; but our two men were on to the other one and he couldn't follow. Instead, he ducked out of their way and ran forward, apparently straight at me. Then Little Zeus, perceiving a mortal threat to his five acres, jumped out and slashed wildly at him with his sword, smashing his wicker shield into pieces and taking a lump out of his arm. That was another mistake. The poor Samian turned and stabbed with his spear at Little Zeus, who of course had no shield to protect himself with. He jerked back out of the way, tripped over his feet, and came down heavily on his backside. The Samian raised his spear over his head – and I stabbed him.

I couldn't believe that I had done it. There was this human body on the end of my spear, looking at me with such utter astonishment that I wanted to smile, and then turning carefully round, like a man who has stepped in something nasty in the street, and looking at the spear-blade sticking out of his side. For a moment I thought he was going to strike at me; then I realised that he had forgotten about everything else except the extraordinary fact of there being a spear right through him. I don't think it was hurting him. He just hadn't expected this at all.

'You *bastard*,' I heard myself saying. 'Really, I'm sorry.'

I think he was going to laugh; then he suddenly collapsed, as if he had noticed he was late for his own death. His weight jerked the spear out of my hands, and his body sagged on to the ground. And there was blood too – so much of it, creeping along the weave of his tunic like the waves on the shore, except not pulling back. I broke a jar of honey once, and stood there watching it oozing out into the dust on the storeroom floor, visibly spoiling in front of my eyes, going expensively to waste. Yes, there was blood all right, and how dark it looks when there's a lot of it. It was a fascinating sight for someone who has learned his Homer, line by painful line, and yes, that sort of blood is black, not red, just as it says in the *Iliad*, and a dead man does fall with a thud, and he does look rather like a felled tree, with his arms spread out like branches. He also looks rather like a man who has fallen over; he has short black hair and long, thin legs and a mole on his neck, and you wonder why he doesn't get up.

Then Little Zeus started praising me in a great voice and thanking me for saving his life, and pledging his eternal allegiance, and that of his children and his great-grandchildren to me and my House for ever, and I turned and kicked him on the shins. And the taxiarch said, 'What the hell was all that about?' and Artemidorus was muttering about having the whole of Samos after us now, and what in God's name did I think I was playing at? And someone pulled the spear out of his body and wiped it on the grass and gave it back to me, and said, 'That's one up to us,' and there seemed to be a lot more noise besides. And for some time they stood there discussing whether we should take him down to the village or leave him up there for the kites and the crows, until they finally agreed on throwing some dust on his face as a form of burial and telling the villagers where his body was in case anyone wanted it.

So we didn't get any tax-money in Astypylaea. From there we went to another village – I can't remember its name – where they tried to play exactly the same trick, except that they claimed that the money had been stolen not by local bandits but Milesian pirates.

The taxiarch listened to the tale, which was well told, and withdrew as before into the village headman's house. Outside in the street we could only hear a few thumps and some squealing, but when they came out again, the headman was rubbing his ears and the taxiarch was grinning. We got five minas in the end, which was three less than the assessment but all the silver we could find.

After that, we met with a different sort of obstruction as we toured round Samos. Instead of ostentatious courtesy and stringy but complimentary goats for our evening meal, we were greeted with barred doors and showers of stones and potsherds whenever we entered a village. It was obvious that the Samians were expecting us, for when we broke into their houses we found that everything of value had been removed. Our taxiarch (who was growing up fast) realised that there was no hope of keeping our movements a secret or arriving unexpectedly at any place; so he thought of another and a better way.

At the next village we came to, he sent us out to secure the headman, whom we found hiding under an overturned barley jar in his house, and sat this gentleman down on a mounting-block in the Market Square. He then explained to him, slowly and loudly, that he was fed up with traipsing through this god-forsaken island in search of what was obviously enchanted silver; he was going to stay right here in this village until it was time to go home, eating and drinking as much as he pleased and letting his men do the same. To pass the time, he added, he would set his men to building a little shrine, as a memento of our stay. As soon as it was completed, he added, he would personally dedicate this shrine to the Luck of Miletus, in memory of a little-known Milesian Hero who had been killed here when some princes of Miletus sacked the village ten or so generations ago. But since he was not an ostentatious man, he would not name himself as founder on the foundation-stone; instead, he would inscribe it with the names of all the villages he had visited, and send a herald to the main cities of Samos inviting all pious men to come and worship there. He stood up, as if his discourse was finished; then he turned round and added, in a nicely matter-of-fact way, that if by some miracle the tribute-money was suddenly to arrive from the villages he would be so busy checking it and drawing up accounts that he would have no time for his pious undertaking, and the other Samians would probably never know of their fellow citizens' religious zeal.

The next morning, we awoke from a sleep curiously untroubled by stray dogs, mysterious falls of rocks and sudden inexplicable noises (which we had come to accept as a way of life in Samos) and set out to quarry stones for the shrine. But when we arrived in the Market Square, we found a small group of harassed-looking Samians holding donkeys on short reins; and on the donkeys' backs were jars overflowing with coined silver. We tipped them out on to blankets and started to count, and the mixture of denominations alone was a feast of entertainment. There were Athenian Owls and Aeginetan Turtles, Horses from Corinth and Carthage, Lions of Leontini and Arethusae from Syracuse; there were Ajaxes from Locris Opuntia, which few of us had seen before, and some very pretty coins with doves on them that nobody could identify. There were even Persian sigloi, stamped with the King dressed as an archer, which must have dated back to before the wars, when Samos was still part of the empire. In fact, it seemed to us that some people had been digging very deep into ancient reserves to find us all this silver; in some cases, a little too deeply, for we found when we made up the final account that we had just over twelve staters a man more than the required sum. But by then, of course, all the silver was so thoroughly mixed up that there was no way of telling which villages had paid too much; and since it would undoubtedly cause bad feeling among neighbours if we tried to sort the matter out, we decided to forget all about it and accept the surplus as a sort of anonymous gift.

The taxiarch put all the money back into the jars and sealed each one with a leaden seal. Then he sent for the headman, who this time came a little more willingly, and sat him down as before in the Market Square. By now quite a crowd of Samians had gathered to see the money, and the taxiarch drew us up in front of the jars before he started to speak.

He started by confessing that up till now he had held a very poor view of Samian loyalty to Athens. He had somehow got it into his head, he said, that the Samians didn't want to pay their contribution to the cost of fighting the Great War of Freedom; that – perish the thought! – the honest men of Samos had forgotten who had freed them from the Persian yoke and given back to them their ancient freedom and privileges. But it was time, he continued, to revise that view. He had learned, from this truthful old man their headman, that leading citizens from all the villages had walked all night along treacherous mountain roads, undoubtedly shadowed all the way by the terrible outlaws and bandits of whom he himself had personal experience, just to be able to pay their taxes. Such behaviour, he said, cried out to be acknowledged; it shone like a beacon in a treacherous and ungrateful world.

He smiled and bowed slightly to the headman, who shifted about in his chair. Yesterday (continued the taxiarch) he had discussed with his friend the headman his plans to build a little shrine to a local Hero. For a while he had been afraid that counting up the tax-money would leave no time for building the shrine; but since everything had been paid so promptly, and since so many

141

able-bodied men were now gathered in the market-place, he could see no reason why the shrine should not be built after all. There would be no time now, he regretted, to send a herald to the Cities, but that could doubtless be done later, after he had gone.

This was our cue to draw our swords and look fierce. For some reason the Samians worked very hard all day and late into the night, by the light of torches which we held for them. It was a pretty little shrine when it was finished, with a sloping roof of tiles, which the headman felt compelled to provide by stripping his own roof, and a charming painting of the Milesians sacking the village, done by a local painter. We held a proper formal service of dedication, with hymns and a little procession, and sacrificed two white kids, also the property of the headman, to the music of flutes and harps. There was dancing too, and a modest amount of wine; and we Athenians enjoyed ourselves tremendously, although the Samians seemed to feel the gravity of the occasion rather more than we did.

I would like to think that the little shrine was still there, high up in the wild country of Samos. But as we marched away over the mountains we saw a plume of smoke rising from the Market Square; and when we stopped and looked carefully, we saw that the shrine was on fire. I can only suppose that some over-zealous worshipper banked the altar fire up too high, and that the sacred flame set light to the rafters.

Chapter Nine

When I was a boy I had something wrong with my eyes – nothing serious; my sight is perfect even now – and my father, who had a horror of illness, used to take me to the house of a horrible old woman who lived in the next village. She professed to cure all illnesses by a combination of prayers to some of the less reputable Goddesses and fierce herbal poultices; though I believe to this day that such cures as she achieved were effected by fear of the remedy. Each time we came away, my father poorer by a four-drachma piece and me with my eyes so red and painful that I could scarcely see the sun, he would slap me cheerfully on the shoulder and say, 'Well, that wasn't so bad, was it?' And I would reply, 'no, it wasn't,' and say a prayer under my breath that I would go blind and so be saved another course of treatment.

But my first taste of soldiering wasn't so bad after all, and I was almost sorry that it was over. I had my arms and armour intact, and a rather tatty crown of laurel leaves presented to me by the taxiarch for saving the life of a fellow citizen, which in spite of certain reservations I wore prominently as I strolled through the Market Square back to my house; and of course nine or ten bosom friends with whom I had sworn oaths of undying friendship, as one does in the army, and most of whom I never managed to get around to seeing ever again. The only one I kept up with at all was Artemidorus, the veteran. Since he was a neighbour I saw rather more of him than

I would have wished. He had guessed (correctly) that his wealthy young comrade-in-arms was a good touch for the use of a plough or a jar or two of seedcorn, and it came as something of a blow to him to find out that I was already married, for he had a spare daughter. It came as something of a blow to me, as well, for I had not given Phaedra much thought while I was in Samos.

I had just arrived outside Philodemus' door and was about to go in when a Libyan slave-boy whom I had never seen before dashed up and tugged at my cloak.

'Get off,' I said, for people were watching. 'What do you want?'

'My mistress says you're to come home with me,' he said urgently. I stared at him.

'Get lost,' I whispered, 'I'm a respectable married man.'

'Are you Eupolis of Pallene?' asked the boy. I said yes, I was, if it was any of his business. He started to tug at my cloak again, and I was afraid he would break the brooch.

'Then you're to come home with me *now*,' the boy said loudly. 'My mistress says so.'

'Look,' I snapped, 'who in God's name are you and what do you want? I'm just back from Samos and I want—'

'I'm your slave Doron,' said the boy. 'You'd better come.'

I shouldered my shield and followed right across the City until we came to the rather grand houses near the old Fish Market; that was where Aristophanes lived, and many other rich, fashionable young men. We stopped outside the door of a large, imposing house, which I remembered as the home of one Execestiades, who had been executed for treason just before my wedding.

'What are we doing here?' I asked.

'You live here,' the boy replied. 'Hurry up.'

I couldn't make head or tail of that, so I spat into my cloak for luck (since I was going into an unlucky house) and followed him.

It was a big, bleak place with a high ceiling, and somebody had been doing a lot of very expensive decorating. There was a silver mixing-bowl on the table, with embossed silver and gold cups all round it; there were Persian tapestries all over the place, and Bactrian rugs on the floor. The couches had bronze legs, and beside the hearth there was a tall, gilded statue of Agamemnon being killed by Clytemnestra on his return from Troy which, I calculated, must have cost the owner as much money as I got from my estate in Phylae in a whole year. In front of the fire two expensive Spartan hounds were sleeping, and there were two birdcages and a baby monkey hanging from the rafters. It looked like the house of an extremely wealthy widow.

The door of the inner room opened, and there was Phaedra, dressed in a saffron gown. 'So you're back, are you?' she said.

'What in God's name is going on?' I demanded.

'Don't stand on that carpet in your muddy sandals,' Phaedra said. 'It cost you twelve drachmas, and you were lucky to get it for that.'

I stepped off the carpet on to the floor. 'Whose house is this, Phaedra?' I asked. 'And what the hell are you doing here? You should be at my uncle's.'

'It's your house, you ungrateful oaf,' she said irritably, 'or it will be after you've got yourself down to the Archon's office and paid for it. Your infernal uncle wouldn't release any of the money in your strongbox.'

'You bought this from the Public Confiscator?' I gasped.

'No,' she said, 'you did. I'm not allowed to buy real property, remember.'

If I hadn't been so astonished, I don't know what I'd have done. As it was, I stood there, with my laurel crown (for saving the life of a fellow citizen) hanging lopsidedly from the side of my head, and tried to find a few appropriate words. While I was searching, Phaedra continued.

'Well, I couldn't go on living in your uncle's house – I mean, the man is unbearable, he keeps ordering me about as if I were a servant or something. And I don't like that goody-goody cousin of yours, Callicrates. I don't think we'll see any more of them from now on.

And it's a good house – expensive, of course, but you can just about afford it, if you're careful for a year or so. Of course you'll be short of ready money for a while; you might have to mortgage some of your vineyards in Pallene, but that shouldn't be a problem. I'm sure my father will take them on, if no one else will.'

'You bought confiscated property in my name? Have you any idea what people are going to say about me?'

'Yes,' said Phaedra, and she smiled.

I wonder now why it took me so long to work it out. Phaedra knew as well as I did that buying up the confiscated property of a man who had been executed was not only ill-omened in the extreme but regarded by all decent men as little better than grave-robbing, and that was why she had done it – to make me look as bad as possible. She also knew that there was now no way that I could get out of it, for she must have used my personal seal to make the contract with the Public Confiscator. If I repudiated a document under my seal, I would for ever after have difficulty buying anything in Athens bigger than a single whitebait.

'It's lucky you came back today,' said Phaedra. 'It's the last date for payment, and the interest rate is quite high, I believe.'

I knew that I was beaten. 'All right, you bitch,' I said, 'how much has this cost me?'

'One talent,' she said, and she giggled.

I sat down on a couch and put my head in my hands. Then another thought struck me.

'And what,' I asked, 'is all this junk?' I waved my arm at all the couches and silverware. 'Where did all this come from?'

'If we're going to entertain my family and my father's friends,' she said sweetly, 'we can't have the place looking like a barn, now can we? But you needn't worry,' she continued, 'they wouldn't give me credit, so all the furniture and so forth is already paid for. I sold my ten acres.'

'You what?'

'My dowry, my ten acres.' She giggled again; she was

146

enjoying herself. 'It hadn't been made over to you formally when you left, if you remember, so my father was able to give a receipt. Of course, we couldn't get anything like the full value for it – who's buying vineyards these days? – but there was just about enough, together with the loose cash you hadn't sealed up before you left. Hadn't you better get across to your uncle's for that talent?'

'Who told you I had a talent?' I yelled at her, but she simply turned and walked out into the inner room. I dared not follow her there, for fear of seeing what wonders of the silversmith's trade she had furnished it with. So I kicked the Libyan boy, took off my armour, and set off for my uncle's house.

Just for fun, I tried fighting the Public Confiscator; the contract was not quite perfectly drawn – I think one of the Gods had been left out of the Invocation Clause – but the lawyers I consulted told me to forget it; no jury would have any sympathy with a man who bought confiscated property and then tried to cheat the State by backing out of a sealed contract.

My uncle solved my immediate financial difficulties by taking a ten-year lease of some of my land in Phylae, which was contributing nothing at the moment and was unlikely to be anything but a burden for the foreseeable future. But he paid me a premium assessed on pre-war yields, which was much the same as giving me the money; in fact, for a long time afterwards he referred to it as my wedding-present. He was able to be so generous because my grandfather's stake in the silver mines, which he had kept back when he transferred the rest of my property, was paying handsomely, thanks to the war. He also lent me enough to buy a share in an oar-blade workshop owned by some friends of his, which turned out to be one of the best investments I ever made.

Now that my new house was paid for, I tried to make the best I could of living there; but I hated the place. For a start, I couldn't help feeling that the previous owner's bad luck was everywhere, and although I sacrificed several times to his ghost, and sprinkled everything

147

in sight with chickens' blood (which did not please Phaedra), the thought of being alone in the house was never agreeable.

Then, of course, many of the people who had known Execestiades refused to set foot in the house, for he had been a popular man and, by all accounts, a good and honest politician. As if to compensate me for the loss of so much good society, Phaedra took to filling the house with her relations and her brothers' friends, none of whom I could stand. On the other hand, I would have preferred to eat and drink with a houseful of Thessalians than spend an evening alone with Phaedra.

You can imagine what my life at home was like when I tell you that I never managed to get around to shouting at Phaedra properly for buying the house in the first place; she always pre-empted me. As soon as I set my foot over the threshold she would be at me with some new catalogue of complaints, so that I was forever on the defensive over some minor domestic trivia. I have always detested arguments and bad temper – I get a headache, and I can't seem to get my words out properly – so I soon took to making tactical withdrawals (like the Athenian generals at Marathon), usually into the storeroom or even the stables, where it was warm and quiet except for the breathing of the horses. I got very little sleep – I think Phaedra slept a lot during the day so as to be able to sit up complaining at night – and of course I had no hope at all of composing any Comedy in my own house. The only course open to me was to be at home as little as possible, which was of course what Phaedra wanted.

So I spent most of my time in the Market Square or at my uncle's, or visiting friends, and the joy of being out of the house added an extra glow to all my occupations. I was making useful friends at this time, and knew most of the leading citizens. It is a strange thing, but people who are gossiped about tend to seek the company of other notorious men, and since the story of my domestic arrangements had long since become a source of lasting delight all over Athens, I never lacked for company or confidences. Once you have got used to being a laughing-stock it is quite a useful attribute, if your skin is reasonably thick. People are not afraid of you, and that tends to break down barriers.

Whenever possible, of course, I went out to the country, especially to Pallene, where Phaedra would not go. There was always something to do on the land, and the work kept me healthy. Because it was pointless trying to replant vines and olives with the threat of Spartan invasions, we concentrated on growing what we could manage to grow in the available time. Many of the crops we tried were rarely grown in Attica (flax and hemp, for example, and some rare varieties of beans and pulses), and I was proud of some of our successes and not too distressed by our failures. In particular I found that beans and lupins were a vastly underrated crop. Because Attica is so dry, and manure of all kinds is worth its weight in gold, most Attic farmers grow beans as green fertiliser; that is to say, they grow them on fallow land and plough them back unharvested before they come to maturity. But I found that you can harvest beans off the fallow without noticeably damaging the soil; the mere act of growing them seems to do the ground a great deal of good. Also, where the Spartans had burnt standing corn, the earth was much lighter and more productive, and I remembered something in one of the old poems – Hesiod, I think it was, or someone like him – that led me to believe that our forefathers deliberately burned off the stalks and helm of some crops to enrich the land. As for water, I managed to organise my neighbours into diverting some of the mountain streams, which never fail even in summer, so that they flowed down through our terraces and so could be used to irrigate. Most people thought we were mad, until we began carting in the produce; then they started lawsuits for illegal conversion of water. I also insisted that all over my estates we ploughed at least five times throughout the year, to work in the frost and the dew. It was hard work and expensive, too – hardly a day seemed to go by when I wasn't down at the smithy ordering a new ploughshare – but the results were little short of spectacular, and I could hardly wait for the return of peace, and the chance to start growing barley again.

And there was hunting, too – the Spartan invasions meant that Attica was alive with hares and deer, and wild boar and even bears were starting to come back – and fowling, and fishing, of course, which had become a very important part of many people's lives since the start of the war. My dislike of the sea meant that I took little direct part in that, but I spent money on fishing-boats and even a small coaster, so that I could take surplus produce round the coast to sell in other parts of Attica instead of having to drag it by land all the way to the City and out again. In short, as you may already have guessed, I enjoyed myself tremendously in the country, and did no harm to anyone.

And, above all, I got back to my play. I found manual labour extremely conducive to composition, and since I carried the entire text of *The General* about with me in my head, I could work on it wherever I happened to be. I'm sure that several of my seasonal workers, if they are still alive, could even now recite you the big speeches from that play, for they heard them often enough, and, being sensible men, were always careful to laugh in all the right places. Sometimes we performed a few scenes for my neighbours, when it was too hot to work and we drifted together under the shade of the nearest trees. Naturally I took the lead, and Little Zeus was my one-man Chorus; the rest of the parts were shared out among the slaves and free hands. I don't suppose I shall ever have a more appreciative audience than those farmers of Pallene and Phrearrhos, who were pleased enough for an excuse to lie still after a hard morning's work, and who hadn't had to sit through three Tragedies before the Comedy. Nevertheless, it was worth watching to see exactly what did make them laugh and what slipped by unnoticed, how far a joke could be drawn before it became boring, and just how long a scene should be.

I suppose I was putting off for as long as possible the horrible day when there was nothing more I could do to it without spoiling it entirely, and I would have to take it to the Archon, like a tenant farmer taking his year's produce to be measured and divided. I dreaded the thought of not getting a Chorus. After all, there were already more Comic poets than Choruses, and new ones coming forward almost every day, as far as I could see. I was starting to bristle with hatred whenever I heard an established poet's name, and often found myself praying that one or other of them would be killed in the war or struck down by the plague. But when I fell to contemplating my *General*, which was something I did far too often for a modest man, I could honestly see no flaw or imperfection in it, from the first joke to the exit of the Chorus. But at other times, after a long struggle with an unwieldy scene, I doubted if anyone, however sick his mind might be, could ever be made to laugh by such dreary nonsense; there was nothing which had not been done a hundred times better a hundred times before. To be brief; there were days when I loved it and days when I hated it, but my play was never far from my mind. It was the one thing I really had to look forward to, yet it was a terrible shadow hanging over me. If it succeeded – would that I could die in that moment! – and if it failed, then I might as well throw myself off the tower in the Potters' Quarter and be done with it all.

To make matters worse, Philonides the Chorus-trainer had not forgotten about me. You may remember that he expressed an interest, that night at Aristophanes' party. Well, I had expected to hear no more from him, but that was not the case at all. In fact, it became quite embarrassing, for I seemed to meet him everywhere – not just in the City, but even in the country, for he had land at Phrearrhos not far from mine, and I always seemed to be running into him on the road home at night – and each time we met he would ask, 'Have you anything for me yet?' and each time I would say 'Well, nearly; but there's still a few things I must iron out . . . ' But instead of putting him off, this seemed to make him all the more eager, and in the end he took to calling at my house in the City, where Phaedra made him as welcome as a beggar with the plague.

I can understand Phaedra's reluctance to have any acquaintance of mine in the house, for she was filling in the long hours of our marriage quite as effectively as I was, if half the rumours I heard were true. Of course, a husband always believes rumours about his wife, and they're very seldom true; but there were so many of them and they all sounded so probable that even the most sceptical juror would have found it difficult not to be convinced.

To start with, I was overjoyed at the thought that I might be able to divorce Phaedra for adultery and be rid of her for good. I remember joking about it, at home in Pallene or at Philodemus' house; we drank toasts to my liberator as if he were a new Solon come to free the serfs, and adapted the words of the Harmodius. But somehow I could never get around to doing anything about it, even though Philodemus and Callicrates offered to fight the case for me.

'For God's sake, boy,' Philodemus would say, 'it's like a gift from Olympus, and you just sit there and do nothing. If it's losing the dowry you're worried about, I've spoken to half the lawyers in Athens, and—'

But I would shake my head and change the subject, and after a while they stopped bothering, looking on me as mad and already lost; or perhaps they were waiting until Phaedra got pregnant and I was forced to take action. I couldn't understand it myself; I only knew that it was something to be done next week, or next month, or after the figs had been harvested.

The day came when, to my inseparable joy and sorrow, *The General* was finished and, try as I might, I could think of no reason why I should not take it down to the Archon. It was as near perfect as it would ever be, I had the backing of several influential people including Philonides himself, and I was old enough to take out a Chorus in my own name. By the way, I realise that I have omitted to describe my coming-of-age celebrations and setting-down in the phratry lists. When I started writing this History I intended to give a full account of it, so that generations yet unborn should know what such a ceremony was like in the heyday of the Athenian power. But to be honest with you, it's such a tedious business that I can't be bothered; so if you wish to read about it, I recommend that you dig out one of the metrical accounts by one of the old lyric poets.

Anyway, I trudged unhappily over to my uncle's house with a big knapsack full of Egyptian paper, commandeered his secretary, and dictated the whole thing at a sitting; then I made the poor boy read it all back to me and corrected the mistakes, and told him to write out five fair copies, while I stood over him just to make sure he was doing it properly. I live in terror of having my words distorted by incompetent copyists. One lapse in attention can ruin a whole roll, in my opinion, and they hate the sight of me at the copying workshops when I come down to see how they are getting on.

When the rolls were finished, cut, dried and folded and properly polished with pumice, I packed them up in little bronze cylinders which I had had specially made in Pallene, with 'The General *of Eupolis son of Euchorus of the deme of Pallene*' and the first line of the play neatly inscribed on the outside, and set off for the Archon's house. My dear Callicrates could see how nervous I was and offered to come with me, but I refused. I wanted to go alone, without even Little Zeus. I felt like Theseus going into the Labyrinth.

It was nearly dark, and I was terrified in case I ran into robbers who would steal the rolls for their bronze covers; but apparently there was a big funeral over on the other side of the City that night, and so the streets were deserted and safe. I arrived at the Archon's door and knocked loudly, to raise my spirits.

A housemaid opened the door and asked who was making such a noise at this time of night. I gave my name and said that I wanted to see the Archon.

'Is it important?' she said. 'He's got visitors. They're singing the Harmodius.'

The thought of going away and coming back the next day was more than I could bear. 'Yes,' I said, 'it's very important, you'd better let me in.'

As I stepped into the house I immediately thought better of it. What, after all, could be more likely to inspire the fury of the Archon than bursting in on him when he was drinking with a few friends? It would be a miracle if he even accepted the rolls. I looked despairingly around the room. To my horror, I saw that the guests, who were all staring at me, included some of the men I had most savagely and obscenely attacked in the play. There, for example, was Hyperbolus, and beside him Cleonymus the Vulture, and Cleon himself, who I knew to speak to and who was smiling at me in a friendly and welcoming way. I stammered out my business, thrust the rolls at the Archon (for some reason I cannot remember his name, although every other detail of that scene is etched on my mind as clearly as my name was inscribed on those confounded roll-covers) and prepared to make my escape.

'So this is your famous *General*, son of Euchorus,' said the Archon drowsily – he had reached that stage of relaxation that is easy to confuse with drunkenness. 'Lie down and have a cup with us. We've all heard about this marvellous play of yours, haven't we?'

His guests murmured that they certainly had, and I started to sweat. It was, I decided, that defile in Samos all over again, except that this time the enemy were well within range.

'Let's have a few lines,' said Cleonymus, wiping oyster sauce from his chin. 'I feel like some poetry.'

'The hell with that,' said Cleon. 'It's early yet, and we have the author here. Let's have the whole thing. You're not busy tonight, are you, Eupolis?'

I started to explain all about this party I had promised to go to. In fact, I was late already.

'Well then,' someone said, 'if you're late already, you'd better not go at all. Dreadful manners to arrive late. Stay here and let's hear your play. Isn't there a scene with an old woman and a pot of lentils?'

I cursed my mother under my breath for ever having

154

given birth to me, sat down on a couch and gulped down the cup of strong wine which somebody passed to me. Then I fumbled the roll out of its cover (whatever possessed me to order those stupid bronze cylinders in the first place?) and drew it open across my knee. Of course, I didn't look at it since I knew the play by heart already, and Cleonymus told me later that I had it upside down.

The opening scene went down very well, and Cleon in particular laughed at the old joke about the size of his private parts – which must have been a politician's instinct, for it was a very unfunny joke and only put in because such a joke was now virtually obligatory in the opening scene of a Comedy. The entry of the Chorus too was rapturously received. It all seemed so horrible, for any moment now the really unforgivable personal attacks would come along, and they would probably cut my ears off with their meat-knives. I couldn't bear to look; instead, I crouched down over the roll and tried to give the play the best reading I could. My favourite lines, which I had nursed since they were little more than a patter of sounds in my head, rattled off my tongue like olives falling out of a punctured basket, and I wished that I had never composed them.

The Cleonymus scene came and went, and the scene where Hyperbolus sells his grandmother to the stone quarry foreman in return for a pound of salt and two cloves of garlic, and still they were laughing. I was just about to start on the Cleon scene when the man himself laid his hand on my arm and asked, 'Am I in this?'

Cleon, the only man in history to have prosecuted a Comic poet. 'Yes,' I said, staring at the writing on the roll.

'Have you got a spare copy?' Cleon asked. I handed him one, and he found the place. Then he motioned to me to continue. Suddenly I heard his voice – he was reading his own part, and roaring with laughter as he did so.

'This is quite good,' he kept saying. 'Do I really talk like this?'

'Yes,' Cleonymus said. 'Get on with it, will you? I'm enjoying this after the beating I took just now.'

Somehow I struggled on to the end, and when I had finished, they clapped me on the back until I thought my spine would snap.

'Eupolis of Pallene,' said the Archon gravely, 'do I take it that you are petitioning me for a Chorus at the City Dionysia?'

'Yes,' I replied. It was not the most graceful speech in the world, but I felt too drained to say anything else.

'Then I shall read and consider your play,' he replied, taking the roll from me. 'Of course, it would be most improper of me—'

'*Most* improper,' said Cleon. 'Don't be so damned pompous.'

'Most improper of me to make any comment,' the Archon continued, 'but if you know of a suitable Chorus-trainer, it might be worth your while giving him a copy now. They like to have time to work out the dances, you know.'

'Actually,' I said, 'Philonides the Chorus-master . . . '

'Oh well then, you're all right,' said the Archon. 'If he's behind you, I don't know why you bothered bringing it to me.' A wicked sort of grin passed over his face. 'Who shall we nominate to finance your play, Eupolis son of Euchorus, of the deme of Pallene? Cleon here is rich enough; do you fancy it, Cleon?'

Cleon laughed. 'It'd be the kiss of death to it if I did. Who else gets a hard time, Eupolis? What about Nicias son of Niceratus?'

The Archon made a very peculiar noise and spilt his wine down his chest. 'You're evil, Cleon,' he said. 'I'll summon him first thing in the morning.'

'Nicias,' explained Hyperbolus, who was the only man present (except me, of course) with a straight face, 'is a good man but he has no sense of humour. None whatsoever.'

Then someone demanded an encore, and this time not only Cleon but Hyperbolus (who would have made a superb actor) and Cleonymus took their own parts, and the Archon was the Chorus-leader, and we went through virtually the whole play all over again. Two of my beautifully prepared rolls were ruined by having wine spilt all over them but by this stage I couldn't care less; and I don't think I'll tell you what we did with those elegant bronze covers.

So, about four hours before dawn, I bade the Archon and his guests goodnight and took my leave of them. I was far more drunk than I had ever been in my life before, and I had no real idea of where I was going. I dropped the torch they had given me and it went out, so I blundered along in the dark, and soon fell over. By now I had no idea where I was, and I didn't really care. My *General* was going to be produced – my Chorus was as good as dressed and trained, and I could almost hear the rumble of those little wooden wheels as the trireme-costumes trundled across the orchestra of the Theatre of Dionysus. I levered myself up out of the puddle into which I had fallen, and continued on my random way.

What happened next is still fairly vague; someone stepped out in front of me and hit me over the head with a stick or a club or something, while somebody behind me jerked my cloak off my shoulders and pulled my purse out of my belt. I fell heavily on my shoulder and lay still, trying not to breathe.

'You've done it now, Orestes,' said the man behind me, and the blood turned to ice in my veins. The man standing over me had been, ever since I could remember, the most feared robber in Athens. 'You've killed him, you realise.'

'Not hard enough for that,' laughed Orestes. 'Come on, move.'

I waited until their footsteps had faded away, and then I tried to move, but I couldn't. My soul inside me wailed, 'This is what comes of your pride, Eupolis, you fool. You're paralysed. They'll have to carry you to the Theatre on a chair.' I could feel tears running down my cheeks and nose, but I couldn't move my hand to wipe them away.

I don't know how long I lay there, sobbing miserably to myself; but some old men on their way to be first in the jury queue tripped over me and saw the blood on my head. They asked me what had happened, and I croaked out the single word, 'Orestes'.

'Don't talk soft, son,' said one of the old men, 'he was hung five years ago.'

That somehow seemed to add the finishing touch to my misery; to have been crippled for life by the great Orestes would have been something to boast about, in the long years of utter stillness that lay ahead of me.

'I can't move,' I gasped. 'Do you understand me, I can't . . .'

'I'm not surprised,' said the old man, 'You're lying on your cloak. That's why your arm's trapped.'

'He's not hurt at all,' said another old man. 'Have you smelt his breath?'

They started laughing and walked on. As soon as they had gone, I made another attempt at moving and was soon standing upright rubbing my head. It was nearly light now, and I recognised the district I had wandered into. Phaedra's house – my house – was just around the corner. I picked up my stick, which had broken under me, and crept slowly to my front door.

There was light under it, and the sound of voices singing inside, but I had no strength to be angry. I just beat on the door with the crook of my stick and leaned heavily against the frame.

'If that's Mnesarchus come back again,' I heard Phaedra call out, 'tell him to go away until he's sobered up. That tapestry cost twenty drachmas.'

The door was opened a crack, and I threw my whole weight against it. 'You paid twenty drachmas for a tapestry, you stupid cow?' I yelled, and fell forward into the room.

There was a sort of a shriek, and Phaedra hurriedly wrapped a tablecloth around herself. The men weren't so quick.

'What the hell do you think you're doing, coming home in that state?' Phaedra said, but her heart wasn't in it. Still, I had to admire her for the effort.

My soul within me reminded me that my sword hung over the door, and I pulled it down and waved it ferociously. 'On your feet,' I snapped, 'all of you.'

There were three men with Phaedra, all undressed and obviously drunk. Two of them I had never seen before, but the third one I had known for a long time.

'You two get out,' I said to the strangers, 'now, before I change my mind. But you,' and I pointed to Aristophanes son of Philip, of the deme of Cholleidae, with the point of my sword, 'stay right where you are.'

The two strangers ran out into the night without even trying to collect their cloaks. Aristophanes tried to hide behind Phaedra, but she stepped aside.

'Thank God you came, Eupolis,' she sobbed. 'He was just about to—'

'I could see that,' I said, and my soul sang within me. 'Go into the inner room and stay there. Don't you dare come out,' I added sternly, 'whatever you may hear.'

Of course, I didn't really intend to kill Aristophanes; for a start, he's much bigger and stronger than me, and if I'd tried to attack him I would probably not be writing this now. But I was enjoying myself too much not to play the scene for all it was worth, and perhaps I played it a little bit too well. Anyway, as soon as I said these words, Phaedra picked up a dish of mushrooms in garlic and cream cheese and threw it at me. I ducked, and Aristophanes dashed past me out of the house. I picked myself slowly up off the floor and felt the edge of my sword.

'That only leaves you, Phaedra,' I started to say, but before I could finish I got a fit of the giggles and let the sword fall to the ground with a clang. 'Now look what you've made me do,' I quoted.

'Oh, very funny,' Phaedra said, and went into the inner room, slamming the door behind her. I picked up my sword and put it carefully back on the wall; then I followed her.

'There's garlic and mushrooms all over your statue of Clytemnestra,' I said. 'Help me off with my sandals, there's a good girl.'

She gave me a look of pure mustard, then undid

the sandal-thongs and threw them into the corner of the room. 'You smell like a wine-press,' she said. 'Have you been fighting?'

'I got robbed,' I replied, 'but they're going to give me a Chorus.'

'There's blood on your forehead,' she said. 'I'll get some water.'

'Don't bother,' I said. 'Did you really pay twenty drachmas for a tapestry?'

She blushed. 'It was a bargain,' she muttered. 'Genuine Sidonian. There's only two or three in the whole of Athens.'

'Crap,' I replied. 'They make them in Corinth by the thousand and the Aeginetans ship them over here as ballast. Twenty drachmas!'

Then she tried to kiss me, but I pushed her away. 'Not until I've made my will,' I said. Her scowl wavered, very slightly.

'I didn't expect you home,' she said. 'If I had, I'd have been waiting for you. With an axe, like Clytemnestra.'

'Are you pleased I've got my Chorus?' I asked, peeling my sodden tunic off over my head.

'So long as it makes you happy,' she said, pouring water into a cup and handing it to me, 'and provided it keeps you out of the house. I trust you're going to wash before you get into bed. I may be a slut, but I'm a clean slut.'

'You're the cleanest slut in all Athens,' I yawned. 'But I'm too tired to wash right now. Besides, it deprives the skin of all those natural oils that make for a healthy complexion.'

'You're no better than a pig,' she said. 'Do you ever wash when you're in the country?'

'Never.'

She let down her hair over her shoulders, like new wine pouring into an ivory bowl. 'You looked a complete idiot standing there in the doorway waving that sword,' she said. 'Honestly, I was ashamed of you, in front of those people. It'll be all round the City in the morning.'

'It's the morning already,' I said, 'and I've got to go and see Philonides the Chorus-trainer first thing.'

'Well then,' she said, letting the tablecloth fall around her ankles. 'You'd better get some sleep.'

'Why bother?' I replied. 'It's too late now.'

Chapter Ten

Now I suppose you will get the idea that that was a reconciliation, and that henceforth all was well within the house. Not so. I don't think we hated each other any less; but I believe we started to enjoy fighting. For a start, we were no longer afraid of each other, and our marriage developed into a sort of running Contest Scene, which is, of course, the heart of any good Comedy. Certainly, I found myself spending more and more time at the house, though that was at least partially because I needed to be in that part of the City, to work with Philonides on the play. Phaedra and I fought all the time, day and night; and yet it was a strange sort of conflict. In fact, it reminded me of those two Spartan hounds of hers, who were always at each other's throats; blood and broken crockery and no end of noise. But when one of them was run over by a cart in the street, the other one refused to eat and died soon afterwards, leaving me thirty drachmas worse off. I don't understand what people see in dogs.

Nicias son of Niceratus was formally appointed as my producer, and I worked out the costings for the production and took them over to him. He was virtually a neighbour, and he lived in one of the best houses in the whole of Athens. His wealth came mostly from the mines, which made some people look down on him, but there was nothing of the silver-king about Nicias. He didn't smell of money, like so many people who make their own fortune; in fact, he didn't smell of anything much. Of all the men I have met in my life, I can think of few

162

that I have admired more and liked less; for Nicias was without question the most boring man in Athens.

He was the sort of man who thinks everything through, slowly, sensibly, carefully, and does nothing until he has satisfied himself that it is prudent (and morally right) to do this particular thing in this particular way. You could see him going through a sort of checklist in his mind, and he was a terror for long, thoughtful silences. Of course, he was a martyr to kidney trouble, but he never let his illness get in the way of his responsibilities (everything in his life was a Responsibility); and although he was obviously in a great deal of pain, he never mentioned it unless he felt it his duty to confess that he would not be capable of doing such and such properly, because of his infirmity. He regarded the production of Comedy (which he could not begin to understand, and found generally distasteful) as a religious as well as a civic duty, and since he firmly believed that he held the bulk of his personal wealth as a trustee for the Athenian people – I am convinced that he enjoyed paying taxes, in so far as he ever enjoyed anything – he was determined that no expense should be spared, and that my Chorus should be equipped and trained to the highest possible standard. But then his prudence and sensibleness came into play; there must be no stinting or false economy, but there must be no waste. Waste is an affront to the Gods, who provide for us. Waste is morally wrong.

The result was that my triremes had genuine Tyrian purple cloaks; but when the cloaks were made, he sent a slave round to gather up all the offcuts and sell them in the market. The Chorus was rehearsed over and over again, on full pay; but his instructions were that anyone who was late was to be fined one obol, and the accumulated fines used to pay for a sacrifice to Dionysus on the eve of the play. As for the actors; the rules said that they were to be paid by the hour, and so every rehearsal was timed with a water-clock, which was stopped as soon as the rehearsal was finished, and the water left in the clock was carefully measured to work out what each man was owed, down to the last obol.

This was insufferable enough, and caused more bad feeling among the company than the usual miserliness and late payment would have done. But Nicias held that his responsibility to the production did not end with regular disbursements of silver. Although he hated speaking in public, he felt it was his duty to make regular speeches of encouragement (with the water-clock running, of course). These speeches never lasted more than a few minutes, and he had a good, polished turn of phrase; but I have never been so bored in all my life.

I can picture him to this day, standing by the altar in the middle of the stage, leaning on a stick, since making speeches always made him feel ill. He would clear his throat, wait for silence, and then tell us how we should always strive to do our best for our City, since between Athens and ourselves there was a perfect harmony of interest. In helping Athens, he would say (over and over again) we were acting both altruistically and selfishly – which, of course, is morally right; a man must do what is good but must also always do what is prudent, so long as he observes that Godlike balance of moderation in both. And he would always end by saying that it is men who make up a city, not walls and houses and temples, and that without good men, all the silver and triremes in the world are nothing but trouble and sorrow. He would then turn quietly away and walk painfully home, leaving us, thoroughly depressed, to try and rehearse a Comedy.

A marked contrast to Nicias' homilies were the addresses of Philonides, which the company dreaded even more. I have heard Sicilian gang-masters, and the foremen in the stone quarries and the silver mines, but even they do not speak to slaves in the way that Philonides spoke to the free citizens of Athens who made up my Chorus. The actors had all worked with him before, but that did not stop them bursting into tears at times and even running out of the Theatre; but when I begged him to stop for fear of jeopardising the whole production, he didn't seem to hear me. During those rehearsals, everything about the play – not least the words themselves – seemed to fill him with unbearable physical pain. Yet when I went to see him at his house after a particularly agonising day in the Theatre, he would smile and pour me wine, and assure me that it was the best play ever written, and that it would be a crime against Dionysus to alter a single word, and how was my lentil crop coming on in Phrearrhos now that I had taken to using seaweed as fertiliser?

During our rehearsals, the doors to the Theatre were firmly barred and slaves with wooden clubs were stationed outside to make sure that nobody got in. But some people did manage to slip past, pretending that they were messengers from Nicias come to count the oil-lamps, or even guests of the author. It was generally known, too, that the other playwrights had their spies in the Chorus, while there was nothing that anyone could do to stop the actors selling whole speeches. I firmly believe they did it more out of hatred of Philonides than for the money; but whatever the reason, I became aware that my rivals, and Aristophanes in particular, were taking a considerable interest in the production.

All playwrights do their best to sabotage the work of their rivals. It is a mark of respect, if you choose to see it in that way, and I do it myself. Even the great Aeschylus used to try and get his rivals' actors drunk on the day of the performance, and everyone knows the story of how Euripides kidnapped the actor Gnatho when he was waiting for his cue in Agathon's *Perseus*, and how Gnatho escaped by wriggling through a hole in the floorboards of Euripides' house, and ran back through the streets in his Tragedy boots, and entered on his cue as if nothing had happened. But somehow, during the rehearsals for *The General*, I had got it into my head that nothing like that would ever happen to me. Of course, Philonides dealt with most of the attempts to disrupt the play, and retaliated with all his characteristic ferocity. It was Philonides who ordered the attack on the poet Phrynichus, which left him with a broken collar-bone; while he nearly killed one of our actors with his own hands for trying to set light to the costumes. But he didn't tell me any of this, of course, and what I heard from other people I dismissed as silly rumours.

165

But I really should have begun to suspect something was up when Phaedra seemed to undergo a sort of transformation. At first, it was nothing more than a smile instead of a glare when I went home in the evenings, and I was probably too preoccupied to notice. But then the statue of Clytemnestra disappeared, and in its place was a fat leather purse full of coined silver; she knew how I hated it, she told me, and Philander's wife had liked it so much. The pet monkey had a mysterious accident at about the same time, and Phaedra began to talk quite seriously about coming to Pallene with me, since, deep down, she felt more at home in the country. She also definitely confirmed that making my will could wait for as long as I liked.

Being young and foolish, I rationalised all this as being just another aspect of my good luck, which appeared for the moment to be unstoppable. Also, Phaedra was shrewd and careful, or perhaps the strain was too much for her; anyway, we continued to have spectacular battles over nothing in particular, only rather less frequently. For my part, I was beginning to feel, at the back of my mind, that it would be no bad thing if they stopped altogether. It was becoming steadily harder for me to work up a good froth of hatred towards her, and in my soul I was afraid that our contests in future might be a little one-sided.

Then she started asking me about how the play was going. This really did shock me, for if she had ever mentioned it before, she spat the name out as if it were a bad olive. At first, it was only a casual, slightly scornful enquiry, just as you might ask a small child how its pet worm was doing, or if it had made any more of those little frogs out of mud and pomegranate-rind. But then she wanted to hear about the costumes for the Chorus (if my Chorus could have purple, why the hell couldn't she?), and was it true that I was saying horrible things about Cleon, who was the only honest man in Athens? From there it was only a short step to asking me to recite some of the speeches; and although she pretended to fall asleep, I could see that her eyes were ever so slightly open, and following me about the room as I went through the moves. In the end, I promised to take her to next week's rehearsal, and she said that would be nice, since she had just been sent a copy of the *Thebaid* by her father and when else was she going to find time to read it, with all the housework she had to do?

As we walked home from the Theatre, I asked her what she had thought of it. She wrinkled her nose, as if she could smell rancid oil.

'What's it supposed to be about?' she asked.

I ignored her. 'What did you think of the Chorus costumes?' I asked.

'I was going to talk to you about that,' she said. 'I thought you said they were meant to be triremes. Or is that another Chorus which comes on later?'

I smiled affectionately. 'I think it's Semonides,' I said, 'who says – I think it's in his *Malignity of Women* – that there's no greater gift a man can have than a stupid wife. Did you like their little wheels? That was a stroke of genius, if you ask me.'

'How long will it be before they can stand up without them?' Phaedra replied. 'Once you've taken those off, they might look quite realistic.'

I stopped and kissed her. 'You've been eating parsley again,' I said. 'If you want to drink in the afternoons, you go right ahead. I can smell it through the parsley, so you needn't bother in future.'

'I wouldn't drink that wine from Pallene if I was dying of thirst in Egypt,' Phaedra said, and she breathed heavily into my face as she kissed me back. 'No wonder people don't come to our house any more. I heard that Amyntas was ill for a week the last time he came to see me.'

'So you're still seeing Amyntas, are you, even though he stole your Phoenician mirror with the ivory handle?' I shook my head sadly. 'And after it cost you so much to get it back from his boyfriend. You're such a bad judge of people, Phaedra, I don't know what's to become of you.'

'Actually,' she said, 'I haven't seen Amyntas for weeks, or anyone else for that matter. Can we go home now?' She yawned. 'I had a good sleep during your play, but I'm still quite tired.'

'It's drinking in the afternoons that does it,' I replied. 'If you're a good girl, I'll show you where I keep the proper wine.'

'Under the figs in the storeroom, and most of it's turned to vinegar,' she said drowsily. 'One of these days I'll get my brother to show you how to seal a jar properly.'

I have just been reading over what I have written, and I notice to my horror that I have been so carried away with my own story that I have said nothing at all about what had been happening in the war. If I were a conscientious man, instead of being naturally frivolous, I would tear the roll across and start all over again. But if I am to be honest for once, I must confess that I remember that part of the war no better than any other Athenian; as a nation we have remarkably poor memories for things that have happened in our own lifetime. We are rather better at the deeds of our fathers and grandfathers; but since we get our information about those times from men who were equally negligent and forgetful in their own day, it stands to reason that if any part of our historical tradition is accurate, this can only be by pure chance, or because we have asked men from other cities what they can remember.

But you have been counting through the years on your fingers, and are sitting there like men at Assembly waiting for the good news about whitebait prices, in the hope that I will say something about Mitylene and Pylos. So I had better say something about that, or you will despair of me and my History, and sell my book to the men who scrape down paper to be used again. Very well, then.

Actually, I did go to Assembly when they debated Mytilene; the first day, that is, not the second, when they changed their minds. I hadn't meant to go; in fact I was standing in the Market Square haggling with a man for a bundle of sheepskins, which I wanted to use as blankets in Pallene. I was so busy trying to save myself a few obols that I didn't see that the constables were coming through the Market Square with the rope dipped in red paint, which is how they used to drive people with nothing to do up to Assembly in my day. The fleece-seller suddenly ducked behind his bales, and when I looked round there was the red rope, heading straight for me. I just managed to get up to the Pnyx before they caught up with me, and so avoided the chant of 'Redleg!' which always greets the last arrivals.

It was there that I heard Cleon speak in public for the first time, and you can imagine the impression it made on me. He was a truly awe-inspiring figure when he had worked himself up into a fury, and although I felt it my duty as a Comic poet to hate him, I found it very difficult.

You probably know more about the Mitylenean crisis than I do, but the basic situation was this. Our subjects in Mitylene, the largest city in Lesbos, had rebelled, and after a lot of trouble we broke the rebellion and regained control of the city. The motion before Assembly, therefore, was what we should do with the Mityleneans, and most of us, at least before Cleon started to speak, would have given the same answer; kill or exile the ringleaders, double the taxes, and leave a garrison. But Cleon, typically, had a much better idea. He wanted to turn an episode which did not, broadly speaking, do us much credit into an opportunity for 'clear thinking and radical action', to use a favourite phrase of his. He wanted us to put to death every adult male in Mitylene, regardless of any plea or excuse. That way, he argued, he would demonstrate not only how dangerous it was to play games with the Athenians, but also how totally unlike other cities we were.

'Who else in the whole of Greece,' he said, in that wonderful, horrible voice of his, 'would dare to contemplate such a dreadful act, the destruction of an entire people? Never mind who else could do it – although there are very few who could; who else would do such a thing? Who would dare?'

Here he paused, and looked around slowly, as if daring someone to interrupt him. 'But you would, Men of Athens, if you have courage to match your position.

And why? Because you are a democracy, the only true democracy in the history of the world. For a democracy which is a true democracy can do anything it pleases, and no constraint of expediency or morality can restrain it. Because the People have no permanent identity, because they are immortal and are influenced by no factor other than their own benefit, the only limit to what they can do is the physical limit of what they can get away with, what they can actually start and complete without interruption or being bodily prevented by others. It is this that gives us Athenians the ability, and the right, to be the servants of none and the masters of others.

'But, I hear some of you muttering, just because we, alone of all men, can put the Mityleneans to death, surely that doesn't mean that we must? On the contrary, Men of Athens. Because we have this unique power, we must exercise it; we must be ruthless in exercising it, or else it will float away from us, like a dream on waking. Otherwise we will create for ourselves mental restraints more deadly than physical ones; we will begin to say, "We *dare* not do this", not, "We *cannot* do this", which would be like binding ourselves in chains because no other man is able to bind us.

'No; if it seems true to us that the best way to preserve our empire in the future is to set it such a terrifying example that no man would ever dare to rebel again, we have no real option other than to set that example, and show the world that Athens will stop at nothing to get what it wants. For you all know the rest. If we lose our subject-states, then we lose our whole way of life, which is that of the landlords of Greece. At present, no man in any of our cities can plough his land or promise his daughter in marriage or buy flour in the market, except by the consent of Athens. I do not mean that we authorise all these things, or that each man must receive a licence written in wax before he does anything; but he knows that he is the property of Athens, just as your chattels are the property of each one of you.

'Supposing Nicias or Callias the son of Hipponicus,

who each has hundreds of slaves, had one slave in particular who not only ran away but incited his fellows to do the same, and cut their master's throat into the bargain. Nicias and Callias are honest, pious men; but would they hesitate to have that slave whipped and tortured to death? Of course not. They are rich enough to bear the loss, and if they did not do so, they would be positively encouraging their other slaves to run away too, and asking to be murdered themselves. And you, fellow Athenians, you have more slaves than anyone else. You can afford the loss, but you cannot afford to give treason a precedent. So if you value your empire and your democracy and your very lives, vote for my proposal. But if you do not, and if you are prepared to hand over your true and only wealth to the Spartans and the Corinthians, then vote against it.'

Of course, we all voted for him, and cheered him until our throats were dry, and went home to tell anyone unlucky enough not to have been present what a feast of oratory and good sense they had missed. But we are Athenians, and so the next day when someone demanded that we reconsider the resolution, we did, and overruled it, too. The general view seemed to be that since we had voted both for and against the motion, we must have got it right either the first or the second time, which was very clever of us.

So Cleon didn't get his way over Mitylene. But this defeat did him no harm at all, no more than all the attacks in the Comedies. The real test of his abilities came much later, at about the time I married Phaedra and went to Samos.

It all started when Demosthenes, a brilliant, dashing and quite remarkably lucky general of ours, made rather a mess of an important and fairly straightforward campaign in Aetolia. He was far too frightened to come home, since he would have been exiled or put to death, and so he hung around in Naupactus waiting for his luck to change. And change it did. Before he knew quite what was happening, he had won a notable victory in Messenia and was able to come home safely.

171

But Demosthenes never knew when to leave well alone, and so he persuaded the Athenians to give him forty first-class warships, to use at his absolute discretion in and around the Peloponnese. For he had seen a place on the Messenian coast called Pylos; once the home of the fabulous King Nestor, but now a god-forsaken place with nothing much to it except a certain shape, which Demosthenes but no one else could see. His fellow generals told him not to be so damned stupid and come and join them in a little recreational crop-burning; but Demosthenes would not be diverted from his arcane purpose. Since he could not openly dissent from the opinion of his fellow generals, he sat down in Pylos and read Homer, and his colleagues washed their hands of him and got on with the war. But Demosthenes' soldiers, either from boredom or because they had had the idea planted in their heads, set about fortifying Pylos with whatever materials came to hand.

King Agis of Sparta, on his way home from burning the best crop of early beans I have ever managed to produce, heard about what was going on at Pylos, and nearly had a stroke. Apparently, he too had seen that natural shape at Pylos, and had been meaning to do something about it for some time. Perhaps my early beans got in his way; certainly he recognised that once a force of determined men got dug in at Pylos, there was nothing on earth that could get them out. He marched as fast as he could, hoping to take Demosthenes by surprise.

Lying next to Pylos is a wooded and uninhabited island called Sphacteria, on to which Agis transferred the flower of the Spartan army, with some idea of using it as a base for attacking Demosthenes without having to risk a sea-battle. The main point about Sphacteria is that there is no water on the island; but this seemed irrelevant, since the Spartans did not intend to stay there for more than a day or so.

Just then, a large Athenian fleet, which Demosthenes had sent for, arrived unexpectedly, and there was a messy battle between the Athenians and Agis's forces on the mainland, both by land and sea. Despite the efforts of a certain Spartan captain called Brasidas, the Athenians won, and the Spartans drew out feeling hard done by. Except, of course, for their best troops, who were cooped up on Sphacteria with no ships and no water.

Demosthenes realised that his position, although it looked good for the moment, was untenable. Unless he thought of something quickly, the Spartans would overcome their profound respect for him and come back, and even his luck was unlikely to hold out much longer. There was no way of knowing how long the reserves of water on Sphacteria would last, and even though he had swept the sea clear of Peloponnesian warships, it would be impossible to stop small fishing-boats slipping out by night and supplying the Spartans on the island.

So he made a deal, which under the circumstances was the best he could do. In return for being allowed to send food and water in to Sphacteria, the Spartans were to hand over all the ships they had in the area as securities (to be returned if the truce was observed) and keep well away while they sent an embassy to Athens to discuss peace terms. The Spartans sent their embassy, which Cleon, who was then under considerable pressure from the moderate faction, sent away again. Accordingly, Demosthenes stopped the food shipments, but claimed some minor infringement of the truce and refused to return the ships. The Spartans attacked at once by land, and Demosthenes, despite reinforcements from Athens, didn't know what to do next. He could see no hope of taking Sphacteria by storm, and if he let the men on the island die of hunger and thirst, he would lose his hostages and with them the best opportunity Athens had yet had of ending the war. In addition, he was running short of food and water himself, in spite of now having seventy first-class warships to fetch and carry for him, and since the Spartans were managing to get some supplies through to Sphacteria, it looked as if the whole thing could still end in disaster. So he sent a full account of his position to Athens and asked for any sensible suggestions.

Cleon, who had turned away the Spartan ambassadors, was now in deep trouble, and all he could think of was to accuse Demosthenes' messengers of lying. It was therefore proposed – I think as a joke – that he be sent out to have a look for himself, and the proposal was overwhelmingly accepted. But Cleon kept his nerve and counter-proposed that Nicias son of Niceratus, who was one of the generals that year, should be sent out with reinforcements to help Demosthenes.

Nicias, being Nicias, stood there like a thoughtful sheep and said that although it was a great honour to be chosen for such an important mission, his infirmity was such that he could not accept it. At this, Cleon tried to be rather too clever. He said that Nicias was nothing special, and neither was Demosthenes, whom everyone was calling the best thing since fried whitebait. Any fool, he said, could have those Spartans off that island and back in Athens in a couple of days. Why, even he could do it . . .

Nicias, who had been sitting there fretting about failing to do his duty in his city's hour of need, suddenly brightened up and said that that was a wonderful idea, and everyone started agreeing with him and cheering at the tops of their voices. Cleon, who knew about as much about the arts of war as I do about sponge-diving, went a ghastly shade of white and started to talk very fast. But nobody would listen to him; the more he gabbled, the more they cheered, until he realised that there was no way out.

So he stood up and held up his hand for silence, and everyone stopped laughing and shouting, to hear what this clever man would say next. Cleon started by saying that he was moved and honoured by his fellow citizens' confidence in him, which was a generous reward for the few small services he had done the Athenians, but which he could not help feeling was misplaced. He had never held a military command before, and although nothing would please him more than to go, he felt he could not risk the lives of his fellow Athenians in this venture. Instead, he said, raising his voice so as to be heard above the groundswell of rude noises coming from his beloved fellow citizens, he would take with him only the few allied heavy infantry who were stationed in Athens, and a force of light infantry and archers, also allies. Then he took a deep breath and shut his eyes, and promised that if he wasn't back, mission accomplished, within twenty days, they could duck him in one of his own tanning-vats and cut him up for sandals. The Athenians roared with laughter and cheered so loudly that they could be heard all over the City; for even if Cleon couldn't hope to deliver, it had been great fun listening to him, and there would be more fun still, first when he made his excuses, and later at his trial.

Twenty days later, he was back; and with him were the Spartans from the island, including one hundred and twenty Spartiate noblemen, in chains. There was a different sort of cheering after that, and although Aristophanes' next play, which was entirely devoted to the most vicious attacks on Cleon, won first prize, that was little more than an Athenian way of telling him how much they loved him, just as they had loved Pericles and Themistocles before him.

In fact, it wasn't fool's luck, as everyone said afterwards. Because Cleon wasn't a soldier, he didn't think like a soldier. He saw that heavy infantry, the heart and soul of any Greek army, are never much more than a liability, and since the object of the exercise was to take as many Spartan heavy infantrymen alive as possible, he couldn't use Athenian heavy troops against them. So he used his brains instead. First he set fire to the woods which cover Sphacteria – Demosthenes had been too clever to think of anything so simple – and when the Spartans came dashing out, like hares out of barley when it's being cut, he harried them with his light infantry and archers until, out of a mixture of exhaustion and frustration at not being able to come to grips with their tormentors, they threw down their shields and surrendered quietly. It was all totally new and barbaric, but it worked, with minimal losses to them and virtually none to us.

That, then, was Cleon, perhaps the most typically Athenian of the City's leaders during my lifetime. It's wrong to think of him as being in the same class as

Themistocles or even Pericles, since those men left Athens stronger than they had found her. But in a way they can be compared; for each one of them taught the world new tricks. It was my duty as a Comic poet to hate Cleon, and I did my best. But I met him many times and could not help liking the man.

I once saw a crowd of people down at Piraeus watching a hawk killing a dove. The foreigners wanted the dove to escape, since it was weaker and more beautiful; but the Athenians were cheering on the hawk. Then, when the hawk had killed the dove and was pulling its head off with its talons, a man stepped forward with a sling-shot and the Athenians started betting on whether he could kill the hawk, since the range was quite long and a hawk is a tough sort of a bird. The slinger had bet three obols on himself, so he put forth all his skill and a moment later the hawk was lying on its back, stone dead, with a great chunk of dove-meat still in its beak. The cheering that greeted the shot reminded me of the cheering that greeted Cleon's return from Pylos, and also the announcement of his death at Amphipolis, rather bravely in battle, against the invincible Spartan general Brasidas, a month or so after my play was performed. He had been trying to repeat his previous stunning success, but this time he had overreached himself, and the defeat at Amphipolis cancelled out everything that he had achieved at Pylos.

I believe Aristophanes went into deep mourning for his death, just as Cratinus had done for Pericles. But unlike Cratinus he continued attacking him in his Comedies for years afterwards, and I remember sitting through a particularly dreary play of his, all about Dionysus going down to Hell to bring back a poet or some such nonsense, and a foreigner sitting next to me asking, 'Who is this Cleon he keeps going on about?' I closed my eyes for a moment, and wondered how I could possibly explain; about Pylos, and the informers, and the Brotherhood of the Three Obols.

'Search me,' I replied. 'Never heard of him.'

Chapter Eleven

Phaedra took to coming to rehearsals with me regularly. So as not to scandalise the company, who were all very superstitious, she dressed up in a boy's going-to-school clothes and sat there with her tablets on her lap, while I told everyone who asked that she was a cousin up from the country.

A week before the Festival, someone took a hammer to the little statue of Hermes outside my house, and pushed a cock with its head and spurs cut off under my door. This didn't worry me at all; I replaced the old Hermes with a new one by a leading sculptor, and we had the cock, stewed in wine, for dinner. I was rather more concerned by the rumours going round that Phrynichus, who had the third Chorus that year, had got hold of one of the big speeches in the Contest Scene, and had adapted it to fit into his play. If his play was called on before mine, they told me, he was going to use that speech instead of his own, so that mine would be jeered off the stage. I consulted Philonides, who said that it had been done before, and so sat down, with a headache and three rolls of scrubbed Egyptian paper, to try and compose a substitute speech. Eventually I got one written, and gave it to the actor to learn. If Phrynichus tried it on, I would be ready for him.

The Tragedies that year included Agathon's *Electra*, Euripides' *Teucer*, and something by Melanthius – there was a scene in it where the hero went off-stage and came back transformed by a God into a pig, with a dainty little pig's mask and trotters, which got a bigger laugh than anything in any of the Comedies, but I can't remember anything else about it. The Comedies were mine, Phrynichus' *Garlic-Eaters*, and Aristophanes' *Veterans of Marathon*. He had two plays that year, for he got a Chorus for his *Wasps* at the Lenaea, which did depressingly well.

Phrynichus was called on the first day. I was told the result of the ballot just before dawn, and sent Doron over to tell Philonides. Of course, I still had no idea whether I would be called on the second or the third day, and I sat through that day's Tragedies in a fever of impatience. For some reason I kept wishing I had Phaedra with me (she was sitting with the other women, of course, on the other side of the Theatre) and at one stage I absent-mindedly reached out for the hand of the man sitting next to me. Luckily he was too wrapped up in the play to notice, since he wasn't my type at all. As Aegisthus or Diomedes or whoever it was droned his way through his cosmic passion, it suddenly struck me that my feelings for Phaedra had undergone an unhealthy change. Instead of wishing she had never been born, I realised, I could feel a sort of smile wriggling on to my face whenever I thought of her, and a warm sensation all over my body. This was only when she wasn't there, of course; it took only a few minutes in her company for all the old, familiar feelings of exasperation and fury to come flooding back. But that was an overstatement too. I felt that we were like two ageing boxers who work in one of those travelling fairs that sometimes pass through the country districts. Every day of their lives, they have to fight each other and put on a show of pain and violence, but if you watch closely they don't hit each other at all; and when the people have all gone, the older one, who isn't married, takes his tunic round to the younger one's tent so that his wife can darn it for him.

Yet all we seemed to have in common, apart from bad luck in having been married to each other, was an unending battle. You know how young husbands and wives are always stretching their minds to think up little treats and surprises for each other – a pretty, old-fashioned grasshopper brooch, or a new way of preparing anchovies; well, we seemed to spend just as much time and effort thinking up new snubs and insults and ways of inflicting annoyance, but never anything that hurt too much. If I heard a fishmonger make some particularly unflattering comment on the appearance of one of his women customers, I would say it over and over to myself under my breath as I walked home, for fear of forgetting it; and whenever a book arrived for me from the copyists, Phaedra would always go through it first and put a little charcoal mark beside any passage concerning Clytemnestra or Medea, or any other heroines who killed or injured their husbands. At night, we rarely did anything but sleep, and when we climbed into bed together we would lie on our sides, each grimly facing the wall on either side. But by the morning it often happened that we had turned to face each other, and usually she was lying on my arm, so that I was woken up by the numbness in it. Then we would start to bicker, still half asleep, until one of us jumped out in a rage and went to wash. And on those few occasions when one of us had the itch, the other never refused, but preferred to make nasty remarks or pretend to be asleep until the clumsy process was over. I was fairly certain that Phaedra had stopped seeing other men (although she denied it vehemently), while I could never see any point in chasing after flute-girls and housemaids, who never wash and are forever pestering you for money.

All this passed through my mind as I sat there, and I quite forgot about the hardness of the seat (I had forgotten to bring a cushion) or the dreariness of the play, or even my fear of Phrynichus. In fact, by the time I came round, the King (or whoever it was) had been killed, or blinded, or turned into whatever he was turned into, and the Chorus were into their second round of lamentation. I dismissed all thoughts of Phaedra from my mind, and started surveying the audience.

It's probably my imagination, but I believe that I can tell just by looking at them whether an enemy line is

179

going to stand or run, or whether an audience is likely to be friendly or not. With audiences, you can work out a great deal beforehand. If it's been a bad year or the enemy have burnt their crops, they will be anxious to be pleased, and will roar with laughter at anything that resembles a joke. But if the vintage has gone off well, or news has just come in of a naval victory, they'll sit there like a jury at the trial of a politician, just waiting for some little flaw or slip. If the play is good they show no mercy to the actors, and if the acting is good, it stands to reason that the play is weak and the costumes were cobbled together at the last minute out of old cloaks and sail-cloth. It's the other way round with Tragedy, of course. People like nothing better than blood and death when they've been gorging themselves on freshly made cheese and new wine; but if there's been a food shortage, or the list of casualties has been read out, the prancing and howling of actors will irritate them beyond measure. This is why, when the fleet sails, the Tragedians go down to Piraeus and offer sacrifices for its safe return, while the Comic poets say a silent prayer to Poseidon for a violent thunderstorm.

But this year had been neither bad nor good; there had been as many victories as defeats in the war (or so we assured ourselves) and if the Spartans had burnt most of the barley, they had missed more than usual. So a great deal would depend on the plays, Comedies and Tragedies, that came on before mine. If an audience falls in love with the first Comedy in the Festival, they don't give the others a fair chance. But if not, then they tend to give the benefit of the doubt to the play which is called on last. If the Tragedies have bored them, they enjoy the Comedies more; but if they are still talking about the Tragedies when the Comedy is called on, they're quite capable of chatting away throughout the opening scene and then blaming the author for not explaining the situation properly.

Of course, the reaction of the audience is not what really matters. What every playwright has nightmares about is the twelve judges. It's a remarkable effect. A play can be booed off the stage, and the actors barely escape with their lives. But if it's subsequently awarded the prize, then by the next day everyone is quoting it as they work in the fields, and declaring it the funniest thing ever, while the play that comes third is universally ridiculed, even if while the Chorus was on stage the audience was choking with laughter and yelling for reprises. And then, of course, there are always those people – I tend to find myself standing behind them in queues – who always disagree with the judges, praising the play that came third and saying that if the prizewinner gets a Chorus next year they'll stay at home and make vine-props.

That year I couldn't recognise any of the judges – in those days they really were chosen by lot from the electoral roll – which I considered on balance to be the best thing. A friend among the judges can be a blessing, but it can also be a disadvantage, while an enemy is always disastrous. I remember staring long and hard at them, trying to prise open their ribs with my eyes so that I could see the shape of their souls, but the more I stared, the less I could see. There was a very old man who kept whispering to his neighbour; I could almost hear him saying, 'When I was a boy, of course, we had Aeschylus and Phrynichus – that's Phrynichus the Tragic poet, of course, not this young man who writes the Comedies.' And the man next to him would nod absently, but he never took his eyes off the stage, and instead of wriggling about in his seat he sat absolutely still, with his hands neatly folded in his lap. He would probably vote for the play with the fewest metrical errors, and I squirmed as I thought of the three fluffed caesuras in *The General*. Another one had his eyes closed, and I was filled with fury; if he dared fall asleep when my Chorus was on stage I would get a sling and knock his eyes out for him. But when the strophe ended, he moved his head and nodded, and I realised that he was paying strict attention. That's the judge for you, my soul said smugly within me; he won't be swayed by smart costumes or clever masks. It's the words he's interested in. Then his head fell on one side, and I could see that he really was asleep after all.

By the time the herald called out 'Phrynichus, bring out your Chorus!' I was drenched in sweat and my heart was pounding like the drum on a trireme when the drummer is setting the pace for the attack. I clamped my teeth together, for I was determined not to laugh, and sat up straight in my seat, praying that Philonides had bribed the Chorus or put sand in the leading actor's mask. Yet when the first big joke came, I felt this strange feeling in my chest and something seemed to well up inside me, as if I had eaten beans and drunk new wine, and I heard myself laughing. A feeling of terror came over me, as I realised that the play actually was funny, and when the audience laughed it was like the sound of hoofs making the earth shake, when the enemy cavalry is coming towards you and there is nowhere to run.

Then my soul spoke quietly within me, telling me that there was nothing more that I could do, at least until the play was over and I could go straight over to Philonides' house and fix those fluffed caesuras and the joke about the sprats. I pressed my feet hard on the stone and pushed myself back in my seat, and soon I was enjoying the play. It was a good play, too, all about a man who wins the war by drawing the sun down into a jar so that the Spartan army loses its way in the dark and marches off a cliff, and there was a hilarious scene with Apollo trying to charm the lid off the jar by reciting passages from Sophocles.

I enjoyed it so much, in fact, that I forgot all about everything else, and clapped as loudly as anyone when the Chorus lined up for the anapaests. Phrynichus' addresses to the audience were always the best part of his plays, and he had an uncanny knack of guessing, at the time he wrote the play, what would be most topical when the Festival came round.

He started off by praising the army and the fleet, and comparing them to the men of Marathon and Salamis; then there was a rather witty invocation to Lady Garlic; then he went into one of his favourite themes, the poets.

First, inevitably, Cratinus, who by now had entered into

his final illness; Phrynichus had great fun with that, saying how while Dionysus and Aphrodite were quarrelling like two wild dogs over his miserable carcase, Hermes, as God of Thieves was sneaking up behind them to secure for himself the greatest stealer of other men's jokes the world had ever seen. Then we were given some marvellous stuff about Ameipsias throwing away his shield at the battle of Delium and having to be rescued by Socrates, who he had made mincemeat of in one of his plays. I was grinning like an idiot by this stage, in eager anticipation of what the poet would have to say about Aristophanes. What I and several thousand others heard was this.

As if it wasn't bad enough (Phrynichus' Chorus-leader said) having these stray polecats jumping up on Dionysus' altar to gobble down the offerings left there by Thespis, there was now a new poet in Athens; a cripple with a perpetual grin and nothing between his legs but a nasty rash. (It's true I sometimes have a rash there in hot weather; God knows how Phrynichus found out about it.) We hear that his play, which you will soon be able to judge for yourselves, has some pretty bits in it. They aren't his own, of course; Aristophanes gave them to him in exchange for his life, when he caught that bald-headed son of a goat up to the hilts in that pretty young wife of his.

It's a strange feeling being insulted in a play, and hearing the people hooting with laughter. The man on one side of me was stuffing his cloak into his mouth and snorting, while my neighbour on the other side had a smile which would have stretched right round the coast from Piraeus to Anaphlystos. I would gladly have castrated Phrynichus just then; but I felt a strange sort of glow, almost like pride, and I wanted to turn to my neighbours and say, 'That's me he's talking about.' And when I've spoken to men I've made jokes about, they say roughly the same thing, and attribute the feeling to the power of the God Dionysus himself. Later, of course, I became hardened to remarks about me in plays, until I only noticed them when they weren't there.

I met Phaedra outside the gate and we walked home together.

'If you really *were* a man,' she said, 'you'd kill that Phrynichus for me.'

I shrugged. 'Why?' I asked. 'Because he agrees with you?'

'I don't care a damn what he says about you.'

'He said you were pretty.'

'I didn't say he wasn't telling the truth,' she replied quickly. 'But how I'm going to hold my head up in public again after that, I just don't know.'

I put my arm around her waist. 'Never mind,' I said. 'He didn't steal my speech, that's the main thing.'

'How did he know about that rash of yours?' she went on.

'You must have talked about it in your sleep.'

'Now all the women will refuse to sit next to me,' she went on, as if I hadn't spoken, 'in case they catch it from me. It's not catching, is it?'

'I expect so. I hope I don't get called on tomorrow. They may not tell me until the morning, of course, and then I'll have to go round the wine shops flushing out the actors. I'll enjoy that,' I pre-empted her.

'Eupolis.' She had stopped in her tracks and was biting her lower lip.

'There's something I've got to tell you.'

'Who's the father, do you know?'

Suddenly she got very angry. 'Why must you always be making *jokes*?' she shouted. 'I'm really sick of it, do you hear? All the time. I just don't think it's funny any more.' She pulled her hand out of mine and turned away. I suddenly felt very foolish, although God only knows why, and I stood there on one leg waiting for her to say something.

'I mean,' she went on, with her back still to me, 'if you hadn't been such a complete waste of time ever since our wedding-day I wouldn't have done it in the first place.'

'Done what?'

'So if anyone's to blame,' she said, rounding on me and scowling, 'you are, you utterly stupid man.' She spat neatly between her feet. 'You pushed me just too far, that's all.'

'What have you done?'

'Go to hell,' she snapped, and started to walk quickly away. I ran after her and grabbed her by the wrists. 'Let go of me,' she said, and pulled her hands free. 'You see,' she sneered, 'you can't even bully me properly.'

'I asked you a question,' I said. 'What have you done?'

'It was all Aristophanes' idea,' she said, 'while I was still seeing him. Do you know,' she went on, 'he's almost as big a washout as you are? Anyway, he wanted me to find some way of wrecking this play of yours. I told him not to bother, it was bound to fail of its own accord; but he's stupid, just like you, and he wanted to make sure. And that's why I started being so nice to you—'

'When? I must have missed it.'

'For God's sake, Eupolis.' She was tight-lipped with fury, and I decided to leave well alone. 'I let you take me to your stupid rehearsals, and you kept on about your stupid costumes for your stupid Chorus. So I listened carefully to what they said about where they stored them.'

'They're over at Philonides' house,' I said. 'He keeps them in his inner room, in a locked chest.'

'I know,' she replied. 'I heard him saying so. So I told Aristophanes, and tomorrow morning, before dawn, he's going round there with his actors and he's going to dig through the wall of the house and steal them.'

It was like being hit by that footpad all over again. I felt my legs go weak, and I couldn't think. 'For God's sake, woman,' I groaned, 'why didn't you just kill me instead? That's a horrible thing to do.'

Then I felt her head under my chin and her arms around me. 'But you deserved it,' she sobbed. 'You deserved it so much. I knew it would hurt you more than anything in the whole world, because you're so stupid.'

The feel of her so close to me was like fire, and my soul filled my arms and my legs with strength.

'How do you know it'll be tomorrow?' I asked her.

'For all he knew, I could have been called on first.'

She shook her head. 'He fixed the ballot,' she said. 'He bribed someone, he didn't tell me who. He wanted you on tomorrow and himself last, to be sure of beating Phrynichus. Eupolis, I—'

'We'll discuss that later,' I said. 'Go home and mix plenty of strong wine. I've got to find Philonides.'

So, when rosy-fingered dawn was spreading across the eastern sky, I was hiding behind a large jar in Philonides' inner room, feeling that mixture of fear and righteous anger that Theseus must have felt when he strode through the Labyrinth in search of the Minotaur.

Philonides himself was crouched uncomfortably behind the costume chest, and positioned at strategic points all round the room were our four actors, Little Zeus, three large slaves from Philonides' household, and a man who had been passing in the street when we arrived, who we pressed into service as an independent witness. Apart from the witness, we were all wearing our helmets and breastplates, and we had heavy olive clubs hastily cut from vine-props.

'Of course,' said Little Zeus (one of whose ancestors had been a famous general), 'the whole thing could be a clever trick.'

'I don't know about clever,' Philonides said. 'Dirty, maybe.'

'No, you don't understand,' said Little Zeus earnestly. 'It could be a false message, a diversion, like Themistocles at Salamis. Aristophanes might want us to be here, while he does something else on the other side of the City. He could be poisoning our Chorus-leader at this very moment.'

Philonides told him to be quiet, but I started to worry, and I picked all the bark off the handle of my club with my fingernails without realising it. The effects of the strong wine we had all drunk at my house were beginning to evaporate, as was the righteous anger. The residue was mostly fear, combined with a feeling that I shouldn't really be there. I had wanted to send someone

186

for Callicrates and Philodemus, but there hadn't been time. And I was sure someone had followed Philonides and me back to my house after I found him.

'Perhaps he isn't coming,' said one of the actors. 'We've been here for hours now, and I'm dying for a pee. Are we getting paid for this?'

'You'll get the back of my hand if you don't shut up,' said Philonides.

'And will you all stop jabbering like a lot of birds? This is supposed to be an ambush.'

At least worrying about the attack kept me from worrying too much about my play, though I had suddenly remembered that we had never got around to fixing the fluffed caesuras. Still, I felt, this would probably not be a good time for a major rewrite, even though we had all the actors with us.

Then I saw Philonides lift his head suddenly, and I heard the sound of a crowbar clinking on the bricks of the wall. Philonides put up his hand and placed a pot carefully over the lamp. In the total darkness, the sound of the crowbar seemed to fill the room, and I started to think of all the battles in tight places that I could remember; Thermopylae, and Pylos, of course. The more I thought, the more uneasy I felt, for in every such engagement that I could call to mind, the attackers had eventually prevailed. We had no idea how many men Aristophanes had brought; he might have his whole Chorus out there, with swords and damp leaves to make smoke. We were well off for heavy infantry, but where were our slingers and archers? And we had forgotten to bar the door; Aristophanes could not expect the house to be empty – what if he were to send a detachment of his forces round to the front of the house, to take us from both sides, as Xerxes had done at Thermopylae? And although we were armed with clubs, they had heavy iron crowbars, and none of us had thought to bring our shields. If only Callicrates was here! If only Callicrates was here, and I was somewhere else.

Then my soul within me told me to be quiet and fight well when the moment came, and I gripped the handle of my club so tight that I pinched the skin inside my signet-ring, which seemed to hurt as much as a sabre-cut. The sound of crowbars was growing louder with every heart-beat, and I was sure I could hear voices, many voices. Not only his Chorus, I said to my soul, but all his household slaves as well, and probably some cooks or other ruffians hired in the Market Square. I felt trapped, like a grasshopper in a jar. Demosthenes himself would have trouble getting out of this mess.

There was a sound of rubble falling on our side of the wall, and a shaft of early morning light came into the room, very faint but enough to dazzle me for a moment. My mouth was dry, and every muscle in my body seemed to ache. More hammering; whole bricks were coming through into the room, and I remember thinking that whoever had built Philonides' house had made a pretty poor job of it. The hammering stopped, and with it my heart.

'Boss,' whispered a voice from the wall, 'I can get my head through the hole now.'

'Get on with it, you idiot.' Unmistakably Aristophanes. 'We haven't got all night.'

'Boss,' whispered the voice again, 'what if there's somebody in there? I mean—'

'Philonides is at Eupolis' house,' Aristophanes said, 'my man saw him go in, they're probably making last-minute changes. And he always sends his wife to the country for the Festival. Can we get on now, please?'

That seemed to satisfy the voice, for the hammering started up again, and more bricks came tumbling in, until I could see a man-sized patch of blue light where there had been only darkness before. I promised a firstling lamb each to Dionysus and Ares the Driver of the Spoil, and waited. There was silence, then a rustling noise, and the blue light was blotted out by moving shapes.

Then Philonides lifted the pot off the lamp and shouted *Io Paian!* at the top of his voice, and there was Aristophanes, frozen like a statue in the lamplight. In his hands were a crowbar and a lump-hammer, and his tunic was gathered over his shoulder like a stone-mason. With him were four men, similarly dressed and equipped. The head of a sixth man, which was poking through the hole in the wall, was hurriedly withdrawn and not seen again.

I aimed a terrific blow at the man nearest to me, but I missed and decimated a terracotta figure of Europa riding the bull, which, Philonides told me later, had belonged to his grandfather. But Little Zeus made straight for Aristophanes and grabbed him round the waist like a wrestler, lifting him up so high that his head banged noisily against the rafters. Meanwhile, Philonides and his men were laying about them with their clubs, shouting ferociously and occasionally making contact. The actual fighting was over disappointingly quickly, and by the time I had picked my club up off the floor, there was no one left for me to hit with it.

Philonides and his men had dumped their four captives on the floor and were tying them securely with scarves and rushes, while Little Zeus manhandled Aristophanes round to face me. Now during our interminable vigil I had prepared a little speech, in case such an opportunity arose. 'Aristophanes son of Philip,' I intended to say, 'what you have done here tonight is a crime not only against the laws of Athens but against our Patron God Dionysus himself. To sabotage one of His plays is no better an act for a free man and a citizen than burning His temple or robbing His priests. But Dionysus is a merciful God, and so I shall leave your punishment in His hands. You may go free, son of Philip, on the following conditions. First, that you make good all the damage you have done here, and lodge a bronze statue of Dionysus the Bringer of Joy in the shrine of Philonides' choice. Second, that you cease to trouble the God with your ill-made plays and henceforth live quietly on your Aeginetan estates without causing annoyance to anyone. What do you have to say?'

It was probably just as well that I did not deliver this address, or my name would have become a byword for pomposity, wherever two Athenians met together. As it was, I had got as far as 'Arist—' when Aristophanes, slipping out of Little Zeus' clutches, made a dash for the hole in the wall and escaped, bumping into me as he went. I tried to catch hold of his tunic but lost my footing in a puddle of lamp-oil, slipped, and sat down painfully on a pair of sandals.

'Pathetic,' grunted Philonides. 'Couldn't catch a fever in the marshes. Right, let's have a look at them.'

He grabbed each of the captives by the beard and stared fiercely at them for a moment. 'Now listen to me,' he said. 'Fun is fun but I can't be doing with nonsense, so when you next work with me, you'd better be very careful. All right, Aristobulus, untie them. I said untie them, you idiot; those scarves cost money.'

'Are those Aristophanes' actors?' I protested. 'We could lock them up, and then—'

Philonides told me to be quiet, and threw each one of the prisoners out with his own hands. 'They'd have done as much for me, I expect,' he said, and sat down on the costume chest.

'But, Philonides—' I protested.

'Now listen, you,' Philonides replied angrily, grabbing me by the arm, 'I have to work with these people, right? And with Aristophanes, come to that. So that's an end of it, right?'

I nodded and he let me go. I went and stood in the corner of the room, feeling rather upset. But Philonides stood up and started to survey the damage to his property.

'Since you let the son of Philip get away,' he said, 'I'm holding you liable for all this damage.' He turned to the witness, who was looking thoroughly confused. 'Have you got that? Eupolis son of Euchorus, of the deme of Pallene. And if I find out which one of you clowns smashed up my best chair, I'll pull his head off.'

There was far too much for us all still to do for any of us to feel tired or elated; there were costumes to be assembled, masks to be lined, and (I'm sorry to say) lines to be learned. By the time the messenger arrived, sent on from my house, to tell me that I was to be called on that day, the Chorus had already assembled and was making one last desperate attempt to come to grips with the major dance routine. Philonides seemed to have put all the events of the early morning behind him, as if such things happened every day, and was frantically chasing after bits of wool and leather strapping for the masks, on which it appeared that the success of our entire enterprise now depended. He seemed to have no use for me whatsoever and finally ordered me to get out from under his feet; he was a busy man, he said, and greatly though he valued my friendship and society, this was neither the time nor the place for amateurs. So I withdrew in a huff, like Achilles, and went home to dump my breastplate and helmet and change my clothes.

The streets seemed to be full of people, some with cushions under their arms, others carrying their children on their shoulders, all apparently making for the Theatre. I thought I heard my name mentioned once or twice, and that made me feel as if I was the King of the Athenians on his coronation-day, or a politician about to be tried for high treason, depending on the tone of voice of the person I was listening to at the time.

Phaedra was looking out of the open door as I came up the street.

'Well?' she demanded, as I pushed past her into the house. 'What happened? Did you get them?'

'More or less,' I replied, slinging my armour under a couch. 'Like a fool, I let Aristophanes get away, but Philonides got the rest of them and sorted them out once and for all. I don't think we'll have any more trouble.'

'Good,' said Phaedra, and she put her arms round my neck.

'Not now,' I said. 'Is there anything to eat in this house?'

She unhooked herself. 'I'll make you some porridge, if you like,' she said. 'You'll need something—'

'There isn't time,' I replied, 'I'll get a sausage or something at the Theatre. What I need now is some clean clothes. These are full of brick-dust.' I poured some water into a bowl and washed my face, which felt as if all the silt of a Nile flood had accumulated on it, and dried my hands on one of the twenty-drachma Persian tapestries. While I was doing so, Phaedra came back in with some clean clothes; but instead of throwing them at me, she pretended not to notice what I was doing and said, 'Here you are.'

I took off my old tunic and she gave me the new one. 'I haven't seen this before,' I said.

'I know,' she replied. 'And do try not to get it too filthy, because it took me weeks to make it and you know how much I hate weaving.'

I stared at it, as if it had been the tunic of Nessus. 'You made it?' I asked stupidly. 'For me?'

'No, for the bath-attendant, but he didn't like the colour. Don't sound so amazed, you ungrateful pig.'

'Bet it doesn't fit,' I said, shoving my head through the collar. It fitted perfectly, and smelt faintly and surprisingly of roses. 'Thought not,' I went on. 'Tight under the arms.'

'Good,' she said. 'So I don't suppose you'll want the cloak.'

'Far be it from me to give offence,' I said. 'I can always take it off when I get outside.'

She came close to me to fasten the brooch round my neck, and I kissed her without thinking. I was starting to lose count of the number of times I had kissed her. 'How's that?' she asked.

'It'll do,' I said.

She had fastened the brooch, but she didn't move away. 'And when do I get shouted at?' she said softly.

'What for?' I asked.

'Oh, for telling Aristophanes about those stupid costumes.' She closed her eyes and raised her head towards me.

'Later,' I said, 'when I've got a minute.'

'You've had your chance,' she said. 'Now, rather more important, when are you finally going to get around to thanking me? For saving the play at the last minute, like a Goddess on the flying machine?' She stood on tiptoe until her lips were very close to mine, and I kissed her again.

'Call that thanks?' she said. 'You didn't even open your mouth.'

192

'I did,' I replied, 'and that's all the thanks you deserve. Now will you please stop climbing up me and let me get on?'

She pulled a face and let go of me. 'Go on,' she said, 'get out and stay out. I can't stand the sight of you.'

'Good,' I said. 'So you won't be coming to the Theatre, then?'

'What, and miss you getting booed off the stage? I wouldn't miss that for all the perfume in Corinth.'

I picked up my walking-stick and looked at my reflection in a polished bronze jar; an idiot, I told myself, but a talented idiot. Then I saw Phaedra's face over my shoulder, and turned round. She pressed her nose against my chest and said, 'Eupolis.'

'Now what?'

'Good luck,' she whispered. 'I know they'll hate it, but I hope they don't throw stones at you. I'm sick and tired of you coming to bed all over blood.'

'Luck?' I said, 'who needs it?' I swirled my cloak round on my shoulders like a cavalry captain at the Panathenaea, and darted a sudden kiss at her, but I missed her lips and connected with her nose instead. She called me a clumsy idiot and giggled.

'When you see me next,' I said, posing in the doorway like a statue, 'I shall be the greatest poet in all Athens, and then you'll be sorry.'

'I'm not exactly ecstatic now,' she said, smiling.

'I shall return,' I continued, 'like King Leonidas himself; with my harp, or on it.' I strode magnificently out of the door, pretended to trip on my cloak, waved, and walked away.

'Do I get a choice?' Phaedra called after me.

As I bounced down the street, I pressed the collar of the tunic against my cheek, and I felt as Achilles must have felt, when he first went out to fight in the armour that the Fire God himself had made for him. Or perhaps I felt more like Hector, setting out on that day when Zeus promised him success so long as the daylight lasted. For although my body was on fire wherever the tunic and cloak touched it, and my heart as well, my soul inside me was still as cold as ice.

The Theatre was filling up when I got there, and after I had bought a sausage and a small loaf from one of the sausage-sellers, I sat down on the end of one of the middle rows and looked about me. There is no sound like the Theatre just before the start of the first play; like a hive of angry bees when they smell the first wisps of smoke from the beekeeper's bellows. Away on the very back rows a drunk was singing a country song, something about the swallow bringing back the good times, and when he had finished, there was a ripple of applause and some cheering. The audience were in a good mood, and I lifted my head and thanked all the Gods.

Someone walking across the stage waved to me, and I saw that it was Phrynichus, who I knew only by sight; a big man with a black beard, and his left arm in bandages. I waved back, just in case anyone was watching, for I didn't want to be talked about as a man who bears grudges. Then I looked around for an omen; but no birds flew overhead, neither on the left nor on the right, and since the sun was sharp I gave up and ate my sausage, which tasted horrible. I decided to save the bread for after the first Tragedy.

I saw Callicrates and Little Zeus and my uncle Philodemus coming down the stairs towards me, but I signalled to them to go away since I wanted to sit among strangers. Philodemus seemed offended, but Callicrates said something to him and he nodded, and they sat down where they were. I could hear Little Zeus saying something in his loud, flat voice, but I couldn't make out the words. I hoped he was praying for me.

Then I saw a bald head with a nasty-looking cut on it walking past a row or so beneath me, and I couldn't resist calling out. Aristophanes stopped and sent on his friends to reserve him a place, and looked up at me, grinning like an ape.

'Hello,' he shouted, 'and how's the cripple with the nasty rash this morning?'

'Couldn't be better,' I replied. 'And how is our two-obol Odysseus getting on, after his bungled shot at stealing the Palladium?'

He broadened his smile until I thought his face would crack. 'This is a very historic occasion,' he said. 'The very last time Eupolis ever leads out his Chorus.'

Just then, I couldn't think of a good reply (I thought of plenty later) and so I threw a nut at him instead. He walked on, laughing at his own joke and waving to somebody important in the front row. I scowled, and it occurred to me that Dolon would have been a neater comparison than Odysseus, but my soul told me to forget it, and I shifted up to make room for a fat man in a leather hat.

I soon found out a great deal about my neighbour, for he told me himself. He was a stranger in town, he said, here on business, but he had brought his wife with him to see the show, and she was sitting over there with the other women, but she had a cushion, so that was all right, and her name was Deianeira, by the way, and he was Pericleidas son of Bellerophon, and his home town was Catana, which was in Sicily but an ally of Athens of course, and very proud of it, too, and he was in the dry-fish business, which was why he was here in Athens, since back home folks were always telling him how Athens was the biggest market outside Persia for dried fish, especially now, with the war and all, although for some reason the Athenians just now seemed to get most of their dried fish requirements from Pontus, which was very strange and hard to believe, since he couldn't think why the Athenians should want to pay two obols a quart over the odds for an inferior product instead of buying from honest-to-God Greeks, especially since there were such strong ties of loyalty and affection between Catana and Athens, which were very important to a man like him, who was just mad about the Theatre, which was really the reason he was over in Athens this time of year, when the best time for dried fish was really later on around the time of the Lenaea, but of course foreigners weren't allowed to go to the Lenaea, which of course he could understand, what with it being a very special and meaningful religious occasion here in Athens, but which was a pity nevertheless for a man who was just wild about the Theatre, like all Sicilians were, although there is no domestic Theatre in Sicily, because most of the cities in Sicily were Dorian foundations, not Ionian, and the Dorians worship Dionysus in a different way, although it didn't actually seem to make the slightest bit of difference to the wine yields, because if old Dionysus got it into His head to make it a bad year then that was that, or so he reckoned, and what did I think?

'My name is Eupolis,' I replied. 'Welcome to Athens.'

Then the herald called on the first Tragedy, and Pericleidas quietened down a bit, once he understood that I knew the story of Oedipus quite well already. I don't remember anything else about that Tragedy, or the others after it, except that I wanted them to go on for as long as possible, provided that they did it quickly. And then the herald called out, 'Eupolis, bring on your Chorus,' and I put my hands in front of my eyes and took them away again quickly for fear of missing anything, and Pericleidas leaned across and whispered, 'Is that you?'

'Yes,' I said.

'Well,' he said, 'isn't that just wonderful?' and he slapped his knees with the palms of his hands for pure joy.

And the actors said their lines and the Chorus danced, and Aristobulus got the Cleon scene right for the very first time, and not one member of the Chorus forgot to do his rowing motions during the Hymn to Poseidon, and when it was all over and the Chorus had danced out again, Pericleidas leaned across to me and whispered, 'Well anyway, I liked it.'

For once, I seemed to have no trouble getting out of the Theatre, for the other people seemed to melt away in front of me, as if they were ghosts. But I could hear them chatting away, as Theatre audiences do, and they were all saying, 'Never mind, we've got the Aristophanes to look forward to tomorrow. Now he really does know how to write a Comedy.' And instead of crowding round me as

I passed by them, the sausage-sellers stood aloof and let me go by, as the gate-keepers shrink back from lepers.

Philonides tried to cheer me up, but I could see that he was furious at having backed a loser and made a fool of himself, while the Chorus were pulling off their costumes and flinging them back into the costume chest as if they were afraid of catching something from them. So I made my excuses and left, and strolled back into the Theatre, which was now quite empty, with only the slaves sweeping up the rubbish ready for the next day. I sat myself down under the big statue of Dionysus and burst into tears.

As I sat there, I heard a voice above me, and I knew that it was coming from the statue.

'Pretty bad, Eupolis,' it said, 'but there's worse to come. No, don't look round; you'll see me soon enough, in the walled orchard, as I promised you. It was a bad play, son of Euchorus. Show me something better next time, if ever you get a Chorus again.'

I listened, but there was no more, and I got to my feet and set off home. The streets were as quiet and empty as they had been that day when I escaped from the stable during the plague, and the only living creature I saw was a dog, who followed me for some time until I threw a stone at it.

Phaedra was waiting for me when I got home, with a cup of wine with herbs and cheese. She tried to put her arms round me, but I pushed her away and sat down by the fire. I needed warmth. Phaedra came and knelt beside me, offering me the wine. I pushed it away, and the cup fell out of her hands and broke on the floor.

'Please don't be upset,' she said. 'It was a good play, really.'

'No it *wasn't*,' I shouted. 'It was the worst play ever written.'

'All right then,' she said, and her voice seemed to come from a long way off, 'you may be right, I don't know. But even if it was, you'll learn from it, and you won't make the same mistakes again. And next year . . .'

Her voice was irritating me, like the buzzing of a fly, and I turned my head away. Had Aristophanes started celebrating already, I wondered, now that the prize was as good as his? Lord Dionysus, I prayed, if you love me and are my patron, let Phrynichus win, not Aristophanes.

'Look,' she said, 'it's not the end of the world, I promise you. Really, you are a good poet, I mean it. Just because this time—'

Suddenly I felt hot, and I pulled at the cloak round my neck so hard that the cloth tore all around the brooch. I wrenched it loose and threw it on the ground.

'Can't you just shut up, for God's sake?' I shouted. 'Why don't you just go away and leave me alone?'

She made a grab for my hand, but I pulled it away. After a moment, she got up from where she had been kneeling, said, 'The hell with you, then,' and went into the inner room, slamming the door behind her.

I didn't go to the Theatre next morning, but in the evening Callicrates came by and said that Phrynichus had won, with Aristophanes coming second, by unanimous vote of the twelve judges. By then I was feeling all stupid and Spartan, and I said something idiotic about thanking the Gods that Athens had two playwrights better even than me. Callicrates very sensibly didn't reply, and he got up to go.

'By the way,' he said, 'we got a message from Phaedra this morning. She says to tell you she isn't coming back till you apologise. I don't know what she's done this time, but if I can help in any way . . .'

I frowned, feeling as if I were drunk. 'Coming back?' I said. 'I didn't even know she had gone.'

'She's at her father's house,' he said, 'she's been there all day. Do you mean to say you hadn't even noticed?'

I started to laugh, and Callicrates, who had been very patient with me, finally lost his temper. He told me to stop acting like a child, and slammed the door behind him. I called after him, but he didn't come back; it was hard to make him angry, but, like everything else he did, he did it well. I sat down by the fire, which had gone out long since, and listened hard to my soul; but nothing came.

The next morning I had two visitors. One was a messenger from Phrynichus, inviting me, as is usual, to his Victory party. I can't remember what I threw at him, but whatever it was I missed. The second was Phaedra's father, dragging Phaedra along behind him like an unwilling dog.

'She's your problem now,' he said, pushing her at me like a man returning rotten fish to a fishmonger. 'I've got guests staying, I don't need her banging about the house. A man should be able to keep his own wife under control.'

He had scratch-marks on his left cheek, just like a set I had seen in my mirror one time. 'I'm sorry,' I said, 'it won't happen again.'

'It better hadn't, that's all,' he said. 'And let me make this clear, young man; I'm not having her giving birth in my house, and that's final. You can clear up your own mess yourself.'

He stormed off, shutting the door quickly behind him, as if he was afraid Phaedra would slip out after him. She stood there looking at me for a long time.

'Did you hear that?' she said.

'I'm not deaf,' I replied. 'Is it true?'

'Yes, it's true,' she snapped. 'I only wish it wasn't.'

'Well,' I said, 'I don't know what you expect me to do about it, since I'm obviously not the father.'

'Of course you're the father,' she shouted. 'And look at me, will you?'

I turned my back on her. 'I'm not the father and I'm not going to accept it. You can do what you like.'

'Fine,' she said. 'I'll leave it out on the hillside for the wolves. Is that what you want?'

'I couldn't care less,' I said, and I closed my eyes and breathed in deeply. 'How long have you known?' I asked.

'Oh, about a week or so,' she said wearily. 'I was going to tell you when you won your stupid prize with your stupid, stupid play. I thought you'd be in a good mood. But trust you to make a mess of that.'

199

'So that's what it's all been about, you devious bitch,' I said, suddenly feeling angry. 'All this—'

'All this what?'

'That,' I said, and I kicked the cloak she had made me across the room. 'You really wasted your time making that.'

'Did I?' She was standing quite still and looking at me, and I couldn't meet her eyes.

'Yes,' I said firmly. 'Look, it's obvious it's never going to work, so I think it would be best if we just kept out of each other's way from now on, just as we did when we started. Don't worry, I'll accept the child. Just don't expect me to have anything to do with it, that's all.'

'That's what you want, is it?'

'I think that would be best for both of us,' I said. 'Don't you?'

'Yes,' she said, 'that suits me fine.'

I stood up and took off the tunic she had made, and put on the one that was covered in brick-dust. It seemed to hurt me wherever it touched my skin.

'I'll send you money,' I said, 'as soon as I get to Pallene. If you don't mind, I'll set off now. I've got everything I need there.'

I walked out without looking back, and rode straight to Pallene without stopping. They were surprised to see me, and as usual asked if my wife was with me. I told them no, not this time, and was there any hot food, because I was starving after my ride. The next day I sent a reliable man and his wife to the city, to give Phaedra the money I had promised her and to stay in the house if she was afraid of being there on her own; also, if she wanted anything, to send a messenger to me, or Callicrates if it was important. She sent the man and his wife back, saying she would get in some of her father's people, if that was all right. I did not reply.

Shortly afterwards, as I have already told you, Cleon was killed at Amphipolis and the Spartans sent an embassy offering peace. There were last-minute hitches and tantrums from both sides, but in the end Nicias son of Niceratus took charge of the negotiations and brought back peace for fifty years, by land and sea, not long after Aristophanes won the first prize at the City Dionysia for his play *Peace*. The war was over at last.

Chapter Twelve

When the Peace was concluded, I was twenty-one years old, a member of the Cavalry class – however hard I tried I could never squeeze more than four hundred and sixty measures of produce, wet and dry, out of my estates, and for reasons best known to himself, Solon set the limit for the upper class at five hundred measures – and shortly to be a father. I could reasonably expect to live for another thirty years, or even longer; my family regularly survives into the sixties, and I had a grand-uncle who made it to eighty-four, to the extreme disgust of his children. It was not as uncommon then as you would suppose for a man to live apart from his wife, if he could afford it, and, apart from gossip, I heard nothing from or about Phaedra. I sent her money regularly, but spent most of my time in Pallene.

There was so much to do there that I had little time to think of anything else. You may have noticed from what I have written that I have always been interested in the life and times of the dictator Pisistratus – I can say such things now, of course, even in public – and whenever I met someone who had a story about him, I would make sure I heard it. From all these stories I was able to confirm my belief that in his time, the Athenians cultivated far more of Attica than they do now, thanks to subsidies and support from the Dictator. I felt that I was in a position to undertake a Pisistratean programme of my own, using the resources of my more productive land to support the recovery of the desert areas. So I bought and hired labour, and set about taking in land on the mountainsides, wherever there was enough topsoil to dirty my fingertip.

It was, looking back, an absurd idea; but I was young and looking for something to do, now that I had turned my back on Comedy. We hacked terraces where even goats hesitated to go, scraping the soil into baskets and lowering it with ropes down to the new working. We built dams like the walls of Babylon just to persuade little trickles of water to drip the right way, but the only moisture that regularly got through to the ground was our sweat. I can't bear to think how much money and food I wasted trying to chip a few acres out of the side of Parnes and Hymettus, but once I had committed myself to it, I was determined not to turn back. In the end it was all done, the vines and olives were planted, and we were able to sit back and watch them wither away and die. Out of twelve acres of terraces that we festooned round the mountainsides, only four are still worked today.

While I was about my fool's errand, Phaedra had her baby, and after all that trouble it was only a girl. Phaedra named it Cleopatra – 'Daddy's pride and joy'; her sense of humour was just as bad as ever – and gave it to one of her father's women to nurse. I didn't go and see it, of course, for I was still maintaining privately that it wasn't mine. But Callicrates went, taking with him a little box of gold and lapis jewellery, which he bought with his own money. His own wife was barren, and he had refused to divorce her. When he next came to see me, he made a point of telling me how like me little Cleopatra looked, but I didn't want to know, so I said that he was probably right – bald, with an idiot grin and a nasty rash. He never mentioned her after that.

It was only after Cleon's death that I discovered that he had been using his influence to keep me off the army lists. I was completely astonished, since I could think of no reason why he should want to help me. I had wondered why I had only been called on once, of course, but I had put it down to luck. But Cleonymus the Vulture, who told me about it when I met him by chance one day in Pallene, said, No, on the contrary, Cleon had liked me, he said, and besides, I was the only poet in Athens he had any chance of getting on his side.

'That was when you still were a poet, of course,' he said, warming his huge hands in front of my fire, 'before that nasty experience of yours.'

I laughed; that was quite easy now. 'Then he made a mistake, didn't he?' I said cheerfully. 'Nobody's right all the time.'

'I don't know so much,' Cleonymus said. 'Now, personally, I think all Comic poets are the scum of the earth, and the sooner you're all sent down the silver mines the better. But Cleon was different. He liked Comedy – said it was worth thousands of votes to him to be made fun of, because it stopped people seeing him as a threat. More fool them, of course.'

'But he prosecuted Aristophanes,' I replied.
'I'd have thought you'd have approved.'

'Murder, yes,' I said, pouring him more wine, 'prosecution, no. It was a terrible thing to do. Impious.'

'Well,' gurgled Cleonymus through the wine, 'everyone makes mistakes. It wasn't the jokes about him that Cleon minded, anyway. That son of Philip is mixed up with some very unsavoury people. You know, long hair and fleece-lined riding-boots and elocution lessons and little trips to Sparta when no one's looking.'

'Your Great Conspiracy again? I thought that was strictly for the Assembly.'

'Oh it is, it is,' said Cleonymus sadly. 'But we're getting away from the point. Cleon thought you were a good poet, Eupolis, and it was his trade to know such things. Now you may have made an unsightly mess all over the Theatre, and I may be old and a nasty piece of work, all told. But I care about the democracy, young man, just like Cleon did; if it wasn't for scumbags like him and me, you'd be taking your orders from a King, not sticking your hand up in Assembly.' He put his cup down and leaned forward, until I felt he was going to roll on me and crush me, like a sow.

'You owe us,' he said, 'just as much as if we had

mortgage-stones all over those new fields of yours. I don't want you to forget it.'

'Get out of my house,' I said timidly. Cleonymus smiled.

'I've been thrown out of better places than this,' he replied cheerfully, and lolled back in his chair. 'I'm not threatening you,' he went on. 'If I was, you'd know it, believe me. What I'm actually doing is encouraging you. Start writing again, that's all I want, and perhaps your friends might see that you get another Chorus.'

'Thanks,' I said, 'but I'm through with all that.'

'Oh well, what a pity. Never mind.' Cleonymus stood up. 'Don't bother letting me know when you change your mind. By the way,' he added, 'you were right about one thing.'

'What?'

'Cleon making a mistake about you. He thought you'd have brains enough to see that he gave you your *General*, that night when you called to see the Archon. I thought that, too. Pity.'

He rolled out, got on his horse, and rode away towards the City, leaving me feeling as if he'd just blown his nose on my head.

After that, it came as no real surprise when, about a month later, I was summoned to the Prytaneum. As I rode I speculated as to what it was likely to be; some sort of punishment for my ingratitude, I supposed. By the time I got to the gates, I had decided that it was probably my turn to pay for the fitting-out of a warship, or (more probably) a Chorus. As I passed the Theatre, I prayed to Dionysus not to let them make me pay for the latest Aristophanes.

I sat on the steps for an hour or so waiting for the Council to call me, and while I was sitting there a man passed by whom I knew from somewhere. I smiled at him, trying to remember his name.

'Hello, Eupolis,' he said brightly, 'how are your new terraces doing?'

'Could be worse,' I replied. The face was definitely familiar – long and thin, with a big nose, and the beard shaved close to the chin. In his middle to late thirties, to judge by the grey hairs. 'Not worth the effort, of course, but then, what is?'

He laughed. 'Quite right,' he said. 'Are they sending you somewhere, then?'

'Your guess is as good as mine,' I replied. 'That, or a trireme, or hemlock, of course.'

He grinned. 'I wouldn't worry,' he said, 'we only execute generals now. Good luck, whatever it is.' He waved and ran gracefully down the steps. As soon as I heard him mention generals, I realised that I had been speaking to the glorious Demosthenes, Cleon's partner at Pylos. I was amazed that he should even recognise me, let alone know about my terraces, for we had never talked to each other before as far as I could remember, and even I wouldn't have forgotten meeting Demosthenes.

Then they called me in, and the palms of my hands started to sweat. For some reason I had got it into my head that I would be called in front of the full Council, and have to stand there while they fired questions at me from all over the chamber; so I was greatly relieved and not at all disappointed when I was shown into a little annexe about the size of a poor man's storeroom. A man I knew, a neighbour of mine from Phrearrhos, was sitting there, and I assumed that he was waiting too.

'Hello, Mnesarchides,' I said. 'Have you been summoned as well?'

'Don't talk soft,' he replied, 'I'm on the Council. Don't you ever listen to what people tell you?'

Now that he came to mention it, I remembered hearing that his name had come up for the year. I smiled broadly and offered my commiserations. He thanked me.

'Well, young Eupolis,' he said, in that voice which even quite sensible people use when they get lumbered with a public office they don't want, 'I'm delighted to have to inform you that you have been selected to accompany our forthcoming mission to Thessaly.'

'What mission to Thessaly? I thought that was all over now.'

'Events have transpired,' said Mnesarchides, 'that

necessitate high-level discussions between ourselves and the present regime.'

'I see.' I could feel his disapproval, but I somehow couldn't force myself to take Mnesarchides in his new role as Councillor seriously; the last time I had spoken to him we had discussed how best to rot manure, and very boring he was too. 'So what do you want me to do?'

'You will accompany Theorus and Strato to Larissa, and report back your findings to the Assembly and to me personally.'

'Personally?'

'That's right.' He nodded decisively, and continued, 'You will receive a drachma a day as compensation, to be paid on your return, and of course should some unfortunate event occur, you will be entitled to a public burial, and your children will receive their first set of armour free of charge from public funds.'

'That's nice,' I said. 'So when do we leave?'

'First,' said Mnesarchides, frowning, 'I must brief you on the purpose of your mission.'

'That would help,' I agreed.

'You will interview the princes Alexander and Jason,' said Mnesarchides, 'about their attitude to sending cavalry assistance should any unforeseen situation arise within the next year. You are authorised to offer five obols per man per day, plus a premium of two talents.'

'Five obols?' I said. 'That's a bit much, isn't it, for a rabble of Thessalian horse-thieves?'

'That is the maximum the Council has authorised,' said Mnesarchides defensively. 'Naturally, we hope that you will be able to come to a more advantageous arrangement.'

'Are you expecting any unforeseen situations, then?'

'We have to provide for every contingency,' said Mnesarchides. 'You leave in three days from Piraeus on the *Salaminia*. You will sail as far as the mouth of the River Tempe, where the princes will meet you with horses and escort you to Larissa.'

'How many cavalry do we want?' I asked.

'Don't specify a number,' he said. 'As yet, our exact requirements are uncertain.'

'Unforeseen?'

'Precisely.'

'But more than a hundred, say?'

'In excess of a hundred, certainly. We can safely authorise in excess of five hundred.'

There was a long silence. 'How are your lentils coming on, Mnesarchides?' I asked.

'Champion,' he replied. 'Good luck.'

I had met Theorus at Aristophanes' party, if you remember, and several times since, and since he had a great reputation for knowing what was going on, I asked him why I had been chosen for the mission.

'Easy,' he said. We were standing on the deck of the *Salaminia*, looking back at Athens disappearing behind us. 'Ask me something difficult.' He yawned, for he was used to sea travel.

'Go on, then,' I said. 'Then I can go and lie down.'

'Well,' said Theorus, 'you're a poet, aren't you? And all these Thessalians and Thracians and Macedonians and wogs like that, they're obsessed with the Theatre. Not that they do anything themselves, of course, because none of them can read or write; but they know all the latest plays by heart, because they send for Athenians to come and recite them, and they're always spouting speeches at you, in those horrible voices, which is very funny because they don't understand a word they're saying. When I was at the court of old man Sitalces, we made up a great chunk of the biggest rubbish you ever heard and swore blind it was from an unfinished masterpiece by Aeschylus. They're probably still reciting it to this day, poor fools. It's all part of them pretending to be Greeks, I suppose,' Theorus said sadly, 'but it'll never work. I mean, most of them look like Greeks, and if you try really hard you can make them talk quite like Greeks, but basically they're animals, like all foreigners.'

'Hang on,' I said, 'you mean I'm on this mission because I had a play produced?'

'Why else?' he said. 'And since all the Tragedians they're likely to have heard of are either too old or – well, you know, not quite sound – and Phrynichus refused to go and Amyntas is ill and Aristophanes is busy with his next and Plato's got toothache, that just left you.'

'You think they've heard of me?'

'I sincerely hope so. We sent them up a couple of copies of that thing of yours that came third a while back – and someone to read it to them, of course – so they'll probably all know it by heart by now.'

I thanked him and went to be sick. It was hard to associate Cleonymus the Vulture and Theorus with my neighbour Mnesarchides in a conspiracy against me, but I have always found sea travel conducive to paranoia, and by the time we arrived in Thessaly I was thoroughly miserable.

The valley of the Tempe is one of the loveliest places I have ever been to. It's where they come to gather the laurel for the crowns they give to the winners in the Pythian games, and no matter where you live, you're likely to find scenery that will appeal to you. There are spectacular rocks and mountains, woodlands quite unlike anything we have in Attica, and good, well-ordered fertile country beside the river. On your left is Mount Ossa, rising almost vertically from the plain; while on your right is Olympus itself. So enchanted was I with the place that I almost expected to see Zeus and Hera standing on the hillside waving to me.

What we did find was a squadron of cavalry, sent by the princes to meet us. Like any good merchants, they had set out their best wares to tempt the buyer, and I must confess that I was impressed by those Thessalians. They were tall men, with big broad-brimmed leather hats and two spears each, sitting so easily on their horses that I was irresistibly reminded of Centaurs; not the grotesque monsters in the carvings, but the Centaurs that you see in some vase-paintings, young and dashing, superhuman rather than subhuman. They said very little, and their faces were strange, too, for many of them were clean-shaven, despite their age, and most of them had bright blue eyes and long, straight hair. I should think Achilles probably looked like that, since he was from Phthia; but I've never liked Achilles, and I liked those Thessalians.

It was hard getting many words out of them as we rode to Larissa; they certainly weren't interested in the Theatre, or in anything much except sheep and Thessalian politics. The latter, I gathered, consisted almost entirely of assassinations among the ruling families. One of our escort told me a bit about what was going on, but I soon lost track, since most Thessalian chieftains seem to have the same names, and when I heard my instructor say, 'And after that, Perdiccas son of Scopadas killed Perdiccas son of Perdiccas, which left Scopadas the son of Thettalus at the mercy of Perdiccas son of Cersebleptes,' I gave up and started counting birds instead. But there was something reliable and straightforward about the Thessalians which made up for their shortcomings as conversationalists, and they had that slow dignity which you often get with unintelligent people. They were the sort of men who don't mind if you say nothing at all for half an hour, and there aren't many like that in Attica.

When we reached Larissa I took it for a village at first. It had walls, and gates, and was really quite large, and the people in the streets, particularly the women, were all well (if curiously) dressed. But it had that small-town feel about it that some people like and others don't. Theorus plainly didn't – he's one of those people who feel uncomfortable if they can't reach out their hands and touch marble – but I admit that I did; if I was ever exiled, I thought, I could find worse places to live than this. Naturally, Strato, the third member of the party, was visibly drooling, but he'd been doing that ever since we'd met up with our escort. I don't think he got very far with any of them.

I expected our hosts the princes to be like their cavalrymen; but they weren't, not at all. When we reached the palace – a large, rectangular building, like an oversized trireme-shed – they came out to meet us, two very fat men in their late twenties. I had expected them to be older, but then I remembered what my friend the cavalryman had been telling me about Thessalian politics, and realised that not many chieftains live much longer than twenty-nine.

There's nothing like meeting foreigners to make you think hard about your own people. Alexander and Jason were dressed in what would have been the height of fashion in Athens among, say, Alcibiades' circle about eight months ago, except that Alcibiades and his friends would never have worn so much heavy gold jewellery. For a start, they couldn't have afforded it, and even if they had managed to get together as much gold as Jason had hanging round his chins, they'd have used it to bribe a jury with instead of having it made into a massive great necklace. When he spoke, Jason used Attic Greek, except that he didn't quite understand where he should change T to S, and his voice was almost but not quite a City voice. Theorus shuddered when he heard him, and I don't think even Strato fancied him much. Alexander wasn't much better; his Attic was almost perfect, but he kept putting on a lisp – more mimicry of Alcibiades, I suppose – and it was rather disconcerting when he forgot to do it. Also, Strato lisps naturally, and I think Alexander thought he was trying to be funny.

The princes, although they were extremely talkative, seemed reluctant to discuss such tiresome matters as cavalrymen and money, although Theorus, who was now sulking and generally behaving very badly, kept trying to drag the conversation round. But Alexander was clearly not going to be cheated of his ration of spoken Attic; and when Theorus asked him bluntly when we were going to start talking business, he waved his hand in a very affected way and said that tomorrow, or the next day, we might have some preliminary discussions. Meanwhile, he said, he had such a nice surprise for us, and we weren't to spoil it by talking about silly old cavalrymen. That seemed to be the last straw as far as Theorus was concerned. He put his feet up on his couch and pretended to go to sleep.

After what seemed like a very long time, we were able to escape, on the pretext of changing our clothes, and

211

we were led off down a long corridor that formed part of the wall of the town. After what seemed like a day's march, we were each shown into a house-sized room crowded with heavily carved furniture and silverware. I put on my best tunic and cloak, looked at my face in a big bronze mixing-bowl (what it was doing there I could not imagine), and knocked on Strato's door to find out what was going to happen next.

'What do you think the surprise will be?' I asked.

'Something dire,' he replied. 'Belly-dancers, human sacrifice, gladiatorial display, poetry reading, you can never tell with these people. Sometimes it's like being at a really boring party, sometimes it's like something out of the adventures of Odysseus. Whatever it is, keep a straight face and smile a lot.'

The main hall of the palace was how I'd always imagined a palace to be, with long tables and benches, just like in Homer, and a fireplace running the length of the room. The roof was high and black with smoke, and they were roasting pigs and deer on spits; I'd never seen so much meat before in my life. The benches were filled with huge, fierce-looking men wearing coarse woollen clothes and enormous quantities of gold jewellery, and they were making an extraordinary amount of noise. Most of them looked like Greeks, but there were men wearing trousers like Persians, or Phrygian felt caps and tiaras, and some of them had breastplates on, for reasons best known to themselves. It all seemed very strange and intimidating to me, but my two companions merely found it distasteful, and muttered that there must be easier ways to earn a living, such as digging coal.

As guests of honour we sat with the princes, and were soon being overwhelmed with food. Among the beautiful and good of Thessaly the belief seems to be that if it moves, it can also be eaten, and if it doesn't, it can't, for the only vegetable I could see was leeks, boiled into a sort of mush and slopped out of a huge silver cauldron. We got wine to drink – lovely stuff from Rhodes and Chios, served neat in hollowed-out buffalo horns – but the Thessalians seemed to prefer a sort of sticky black stuff which they apparently make from rotten honey. No one offered us any, which was a great relief. If this was the lovely surprise, I thought as I started on my third helping of roast venison, it could be worse. But it seemed a terrible waste somehow, and I wished I could find some way of hiding some of the roast meat inside my tunic and taking it back to Athens with me.

Eventually the stripped ribcages were cleared away, and the entertainment began. I think the Thessalian nobles seated below us were dreading it almost as much as we were – in Thessaly, I am told, they like to while away the evenings by grabbing hold of the smallest person present, tying him to a pillar, and throwing bones at him. Anyway, Prince Jason called for silence by hammering on the table with his goblet, and the roar of voices dwindled away like water out of a punctured skin.

'Men of Thessaly,' shouted Jason – and I was amused to see that he used his proper voice for addressing his peers – 'today we feast three honoured guests from Athens in Attica.' Loud cheering and much banging of tables. 'They come to seek our aid in their war against the Spartans of Laconia. They, who are invincible by sea and excellent above all men for their armoured infantry, beseech us as friends to send them cavalry. What is your opinion?'

More cheering, banging on tables, waving of arms, throwing of bones. While all this was going on, I leaned over to Theorus and asked what Jason meant by our war with the Spartans. Hadn't they heard about the Peace?

'Don't be an idiot,' he whispered back. 'The princes know all right, but obviously they haven't told this lot. I don't think most of them would understand the meaning of the word, and those that do probably don't hold with it.'

'I thank you, men of Thessaly,' said Jason. 'Now, to celebrate the presence amongst us of three such noble guests, I command you all to assemble in the Field of Zeus tomorrow three hours after sunrise. That is all.'

He sat down; muted cheering, no banging of tables. 'Savages,' muttered Jason under his breath, and picked up a roast rabbit that everyone else had overlooked. 'You can't imagine, my dears,' he said through a mouthful of rabbit, 'what a trial it can be living among these barbarians. How I long to see Athens again – the Market Square, the Necropolis . . . '

Alexander giggled. 'You mean the Acropolis, silly.'

'Just my little joke,' Jason replied irritably. 'You're the silly, for not spotting it. And of course,' he said, turning his head and looking straight at me, 'the Theatre. You can have no idea how I long for the Theatre.'

Strato kicked my ankle under the table. 'You're interested in plays, then?' I asked.

'I live for the Drama,' replied Jason, and to emphasise his sincerity he stopped eating for a moment. 'Which is why today is the happiest day of my life. To have, under my roof, the great Eupolis, greatest poet of his age – well, if I died tonight it would be like the answer to a prayer.'

To judge by the way Alexander was looking at him, his prayers could easily have been answered. I took a long pull at my wine, and thanked him for his kind words. Jason stood up and bowed, and then sat down again, and started firing questions at me – did Euripides really not believe in the Gods, and was Moschus as brilliant as everyone seemed to think, and what was Theognis going to do next, and could we expect anything more from Sophocles, and what was Agathon *really* like, and was Phrynichus (who Jason had obviously got confused with the old Tragedian of the same name) ever going to give us an *Oedipus*? I replied as best I could, but for the most part I had to make it up as I went along; for Theorus and Strato really did know all these people, and were bound to tell them what I had said as soon as we got home.

'And now,' said Alexander, after Jason had choked on a mouthful of roast pork and so fallen silent for a moment, 'do tell us all about the Comedy, which is what we're really interested in. I mean, the Tragedy is all very well, in its way, but . . . '

So I had to go through the same procedure all over again with Ameipsias and Plato and Cratinus and Aristomenes and Aristophanes – I didn't mention Phrynichus, so as not to upset Jason – until my voice was hoarse and my head was dizzy with nodding. By the time the princes were drunk enough to be carried away, I had had enough of the Theatre to last me a lifetime. But they lasted long enough to demand a précis of the plot of my own next play, and I had to improvise furiously.

I slept well that night, despite having the feeling that I had got myself locked into the treasury of a temple, and when we were summoned next day I felt relatively restored, which was just as well.

The Thessalians don't eat much during the day, but as Athenians we were expected to be starving hungry as soon as we opened our eyes; so there was roast venison and boiled beef to be got through before we could proceed to the surprise at the Field of Zeus. Theorus managed to get hold of one of the skin-and-bone dogs that are everywhere in Thessaly, and we fed most of the food to it, but it couldn't eat it all.

The Field of Zeus is about an hour's ride north of Larissa, and it has a spectacular view of Olympus. To get there, however, we rode through what our escort told us was typical Thessaly: rocky, bleak and miserable, and populated by starving people who are effectively the slaves of the ruling families. Just as I had never seen such wealth as I saw in Larissa, I have never seen poverty like that of these Penestae, who are of the same race as their masters, and theoretically citizens. They would run up to us as we rode past begging for food (I don't think they knew about money), and the cavalrymen would knock them aside with the flats of their sabres. The cavalryman next to me said that there was quite an art to it and offered to teach me if we ran into any more of them, but I said I had a pulled muscle in my shoulder.

The first thing we saw when we arrived was a sort of horseshoe-shaped earthwork. Whatever it was, it wasn't quite finished, because there were men scurrying about with baskets of earth on their shoulders and other men, on horseback, shouting at them and hitting them with olive branches. Then Alexander and Jason rode up, on enormous white stallions, and welcomed us to the Theatre.

I nearly fell off my horse.

'Next year,' said Jason, 'we shall line it with stone, and then it will be just like the Theatre of Dionysus.'

I doubted that somehow, but I remembered that I was here to further the interests of Athens, and said on the contrary, it would be better. 'In fact,' I went on, 'I wish that I could put on a play here. It's so . . . ' I couldn't think of anything to say, so I waved my hand in the air instead.

Then Jason giggled, sounding just like one of the conduits at Nine Fountains when it gets blocked with leaves, and I felt a terrible sense of foreboding.

'Then your wish is about to be fulfilled,' Jason said. 'If you would care to take your seat, we'll see what we can do.'

I got slowly off my horse and followed him down into his earthwork – I refuse, even now, to call that overgrown sump a Theatre. Alexander was already sitting there, in a great big carved oak throne. He was obviously livid that the Theatre wasn't ready yet, and there was a man on his knees in front of him, who I took to be the overseer of the work.

'This miserable dog,' growled Alexander in his own Thessalian voice, 'has betrayed his trust. He swore by the head of Poseidon that all would be ready, and he has broken his oath. Very well, then; his blood shall—'

'No, don't do that,' said Theorus suavely. 'It's terribly unlucky, you know. Isn't it, Eupolis?'

'Terribly,' I said.

Alexander shrugged his shoulders and became all Athenian again. 'But it's so terribly naughty of him,' he whined. 'He knew we were expecting honoured guests, and just look at it.'

'It's perfect,' I assured him. 'Don't change a thing.'

'Well, if you think it's right, it must be right,' chirped Jason. 'So why don't we all sit down and let the revels commence?'

The Thessalian lords who had been at the feast last night were filing in and saluting the princes; they looked as miserable as I felt. Finally Alexander called for silence

216

and warbled out, 'Eupolis, bring on your Chorus!'

I once saw a play by Cratinus which was a burlesque on the blinding of Oedipus, and although I enjoyed it, I wondered what Oedipus himself would have made of having his Tragic sorrow made into a Comic travesty. By the end of the opening scene of my *General*, as performed by members of the flower of Thessalian youth, I knew the answer; he would have loved it. To start with, I didn't know where to look; I was so embarrassed, especially with Theorus and Strato sitting there looking like a couple of owls, that I would gladly have cut my own throat if I could have borrowed a razor. But when the actors started forgetting their lines and I had to prompt them, I actually started to enjoy myself. It helped that the entire company, Chorus as well as actors, hadn't the faintest idea what any of it meant, and so recited their parts with a sort of Tragic profundity. They had tried their best to make trireme costumes out of old goatskins and the staves of buckets, but the people wearing them had no idea what they were meant to be, and apparently nobody had thought it wise to tell them; so they must have assumed that they were some sort of sacred vestments, and moved accordingly. As the play went on, I could see exactly what was wrong with it; why the dialogue was so flat, and why the Choruses had failed so utterly. There was, quite simply, too much of everything; twenty years of wanting to be a Comic poet jammed into one little play. That was why the jokes had flown over everyone's heads; like Xerxes' arrows, they had blotted out the sun. As for the choruses, they were far too complicated for anyone short of Athena herself to follow at first hearing. Written down, of course, and read slowly at leisure, it quite probably seemed to coruscate with wit. On stage, it was a meaningless torrent of words.

So, when the Chorus had floated gracefully off, there was real feeling in my voice when I thanked the princes.

'It was marvellous, really,' I said. 'You don't know how much pleasure that gave me.'

Jason seemed rather taken aback – I think he had prepared a little speech of apology – but Alexander beamed, and said that it was an honour. I replied that no, it was an honour for *me*, and I think we'd be there yet if Jason hadn't got bored and suggested we eat something.

I had a Thessalian appetite for my food, but my mind was full of Comedy again; it was as if some God had inspired me, and all I wanted to do was sit down somewhere quiet and start composing. It didn't matter that I had no plot or theme or characters – mere details. What mattered was that the cloud of the *General* had been lifted from my shoulders. And then, as if a second God had joined the first, I remembered what Cleonymus had said when I spoke to him in Pallene; he could get me a Chorus, and then everything would be all right.

Don't ask me to remember how much we paid for the cavalry in the end – it was something like four obols a day and one talent, and we got past the Assembly on our return without too much trouble. The next thing I can remember is sitting under my fig tree at Pallene, with half an opening scene in my head searching frantically for a name, and someone in the fields above the house calling out the name of my steward, who was called Maricas. Not long after, I took three rolls of Egyptian paper to the Archon, and was granted a Chorus.

Maricas won first prize at the City Dionysia in the year that Ameipsias came second with his *Wineskins*. Aristophanes won third prize with *The Two Brothers*.

Chapter Thirteen

I hadn't expected to win first prize with *Maricas*, and so I hadn't thought of a suitable place to hold my Victory party. The true horror of my situation only dawned on me at the Cast party, immediately after the performance (I had been called on last), and for a while I sat with my head in my hands, trying to think of some way out of the mess. As I saw it, I had three options; not to hold a Victory party at all (which was unthinkable, like fighting a battle and not raising a trophy afterwards, or growing corn and not harvesting it); to hold it at Phaedra's house; or to find somewhere else. I had just decided to beg the backer – a cumin-seed-splitting, parsimonious old fool called Antimachus – for the loan of his pottery warehouse in Piraeus, when a messenger came looking for me. It was Phaedra's slave Doron.

'My mistress asks me to tell you that she's visiting her father in the country,' he said, 'and so the house will be empty for three days. She asks you not to let your friends be sick on the couches.'

At the time, I raised my hands in thanksgiving to Dionysus and started issuing invitations immediately; but as I was being carried home to Philodemus' house, my soul pointed out to me that this was a generous gesture from someone whom I had not treated well. Mind you, I think that I had drunk so much wine that some of it must have seeped through into my soul, for it was being unusually sentimental that night.

After a few hours' sleep I was up and busy, sending all Philodemus' household, Callicrates, and even Philodemus himself out into the City with invitations, which were on no account to be refused. My own role in this Xerxian campaign was quartermaster, and I filled my purse with handfuls of money and set off for the market. The sunlight hit me like a hammer as soon as I set foot outside, but I persevered manfully and bought up every drop of wine in Athens, together with a good stock of food, mostly fish, in case people should forget to bring any of their own. Then I descended on Phaedra's house, with a train of porters behind me that seriously disrupted the movement in the streets, and got to work.

Phaedra's house, which I had not seen for some time, was a splendid setting for a party with all its expensive and ostentatious fittings. There were more couches and chairs than in Aristophanes' house, and enough mixing-bowls to mix the Aegean with Ocean. Phaedra had removed every feminine object from the place, and the floor was scrupulously clean and dry. But outside the back door, I found a cache of empty wine jars, all ready for the jar-collector, and I wondered how on earth she had managed to empty so many.

Needless to say, I hadn't expected the prize guests – what you might call the collector's items – to turn up, for I had invited men who I had never even met. But they came. Everyone came, from Cleonymus and Theorus down to my nearest neighbours at Pallene; even Cratinus came, although he was very ill indeed and had to leave early. Only Socrates son of Sophroniscus didn't come, at which I was secretly relieved, for he never seems to get drunk and monopolises the conversation. Oh no, it wasn't one of those cosy little parties where seven or eight close friends sit in a semicircle and talk about the Meaning of Truth, which is how people celebrate victories nowadays. It was a good old Athenian thrash. The formal drinking-rules I had devised, the subtle order of courses and succession of toasts and libations, were abandoned like the shields of an infantry-line when the cavalry attacks it from behind. I have heard many times how Atlantis was overwhelmed by the sea, but I could never visualise it properly until that night.

It was touch and go at times, but I stuck it out to the last drop. About an hour before dawn, the only people still capable of speech were me, Callicrates, Philodemus, Euripides and Cleonymus, and we were talking about the Soul; we had decided that it couldn't possibly live in the liver, where everyone thinks it lives, but that it couldn't live in the chest, since that's where the heart lives and the two never seem to agree. That left the head (which is absurd), the groin or the feet, and I can't remember what we finally decided.

The next morning I left the slaves to scrub the floor and make good the damage, and rode off to Pallene. Cleonymus rode part of the way with me, and I screwed up my courage to thank him. He made a noise that was something between a laugh and a sneer, and changed the subject. Of all the men that I have ever liked, I think he was the most repulsive, with the exception of my dear Cratinus.

I spent my first few days at Pallene going round my rapidly crumbling new terraces, to remind myself that I was not successful in everything, and then settled down to work. The old Tragedian Phrynichus, who wrote his best plays in Themistocles' time and was once prosecuted and fined because his *Sack of Miletus* depressed everyone so much, used to say that when a playwright sat down to watch his Chorus being led out, he should already have his next opening speech perfect in his mind; and I have always tried to follow this advice. When a play is presented and the actors run out to speak the first words, you know that that is the first and last time that that play will ever be heard. It's like raising a son who is the pride of your heart to run in one race at the Games; even if he wins, you know that you'll never see him again. So I have always had another play in my mind, and as soon as I hand my words over to the actors I do my best to forget them utterly. Likewise, I am always striving to do better, as if my last play were my own most deadly rival.

I had rivals enough as it was. My next play, *The*

Man With Two Left Hands, came second, well beaten by Hermippus and only narrowly beating Ameipsias, at a Lenaea for which Aristophanes, Phrynichus and Cratinus had not contributed anything. My *Vines* and *Cities* were only saved from third place by the brilliance of the costumes – I paid the vase-painter Phrygus to do them, out of my own pocket – and Aristophanes narrowly beat my *Corinthians* at the Dionysia when Aristomenes' *Heracles* was booed off the stage. I had resigned myself to a future of second prizes when I won, quite unexpectedly, with *The Flatterers*. After that, I seemed to lose that sense of urgency which had been driving me to compete as often as possible. Although I was never without a play in my head, I found that I could bring myself to wait for a while, instead of forcing myself to complete it in time for the next Festival. I have had a good run, all in all; I have led out seventeen Choruses and won seven first prizes, and only once come third. As for my reputation with posterity, I no longer worry about it. The other day, for example, I came across a book of Aristophanes' plays, with the copyist's scribble all down the margins and on the back of the roll, in which some fool had written that Aristophanes' *The Acharnians* beat a play called *The New Moons*, which was there ascribed to me. I have never written a play of that name, and if the copyist had had the sense to ask someone who knows me, he would have found out that I was far too young to have been given a chorus that year; as you may remember, *The Acharnians* was the play for which Aristophanes gave the party I went to. But I couldn't be bothered to look up the copyist and make him correct the mistake, even though this *New Moons* of mine was supposed to have come third. Twenty years ago, of course, I would have cut his head off for saying such things about me.

It wasn't long after *The Flatterers*, at a time when I was as near content as I have ever been, that I heard that my daughter Cleopatra had died, quite suddenly, from drinking bad water. By the time the news reached me the funeral had already been held, since I was staying with a friend at Araphen, and nobody knew where I was. My host commiserated with me and sent away the guests he had invited, but I must confess that my principal feeling was relief. I suppose that sounds very heartless, especially nowadays, but I had never so much as set eyes on the child, and somehow, given the circumstances of her birth and that stupid, insulting name that Phaedra had given her, she seemed to represent the division between us. You know the story of the Hero Meleager; how when he was born the Goddess prophesied that he would live only as long as it took a certain log on the fire to burn, and how Meleager's mother grabbed up the log and kept it safe, until one day many years later, she flung it on the fire in a fury and so brought about her son's death. Well, it had somehow got into my mind that as long as Cleopatra was alive, I could not bring myself to see Phaedra again, even though I had long since come to accept that Cleopatra was my child. Now she had died, as suddenly and inexplicably as Meleager. I felt no guilt for her death; but it seemed to me that there was a purpose to it. If I was one of those people who believe in what they say at the Mysteries, I would no doubt explain it all as the innocent child sacrificed for the good of the People; but I could never be doing with that sort of thing.

So I took my leave of my host at Araphen and rode to the City, only to find that Phaedra wasn't there. The doorkeeper at the house said that she had gone to stay with her uncle, out near Eleusis, and wouldn't be back for a month. I thought of going to Eleusis after her, but I had business in the City which couldn't be put off, and so I decided to wait until she got back. I moved into the house, and asked the servants how Phaedra had been getting on.

They were reluctant to talk to me at first, but when I had convinced them that I wanted a reconciliation between us, it was hard to make them stop. Their mistress had been terribly unhappy, they said; she had stayed in the house, spinning her wool and weaving cloaks and tunics for me in the hope that one day I would come back. She hadn't touched a drop of wine – wouldn't have it in the house – and had been to see all my plays. I was deeply touched by this, until I found the remains of several broken wine jars on the ash-heap, which made me suspicious. So I asked the servants to show me the clothes Phaedra had made for me; there must be several chests full of them by now. They looked mustard at me and admitted that they had been exaggerating slightly, about both the clothes and the wine. But they swore by Styx that there had been no men in the house at all, and offered to be tortured if I didn't believe them.

Then a messenger arrived from Eleusis to say that Phaedra wouldn't be back for another couple of weeks at least. He was rather surprised to find me there, and didn't want to say any more, but a four-drachma piece did wonders for his sense of loyalty, and he told me what had happened.

Phaedra had gone with her aunt and some other women to make some offering or other at one of those little country shrines; it was more an excuse for a picnic than a religious occasion. They had made their offering and eaten the rest of the food, and the groom was just harnessing the donkeys to the cart when one of them was stung by a fly and went out of control. Phaedra, who had been putting the picnic things in the cart, had been kicked in the face, and her jaw had been broken. They had done what they could – the eminent doctor Eryximachus had been staying near by, and they had sent for him to set the fracture – but the bone had been too badly damaged for much to be possible. Phaedra, said the messenger, would never look the same. She would have a sort of permanent smile; just like that, he said, pointing to me without thinking, only on the other side of her face . . .

I burst out into uncontrollable laughter, until everyone was quite angry with me, but I just couldn't help myself. The thought that my beautiful Phaedra would henceforth be as repulsive as her husband – a matching pair, in fact, except that presumably she still had some hair – was a sort of pure delight, such as you feel when you recognise the intervention of a God. It was not that wonderful feeling you get deep inside you when you hear of the misfortunes of an enemy; there was nothing vindictive about it at all. When I had control of myself again, I told the messenger to go back to Eleusis as quickly as he could and tell Phaedra that I was on my way, and that if he said anything at all about my reaction to his news, I would make sure he spent the rest of his life in the silver mines. First thing next morning, I set out for Eleusis with Little Zeus riding with me, since it would be just like my luck to run into bandits at such a time if I went on my own, and I was determined to go straight there. But my soul made me stop off at Callicrates' house to pick up the gold and cyanus necklace which I had been given as a parting gift by the princes in Thessaly. It was the most valuable single object I owned at that time.

I once bought a tripod from a Syrian; it was a wonderful thing, with bronze lion-heads all over it and inlays of lapis and glass. It was far too expensive, and when a man offered to buy it from me, I sold it to him gladly, since I had been worrying about spending so much money ever since. But almost as soon as I had delivered it, I regretted what I had done, and finally I went to the man who had bought it and begged him to sell it back to me. He was a shrewd man, and asked rather more for it than he had given me, but I paid what he asked and took the tripod back with me. When I got it home, I saw that one of the little bronze lion-heads had been broken off and most of the lapis had been dug out with a small knife, probably to be used for earrings. But I didn't feel that the damage spoiled my precious tripod; it made me value it all the more, and I never had it repaired.

It was nearly dark when I reached Eleusis, and Phaedra's uncle, who was called Parmenides, was standing by the door.

'I don't know what you want here,' he said. 'I'd have thought you'd done enough damage without coming to gloat.'

Parmenides was shorter than me, and I wasn't afraid of him. 'Does this look like gloating?' I said, waving the Thessalian necklace under his nose. 'Where is she? I want to see her.'

'She's told me not to say where she is,' said Parmenides firmly, as if his house was as big as the Labyrinth. In fact it was quite small, and I could see over his shoulder into the main room. She wasn't there, so she had to be in the inner room or upstairs.

'Don't worry,' I said, 'I'll find her. I'll just have to break down all the doors, that's all. Right, Little Zeus, you'd better start looking round for something you can use as a hammer.'

Little Zeus' face lit up, for he dearly loved smashing things; I think he thought it was rather aristocratic. He pushed past Parmenides and picked up a big bronze lampstand.

'She's in the inner room,' said Parmenides, 'and if you break anything I'm calling a witness.'

I thanked him and strode like the avenging Odysseus to the inner door. As I put my hand on it I heard the bar go up.

'Let's see that lampstand,' I shouted, but before Little Zeus had a chance to move, Parmenides was standing beside me hammering on the door with his fists.

'Phaedra,' he shouted, 'this is your uncle. Open this door immediately. I won't have violence in my house.'

That didn't have much effect, and Little Zeus stepped forward, with his Heracles face on and the lampstand in both hands, but I pushed him back. He shrugged and put the lampstand back exactly where it had been, for he was a most meticulous man.

'For the last time, Phaedra,' Parmenides was saying, 'will you open this door, or do I send for the carpenter?' I left him to it, and crept out through the door. I went round to the back of the house and sure enough, there was a nice big window. The shutters were drawn but not barred, and I gingerly pulled them open, so as not to make a noise. Then I climbed in.

Phaedra was leaning against the door, obviously preparing to resist the onslaught of the lampstand to the last drop of blood. She hadn't heard me come in so, treading as carefully as if I were walking on ice, I made my way over to a chair beside the bed and lowered myself into it.

'Hello, Phaedra,' I said.

She jumped about a man's stride in the air, whirled round and stared at me. 'You left the window open,' I went on. 'Leonidas wouldn't have done that, and neither would Demosthenes. You're slipping.'

I got up, went to the window, and closed and barred the shutters. I didn't want any interruptions.

'Go on, then,' she said, and her voice was slow and painful. 'Have a good look.' She thrust her face at me, as if she were a soldier on parade presenting his shield for inspection.

I needed no invitation. It looked much worse than it really was, because of the bruises, but I could see that it was the sort of disfigurement that could ruin somebody's life, especially in Athens, where we are obsessed with beauty. But I'm proud to say that I didn't shudder, or spit in my cloak for luck. Instead, I stood up and turned my own face to her.

'They say husband and wife get to look like each other in time,' I said. 'I'm sorry it had to happen to you.' Then I pulled the necklace out from under my belt and fastened it round her neck, and I kissed her.

'Idiot,' she said. 'What do you mean by it, creeping up on me like that?'

I put my arms round her. 'You've put on weight,' I lied.

'No I haven't,' she replied. 'And take your hands off me.'

'Does it hurt?' I asked.

'Yes,' she said, 'and that last play of yours was the worst yet. I was so ashamed that I didn't go out for days.'

'What did you do all that time,' I asked, 'stay in and catch up on your drinking?'

'Who says I can afford wine, on the pittance you send me?' She tried to smile, but it hurt her too much. 'Is it very horrible?' she asked.

'No.'

'Liar.'

'You look like Medusa,' I said. 'Both before and after she was transformed.'

Even she could think of no answer to that, so she looked down at the necklace and stroked it. It was the first thing I had ever given her.

'Where did you get this piece of junk from?' she said. 'If you expect me to appear in public wearing it, you're very much mistaken.'

'The hell with you,' I said.

'And how dare you be so rude to my uncle?'

'The hell with him too.'

'And now I expect I'll have to put up with you under my feet all day long,' she whispered, 'not to mention your disgusting friends.'

'It'll be just as bad for me,' I said, 'coming home and finding your lovers hiding under the—'

It was the wrong thing to say. 'That's not really likely, is it?' she said, pulling away from me. 'Not unless I take to sleeping with blind men.'

'I'm sorry, Phaedra, I didn't think.'

She tried to laugh. 'What's up, Eupolis,' she said, 'lost your sparkle? Or are you so big in the Theatre now that you can't spare a clever insult for your poor, ugly wife? Don't say you're running out of jokes at last.'

'You know me, Phaedra,' I said, 'Eupolis the song-and-dance man. Always good for a laugh, young Eupolis, especially if you kick him hard enough.'

She sat down on the bed and took off the necklace. I think she was going to throw it on the floor, but she just sat there with it in her hands, as if it was a dead bird. 'Just what do you want from me?' she said.

'I don't know,' I replied.

'Well it can't be much, can it?' she said. 'Look at me, will you? I'm an ugly woman with a dead child, and nobody can bear to have me in the house. I can frighten the thieves away for you, but not much else.'

'You're all I deserve,' I said, sitting down beside her. I wanted to take hold of her hand, but I was afraid to. 'Listen to me for a moment, will you? You know the story of how, when the Gods made the first man, he was so happy and content that they were afraid he wouldn't need them any more, so they went away and made the

228

first woman? Well, I think the Gods made us marry each other so that we'd each have someone else to hate instead of ourselves. They even gave us both crooked faces, to make sure we never go off with anyone else. That's why I think—'

'Oh do shut up,' said Phaedra, 'you're giving me a headache with all your whining.' She gave me a look that I'll never forget; contempt and pity and something else, too, which made her look more lovely than ever before. 'You never know when to stop talking, do you?'

'Will you have me back then?' I asked.

'I don't remember throwing you out in the first place,' she said. 'It was you who went prancing off to Pallene and digging holes in the mountains rather than sleep with your wife. It was you who wouldn't touch me on our wedding-night. It was you, I seem to remember, who wouldn't even come to see your own child.' She shook her head and sighed. 'Oh, Eupolis, why are you such a complete fool?'

'Because your father couldn't get you a proper husband,' I said. 'Don't you remember?'

'Come here,' she said softly. 'No, not like that, with my uncle listening at the door and my face all full of splinters. Just come here.'

The next day, we drove back to the City in Parmenides' cart, and we quarrelled all the way.

Chapter Fourteen

My son Eutychides ('son of a lucky man' – Phaedra's idea) was born just over nine months later, in the year when Alcibiades was elected General for the second time. He was a small, sickly child, although he hadn't inherited his parents' idiotic grins, and nobody expected him to survive longer than a week. But he did, and as soon as he looked big enough to last we got him the best nurse money could buy.

Naturally, Phaedra and I quarrelled bitterly over him from the day he was born. I was all for having him brought up in the country, among the goats and the olive trees, as I had been, away from the fads and trends of the City; that way, I said, if later on he wanted to live in Athens and take part in City life, it would be his own choice. But a man who has been brought up in the City is never really at home in the country, I said. He hasn't learned to use his eyes and ears, and he never values his neighbours properly. But Phaedra said that I could do what I liked, but her son was going to be brought up a Cavalryman, with a proper education in polite society, so that he would one day be a General. We compromised; she was to have her own way, and in return, she wouldn't shout at me about it. In fact his upbringing was quite different, as you will see.

Now on the one hand we were still theoretically at peace with Sparta; on the other hand we seemed to be at war with everyone else. But it was the sort of war that seemed to do nobody much harm – that is to say, it

230

stayed well outside Attica, so that we were able to farm in peace, while there was plenty of employment for anyone who needed it, particularly for the fleet. There were still the annual State funeral celebrations for the heavy infantrymen who had been killed on active service, and every year I lost another fifteen or twenty men who I had come to consider friends. On the other hand, I inherited another twelve acres, being the nearest surviving heir to some dead cousin or other, which brought me perilously close to the five hundred measure mark at one stage. Most of my wealth comes from plague or war, yet it was all honestly acquired. Perhaps that is why I have never striven after money and property as so many other men do; I have simply continued to live, and the Gods have crowned me with flowers. Yet because I was not born rich, I have never felt the need to become richer still. My attempts to improve the yield of my land was more instinct than anything else. After all, it is not as if I were a Corinthian or lived in Persia, or needed money for a political career; there is not very much that I want that money can buy.

At long last, Athens had put the effects of the plague behind her. The tribute-money from the empire was coming in promptly every year – and each time I went down to read the Tribute lists, I thought of that little shrine in Samos – while our own produce in Attica, though still below pre-war levels, was like an unexpected bonus after all the years of war. Wise men say that the earth needed a good long rest after years of being driven too hard by a population too large for it to sustain, and that the Spartans had provided her with it. Men were talking about returns of fifty gallons of wine an acre in some parts of the country, which had not been heard of since the days of the dictator Pisistratus, and as soon as the new vines, which we were putting in every day to replace the ones cut down by the Spartans, started yielding, we all expected to be as rich as kings. But none of us expected to see the olive trees yield much in our lifetime; it takes nearly a generation for a tree to be of any use in Attica.

That reminds me; to celebrate the birth of my son

and to get rid of the man generally, I fulfilled my oath to Little Zeus and planted out his land in the best vines. I had been meaning to get around to it ever since the war ended, but there had been a lawsuit about them – I wrote Little Zeus some good speeches, the first time I ever tried my hand at such work – and that had dragged on for some time, and then I was busy with a play. Then two of Little Zeus' brothers were killed at sea, and neither of them had children, so there were more lawsuits. Eventually it was all cleared up, and Little Zeus was master of nine and a bit acres of good but empty land. I planted out the whole lot, for which the man was embarrassingly grateful, lent him enough money to tide him over until his first vintage, made him promise to come to me if he needed help, and wished him good luck. When I next passed by his holding, I was amazed at the transformation. What had been a useless little drip of a stream coming off the side of the mountain had been hacked into a model irrigation channel, with branches off it right across the estate. Every vine was nicely propped and expertly pruned, and every inch of ground between the trenches had been ploughed for barley. There was not a stone to be seen anywhere, and from behind an ambitious-looking half-built wall I heard an unmistakably loud voice reciting the Entry of the Chorus from Aeschylus' *Persians*. I called out, and Little Zeus, looking bigger than ever, came running over.

'Well,' I said, 'I don't think I've ever seen a better vineyard.'

He nodded enthusiastically. 'I know,' he said, 'it's the best in Attica. And there's more.' He pointed away over towards the mountainside. 'I've taken in another acre, waste land that nobody was using.'

I stared. 'But that's all bare rock,' I said.

'You did it,' he said. 'Everything here I learned from what you did in Pallene and Phrearrhos. Whenever I felt myself getting discouraged, or I couldn't think what to do, I said to myself, What would Eupolis have done? And then it all became clear in my mind.'

I didn't know whether to laugh or cry. 'But you've achieved more here than I could ever have done,' I said. 'I mean, it's extraordinary. Where did you get the men from?'

'Oh no,' he replied, 'I did it all myself. I didn't want to spend more of that money you lent me than I had to, because it'll be at least a year after my first vintage before I can pay you back, and—'

The thought of him half-killing himself up the mountain just to pay back what I thought he had understood was a gift was almost more than I could bear. 'For God's sake,' I said, 'don't worry about it.'

He smiled beatifically, as if he had seen a God. 'That's just like you,' he said, 'but it's a debt of honour. Now, if you've got a moment, I'd like your opinion on these trellises. Should they be a finger higher, do you think, or are they too high already?'

I almost expected to find a little shrine of the Blessed Eupolis somewhere about the place, and I was glad to get away.

Little Zeus wasn't the only man working hard at that time, and with the return of prosperity, men started to think hard thoughts about Sparta. The general opinion was that we as a city, and Nicias in particular, had more or less let them name their own terms. It went deeper than that, of course; deep down, everyone was convinced that Athens would never be safe until Sparta was a heap of rubble and her people were exterminated. But if we were actually to destroy Sparta, so the argument ran, we needed to double or even treble our strength, in terms of ships, money and above all, manpower. We needed to enlarge the empire, and that must be our next priority. There was little room for expansion in the east, although some people spoke grandly of casting the Great King of Persia from his throne and stamping Sparta flat under the heels of Egyptian and Median levies. But that was foolish talk; the King was much too powerful, and besides, what we needed was Greeks. So men's eyes began to turn west, to the Greek cities of Italy and Sicily, and even further. People started to remember the stories they had heard from their fathers; about the man called Colaeus who was blown off course sailing west, and came back with his ship loaded down with silver, or the Golden Islands on the edge of the world, which are so far over that the sun sets in the east. There were more sensible stories, too, about the wealth of the west; not just corn, although the whole region is incomparably fertile and nothing is grown but wheat, but also metals and timber, hides and wool, gold, silver, amber and precious stones – everything that the east has to offer, but guarded only by a few fat Greeks and sub-human savages. From Italy, men were saying, we could conquer the land round Massilia, where it rains so often that men dig ditches not to gain water but to get rid of it; and we could go south, to Carthage and Cyrene, and down into the hot country where there are people blacker even than the Libyans. The Pillars of Heracles were not the end of the world, as our fathers had taught us; the Phoenicians had gone beyond them, and found tin and copper, and huge animals with thick hides suitable for making shields. There was no limit to the opportunities that awaited us, just as soon as we had secured ourselves a base.

It occurred to me that if we could take over so many distant lands without exerting ourselves too much, it was curious to say the least that we had so much trouble in dealing with a little city not two hundred miles away, where they use iron spits instead of money. What appealed to me was the argument I heard from Cleonymus and his friends. They asked who among the Peloponnesian Alliance had the most warships? Corinth, of course. And wasn't it true that Corinthian ships carried most of the corn imported into the Peloponnese? True indeed. And where did the Corinthians get the corn that they supplied to their allies? Wasn't it from the golden plains of Sicily, and most particularly from their allies the Syracusans? And didn't we have allies in Sicily already, good, trustworthy places with plenty of money, who lived in fear of Syracusan aggression? What better pretext would we need for interfering in Sicily than coming to the aid of our own cities there? But there was more; these cities had actually offered to

234

pay for the war out of their bottomless reserves of coined silver. The war would not cost Athens an obol; yet if we were successful (and how could we fail?) not only would we seize the immeasurable wealth of Sicily for ourselves, but we would also cut off Corinth, and through her the Peloponnese, from their main source of imported food. Corinth would be ruined and would have to defect to us, the Peloponnesians would lose their food supplies and their fleet, both together, and with absolute control of the sea and the Isthmus of Corinth in our possession, we could simply starve them to death.

It was not, they went on, as if Sicily was an unknown land to us, for we had fought wars there only a few years ago. True, we had not been successful, but neither had we failed; and the forces we had sent out then were small and poorly equipped, and fools had led them, men like Laches. Some people said that Syracuse was a great city, strong and well armed; but they were living in the past, in the time of the Persian Wars. Then, it was true, the power of the cities of Sicily had been equal to that of all the other Greeks put together, when the dictators Hiero and Gelo had been in control. But they had worn themselves out in wars with the Carthaginians, and the dictators had been deposed and replaced in Syracuse by a ramshackle democracy, who were constantly fighting with the aristocrats for control of the city. With two sides to play off against each other, in the way which we Athenians know better than any other nation in the world, it was highly probable that we could gain control of Syracuse, which was effectively control of Sicily, without having to fight a single battle.

These arguments were put forward at a time when the urge to be doing something was at its height. Without them, I believe the fever would have broken – there would have been some scandal or crisis, and everyone would have forgotten all about the world to the west of Piraeus – but by giving a realistic shape to their hitherto quite nebulous ideas, the propounders of the Sicilian project were able to harness the dreams of the Athenians, just as Aeolus once tied up the Four Winds in a sack.

There were people who opposed the idea, of course, but most of those were lovers of words who oppose things just to provoke an interesting debate. They were not short of arguments, of course; no Athenian ever is. Some of them recalled the Great Armada to Egypt, just after the Persian Wars. That was when we sent the best part of our army and our fleet to help Inaros and Amyrtaeus, the Kings in the Marshes, against the Persians. The motives were almost exactly identical, except that the enemy then was Persia. By seizing Egypt, it was argued then, not only would we become masters of the richest country in the world, and add the mighty Egyptian fleet to our own, but we would also cut off the Persians from their principal source of food. Then, with Egypt as a base, we proposed to overrun the east and take the Great King's sceptre from his hands, with which to crush our real enemies the Spartans into dust. What happened was that the Armada, both land and sea forces, was wiped out in the biggest disaster ever to befall the Athenians.

But that was different, came the reply. Then, we had taken on the whole of the Persian empire; now, we proposed to deal with one or two cities. Then, we had been fighting a land-locked country, and our fleet had not been much use to us; now, we were sailing against an island. Then, our only allies had been two bandit chieftains and our enemy the best-organised system of government the world has ever seen; now, we had rich and substantial allies in the country we proposed to invade, and our opponents were in a state of virtual civil war. Then, the Persians had the manpower of all Asia to call upon; now, the Sicilians could not hope to receive any assistance from our enemies, since everybody knew that the Spartans never went to war outside Greece. In fact, the superficial resemblances between the Egyptian disaster and the Sicilian project served only to highlight our wonderful prospects of success.

And so on, day after day, wherever two Athenians met together. For we Athenians love to have something to look forward to, and something to discuss; and since everyone enjoyed talking about Sicily so much, they fell

236

in love with the project itself. I have said that we had all been working hard since the end of the war to get our fields and vineyards productive again; well, that was part of it too. Athenians love working hard in short bursts, but the prospect of working hard at the same thing for the rest of their lives fills them with gloom and misery, and they start to consider themselves little better than the slaves of their own land. On the other hand, they had done most of what they could usefully do already – the vines and olives and figs were planted, and it would be years before they could enjoy the fruits of that work. What they wanted now was some new project, preferably with unlimited scope; something which they could hand on, unfinished, to their grandchildren.

Above all, I believe, it was the complete safety of the enterprise that thrilled them so much. For even if we lost the war, what harm could possibly come of it? After all, the Syracusans were hardly likely to leap aboard their ships and come after us; and even if they did, we always had the City walls to keep us safe. There was no power on earth capable of storming the City, and so long as we had the fleet, no siege could starve us out. As to the cost of the war, hadn't we been assured that Egesta and Catana and all those other fat, wealthy Sicilian allies would pay for the whole thing? Hadn't our men been to those cities and been entertained in private houses there, and seen that every vessel, from the mixing-bowl to the chamber-pot, was made of solid silver? Hadn't they been shown the floors of the temple treasuries, knee-deep in four-drachma pieces?

Now the trouble with being a Comic poet is that you see everything in terms of individual people; if you don't like an idea, you look for some person, some notable public face, to attack. And then you don't attack his policies or his public work – that would make terribly dreary poetry. No, you go for him personally, and in particular his sex life, for it seems to be a generally held belief that what a man does in bed is a perfect paradigm of all his other activities. Now it so happened that the man behind the Sicilian project did all sorts of funny things in bed with all sorts of peculiar people, and so I started to feel instinctively suspicious.

The whole thing, you see, had been Alcibiades' idea. The best Alcibiades story I know, as it happens, has nothing to do with his sexual activities; if I find time, I shall tell you some stories about those later. No, this story originated as a Pericles joke, and I got it from Cratinus, so you may feel quite free to laugh if you so wish.

When Alcibiades was about twelve or thirteen, his lover was no less a man than Pericles himself; and it was about the time of the Euboean crisis. Now Pericles, as you know, was faced with the problem of presenting his annual accounts, as General, to Assembly; there was a truly staggering sum for which Pericles could find no explanation which he could give to the Athenians without ending up on the wrong side of half a pint of the best hemlock. At the time, then, he was terribly worried about this, and even talked about it in his sleep.

Now Alcibiades has always liked to get his full six hours, or even more if possible, and he found this extremely upsetting. So one night, as Pericles was lying there muttering, 'I must find some way of giving my accounts, I must find some way of giving my accounts,' Alcibiades shook him by the shoulder and woke him up.

'You're looking at this from the wrong angle,' he said. 'What you've got to find is some way of *not* giving your accounts.'

Pericles said something memorable, like 'Shut up and go to sleep,' but when he woke up he had the most marvellous idea. He simply put the whole sum down under 'necessary expenditure', and provoked a major international crisis to divert attention. In that way, Pericles escaped not only with his life but unimpeached, and was able to lead us through the first part of the war.

That story is typical of Alcibiades; first, that he should see that the way to deal with an insoluble problem is not to try and smash it open but to walk round it and leave it alone; second, that he should exercise his brilliance not for the good of the City but so that he could get his full quota of sleep; third, that he should be in bed with the leading man of the day. I confess that I have never liked Alcibiades, and the reason I dislike him is the reason everyone else adores him; because he's the best-looking man in Athens. I tend to resent good-looking people. The Athenians, as I have said before, believe that the beautiful are good and that only the good are beautiful.

Alcibiades must have thanked the Gods that the only person prepared to make a real stand against him was Nicias son of Niceratus, because even his best friend (if he had one) could not pretend that Nicias was a thing of beauty, particularly when his kidneys were giving him trouble. I think Nicias started off as much in favour of the idea as everyone else; but then he saw a few inconsistencies in the project as outlined, and felt it his duty to point these out. Now everyone listened when Nicias spoke, even though it was generally agreed that he was the most boring and depressing speaker in Athens; I think they listened because they reckoned that something that tasted so horrible must be doing them good, like medicine. Whatever the reason, Nicias spoke and they listened, and Alcibiades started to worry. You know how the Athenians are, being a democracy; the more they love a man, the more they want to see him destroyed. Alcibiades had no wish to meet with the same treatment that they had handed out to Themistocles, Pericles and Cleon. He also knew about Nicias' obsession with duty. If Nicias was somehow bounced into joining him as co-leader of the Sicilian project, with some nonentity as third partner so that Nicias would always be outvoted, that would put an end to all opposition; with Nicias on the team – thorough, meticulous, conscientious, screamingly dull old Nicias – even the most timid and cautious people could not help feeling absolutely safe.

So Nicias was appointed as second General; and he panicked. The only way he could think of to discourage the Athenians was to rely on his reputation and give them a ghostly inflated estimate of the resources that the project would need if it were to be absolutely safe, in the hope of scaring the people off. So he prepared an enormous schedule, and read it out. The project would need scores of ships, he said, virtually every ship we had, and most of the male population of Athens would be needed, either as soldiers or sailors. And you couldn't expect these heroes to go forth and conquer for the usual rates of pay; you'd have to give them a whole drachma a day, at least until the Sicilians started paying their share. Then there would be supplies and materiel; so many hundred thousand arrows and throwing-spears and sling-bolts, so many pairs of sandals and cloaks (thick, military) and cloaks (lightweight, military) and helmet-plumes and spear-covers and rowlock-pads and coils of rope and jars of sardines (fresh) and jars of sardines (dried); all of them at market price or above, because of the urgency, so there would have to be property taxes to raise the money. In short, he said, Athens would need to prepare the greatest army and navy ever assembled outside Persia; she would have to put forth almost her entire strength.

He finished his speech, in the confident expectation of silence broken only by discontented grumbling. What he got was a roar of approval and an almost unanimous vote in favour. I remember the expression on his face as if it were yesterday, like a man struck by lightning in the evening of a cool summer day. What he hadn't reckoned with was the almost unnatural gregariousness of us Athenians; when something nice is happening, we don't want to be left out, and for weeks people had been tortured by fears that they would be left behind. Now Nicias had said that there would be room for everybody. Everybody was going to go to Sicily!

Except me. I found out later that the person drawing up the enlistment roll was an unimportant little man who I had made some passing remark about in a Comedy. This had so enraged him – he wasn't used to it, I suppose – that he decided out of spite to leave me off the roll.

I remember how furious I was when the roll was read out, and how I stumped back home, kicking a stone in front of me all the way. I was nasty to Phaedra, refused to eat any food, and went to bed while it was still light.

I lay in bed for hours, unable to get to sleep, and mused on the unfairness of life. About the only person I knew who wasn't going was Aristophanes son of Philip, and the only reason he wasn't going was because he was a coward and had bribed someone at the draft board. And now, I supposed, people would think that I had done the same. Only a few days before, I had been to see Little Zeus, and he had been anxiously going over his property to see if he could manage to squeeze another cupful or so of produce out of it to bring him up to Heavy Infantry status, so that he could go to Sicily too – for if he went to Sicily, he said, he could probably make enough in pay and plunder to pay me back what he owed me. Knowing him, he had probably managed it, so he would be there. So would everybody in the world, except me and Aristophanes.

But Callicrates wasn't going, said my soul. He was slightly too old for military service, and had refused to lie about his age, saying that a man who strove too hard to get mixed up in a war probably had something wrong with his brain. The more I thought about it, the more I was comforted, in a way, for most of the people I valued most were too old to fight. This set me worrying in a different direction (why did I only make friends with old people, and what would become of me when they died?), and between the two conflicting streams of anxiety I fell asleep.

I was woken up by the most appalling noise. Phaedra woke up too, and threw her arms around me out of pure terror, and as soon as I realised it was her and not the heavily armed Syracusan cavalryman I had been having a nightmare about, I felt rather brave and told her not to worry, I would protect her.

'Marvellous,' she said. 'What from?'

'Whatever made the noise,' I said.

'Idiot,' she said, unwinding herself from me, 'go back to sleep.'

There was another terrible crash, right outside our front door, and a lot of confused shouting. My first instinct was to hide under the bed, but that would have been the sort of behaviour one would expect from a man who *wasn't* going to Sicily. Besides, I didn't want to appear a coward in front of Phaedra, or life would be intolerable for the next week or two. So I pulled on a cloak, found my sword, and poked my head out of the front door.

The first thing I saw was my little statue of Hermes, with its head and phallus smashed off, lying on its side. I am not a brave man, but I had paid good money for that statue after its predecessor was wrecked, and I wanted a word with the person responsible. I looked up and down the street, but there was no one in sight; just moonlight, a few stray dogs and a little pool of fresh vomit. Just like any other night in the violet-crowned City of the Muses.

A sensible man would have cursed freely and gone back to bed. Instead, I looped my cloak round my arm, gripped my sword firmly, and set off in pursuit. For I could hear smashing-noises just round the corner; the assassin had not got far. Walking quietly, on the sides of my feet, I crept round and saw a gang of very drunk-looking young men dismembering the statue outside the house of one Philopsephus, a grain merchant.

There were rather a lot of them, and some of them were quite big, and drunks can be terribly violent. I decided that Callicrates was right; only a fool would strive too hard to get mixed up in a battle. I started to retire, but unfortunately I had left it rather late for that. One of the jolly stone-masons had seen me, and was yelling to his friends.

How do drunk people manage to run so fast, I wonder? Before I could cover the few yards to my door they were on to me, and I brandished my sword at them as if I were Achilles himself. One of them made a rude noise and took it away from me, and another one grabbed my arms from behind.

'I said no witnesses,' said a voice behind me, slurring its words somewhat. 'We'll have to cut his throat, whoever he is.'

'Good idea,' said the man who had taken my sword. He was a tall man with a bald head, and I recognised his voice.

'That would be typical, Aristophanes son of Philip,' I said, 'using a drunken brawl as an excuse to murder your chief rival.'

'Oh, for God's sake,' said Aristophanes, 'it's not you again, is it?' He peered at me and made a sort of whining noise, like a dog after a titbit. 'Gentlemen,' he protested to his friends, 'this is too much. Every time I have a little bit of fun in this city, this little creep pops up and gets under my feet. It's getting beyond a joke, it really is. Please take him away and cut his head off.'

'Who is he, then?' asked the man behind me.

'My name is Eupolis,' I said, 'and as a poet I am under the direct protection of the God Dionysus. Anyone who so much as nicks my skin will be condemned to drink nothing but water for the rest of his life.'

Someone giggled, and soon they were all roaring with laughter, the way drunks do – all except Aristophanes, who was begging them to kill me. It would be such fun, he pleaded; they could cut off my head and put it in a bag, and use it for turning people into stone.

'And now,' I said confidently, 'if I may have my sword back, I will leave you to your work, which I can see is of considerable public importance.'

'That's right,' someone said. 'Got to stop the fleet sailing. Can't have Alcithingides prancing round Sicily nibbling all the cheese off the cities. Going to burn the fleet soon as we've finished here.'

'What a splendid idea,' I said. 'Then no one can go.' I prised my sword out of the hand of the man holding it (I recognised him too; in fact I knew most of them now I could see them clearly – all people who weren't going to Sicily, which probably explained why they had been having a party) and walked quickly away without looking round. The sound of breaking marble indicated that they had resumed their work. I shut the front door behind me, and put up the bar.

'Well?' Phaedra called out. 'Who did you kill? You were gone a long time.'

'They'd gone by the time I got there,' I replied. 'You were worried, weren't you?'

'No I wasn't,' said Phaedra. 'Who cares a damn what happens to you?'

I tossed my sword into a corner. My little brush with danger had taken most of the sting out of not going to Sicily, and my own moderate cleverness in getting out of the danger had left me feeling rather cheerful.

'Come here and say that,' I said.

The next day, nobody was feeling very cheerful. You must understand how superstitious people were then, before Philosophy became so fashionable, and how everyone was terribly edgy because of the sailing of the fleet. So when they woke up and found that someone had been smashing up statues of the Gods (apparently the jolly stone-masons had made a clean sweep of most of the little Hermeses in the City), they were appalled and took it as an omen. Hermes, they said, was the God of Escorts – He goes with us when our souls travel across the Styx, and watches over all embassies and perilous journeys – and now all His statues were only fit for the lime-kilns; the God was angry with us. I think the main reason for the panic was that nobody knew who had done it, because everyone (except me) had been asleep; either they were sailing the next day with the fleet and had had an early night, or they had been to good-luck parties and were sleeping it off. So it was anybody's guess who was responsible, and under such circumstances, anybody tends to guess at hidden conspiracies. By dawn, the general view was that the anti-democratic faction, whoever they were, had done the deed in order to bring disaster on the fleet and then, by some undefined means, seize control of the State. It was all very worrying.

Put together three or four worried Athenians, and they will immediately demand that the General be impeached. The General at this time, of course, was Alcibiades; and thanks to the inscrutable processes of the democratic mind, it was assumed, without question, that since the expedition was Alcibiades' idea and had been conceived and organised by him, he must have sabotaged it. After all, people said, Alcibiades is always going to parties and getting drunk, and people who get drunk smash up statues. Therefore it followed, as night follows day, that Alcibiades, single-handed or with accomplices, smashed up the statues.

Now I knew for a fact that he hadn't, but even I am not so stupid as to open my mouth at such a time, and so I kept quiet. After all, I had no great love for the man, and given his career to date it was inevitable that he was going to be put to death sooner or later, so why not now? Besides, I am an Athenian and so must always find someone to blame for my misfortunes; and I think that deep inside my soul, I was blaming Alcibiades – if he hadn't organised it, there would be no fleet for me not to sail with. It was the wrong thing to do, of course, but I was amply punished for it later.

So the Athenians were in a difficult position. Unless they impeached Alcibiades, they couldn't execute him for blasphemy; but if they did that, there would be no Sicilian project and everybody would have to go back to work. There was a frenzied debate about it in the Assembly which amused me very much, with everybody calling everybody else a monarchist and accusing each other of betraying naval secrets to the Persians, and finally they reached an Athenian compromise. Alcibiades would lead the fleet to conquest and glory in Sicily, and they would try him for blasphemy on his return. This would give his enemies plenty of time to buy the requisite witnesses, and everybody would have two treats to look forward to instead of one.

Do I sound as if I hate my city and this monster we used to call democracy? I don't. I suppose I felt for Athens in those days the same tortuous jumble of emotions as I felt for Phaedra; even when she behaved most terribly, she fascinated me utterly, and I would not have had a different city, or a different wife, for all the wealth of King Gyges. All my life I have loved the Festivals, where three Tragedies are followed by one Comedy, and the horror and the humour get mixed up in your mind until you can barely tell them apart. Now I am a worshipper of Comedy: I believe in it absolutely,

245

as being the purpose of the world and of mankind, and I believe that Zeus thinks as I do, which is the only possible explanation I can think of for most things that happen, and so I winnow out the Comedy and let the wind blow everything else away. Now tell me, where else in all the kingdoms of the earth could Zeus and I find a richer Comedy than in Athens, where men used to conduct their affairs in the way I have described to you? And of all the little Comedies of Athens, what could be better than the Comedy of bad-faced Eupolis and his bad-faced wife?

Dexitheus the bookseller, who is a man of taste and discrimination, tells me that I should stop here. He thinks that this first part of my life makes a complete story in itself, dealing as it does with Athens before its downfall. He feels that in what I have written so far I have so perfectly blended Tragedy and Comedy that to add any more would be a display of sacrilegious ingratitude towards the Muses who have so clearly inspired me up till now, and that the next part of my story, which deals with what actually happened when we got to Sicily, would therefore be best published under separate cover. Now I have known Dexitheus since before the holes in his ears healed up and everybody thought he was just another ex-slave on the make, and so I can honestly say that the fact that he can make two drachmas by selling two short books but only one and a half by selling one long one has not influenced his advice to me on this matter in any respect, and I am bound to say that on the whole I agree with him.

I shall therefore leave you at this point and catch up on my sleep, which I have been neglecting lately. If you want to find out what happened in the end, and what became of the greatest expedition ever mounted and the most perfect democracy the world has ever seen, I recommend that you buy at least three copies of this book, and advise all your friends and relatives to do the same; that way, Dexitheus may feel justified in asking me (and the Muses, of course) to exert ourselves just one more time.

One last thing. I was talking to a man of my age yesterday night, and he assured me that the fighting-cock killed by Ajax Bloodfoot wasn't called Euryalus the Foesmiter at all. He is positive that I've confused the bird I saw (which, according to him, was called The Mighty Hercules) with the bird that eventually did for Ajax Bloodfoot about three months later. He may well be right, at that; so, since this is meant to be a work of history, I record his opinion on the matter as well as my own and leave the final choice to generations yet unborn.

NATIONAL UNIVERSITY
LIBRARY   SAN DIEGO

NATIONAL UNIVERSITY
LIBRARY
SAN DIEGO